BELVEDON

Isobel Birch

This novel is a work of fiction.

Any references to real people and historical events are used fictitiously. Other names, characters, places, and events are products of the author's imagination. Any resemblance to persons living or dead, actual events, or places, is entirely coincidental.

Copyright © Isobel Birch 2024
ISBN: 9798865150237

All rights reserved. No part of this publication may be reproduced, stored in a retrieval system, or transmitted, in any form or by any means, electronic, mechanical, photocopying, recording or otherwise, without the prior written permission of the publisher.

Cover image: Fotor.

Dedication

To the memory of my parents who gave me
an enduring love of the arts, in all their forms,
and to my family for their loving support.

Prologue

Yorkshire, England 1768

The grouse moor was a wild and lonely place. Untamed. Bleak in winter, with short days and dark oppressive skies. Frequent thunderous rainstorms lashed the land, driven by fierce, unrelenting winds. Snow fell, white to the far horizon, heralding the cold bone deep chill, which even a roaring fire could not dispel. Damp pervaded. His outdoor coat and sturdy leather boots never truly dried, until the softer winds and milder days of Spring, slowly crept in.

Summer had always been his favourite season, when the sun rose high in the sky, bringing warmth, brighter light, and longer working days. Then the moor teemed with wildlife, hunting, or foraging for food: hawks circling, birds on the wing, lively hares, slithering adders, and the red grouse.

He loved the moor, and he loved the heather when it bloomed in the late summer months, twiggy with tiny narrow leaves and a mass of bright pink flowers.

Here was his life, his working year, managing the landscape, protecting the birds and keeping on top of the predators.

Autumn, when it came, was the season of death.

The noble family, who owned this vast expanse of heathered moorland, came every year to their hunting lodge at Belverdon, to shoot and party wildly with friends. This autumn was no different.

The Duke and Duchess of Aven were in residence, a most lofty and austere couple, who barely tolerated each other and never had, their two noble families united solely for wealth and status. A sadly passionless arrangement, so obvious, that in their youth, bets were placed upon the likelihood of the pair being together for long enough to produce an heir, yet produce an heir, they had.
Their eldest son, Thomas, now twenty-four, styled the Marquess of Deane, and soon to become a father himself, had since infancy born such a striking resemblance to the Duke in looks, all doubts and suspicions as to his noble lineage had been firmly cast aside. He too had travelled to Belverdon with his beloved wife Elizabeth.

William Foster, nineteen years of age, married at eighteen, apprenticed gamekeeper on the vast Belverdon estate, knew little of their wealthy lifestyle or family life.
He lived high on the moor, in the same stone cottage his parents and grandparents had occupied before him, all born at Belverhead, a stark and uncompromising place, where even in death, they rested beneath torrid skies, roaring winds, and ground soaking torrents.

Death had taken his parents early, before his seventeenth year, and loneliness had been his lot until Letty had agreed to marry him.
He had painted a sorry picture of the cottage, the isolation, the cold and damp, but to his immense joy she had not been put off, and they had worked together to make the cottage

more homely. Even so, he knew she had sacrificed much to be with him, and worried she was too often alone.

He had tasks allotted to him, orders to follow and reports to make. He spent his days walking or riding the moor, always knowing where the healthy red grouse he nurtured were to be found, and how many they numbered. He readily shared the information, yet he took no active part in the organisation of the Autumn shoot. Others, more senior than himself, with greater experience, had the task of ensuring all went well. They were the ones who dealt in guns, dogs, and slaughter.

One day, he thought sadly, there would be no grouse left. You could not keep shooting the best stock and expect them to go on forever reproducing so abundantly, when so much was against their survival, right from the moment their eggs were laid. He observed much, but no one cared what he might think, or what he might say. This year's birds were all that mattered to them; numbers, nothing more. He sighed but did not linger. Rain was on its way, the light was fading, and he had matters at home to take care of. His beloved Letty needed him, close as she was to giving birth to their own first child.

Ten days later, he gently laid the swaddled body of his tiny daughter Sally in the grave he'd dug for her, within the walled moorland graveyard at Belverhead, where his parents and grandparents also lay at rest. There was no clergyman to say a prayer over her, so he tucked a small wooden cross inside the swaddling, close to her heart, before gently covering her with earth, until he could see her no more.

He used his shovel to fill the rest of the grave and scattered a handful of pebbles to mark the place where she lay.

'May the Lord God take you gently in his arms to heaven,' he said with bowed head and broken heart, before leaving the

desolate place and making his melancholy way home; melancholy, not only for his own loss, but for his distraught wife, who felt the death of her child so keenly.

The tired old nag he rode plodded along, taking him ever nearer to the empty cradle he'd laboured over with such care, to the patiently knitted blankets, the lovingly sewn baby clothes and the shattered hope. Back to his sweet Letty who worked hard, never complained, and deserved better from life.

The landscape was as desolate as he felt. Mournful eerie sounds, like the whispers of lost souls, carried from near and far on the restless wind. He fancied he heard a baby crying and thought it to be conjured up in his grief. His mind had not let go, was still disbelieving, desperately hopeful, longing to relive a cherished memory. Such a welcome, joyful sound when Sally had entered the world. Now in death, silenced forever, her tiny body unable to thrive for no reason he could see nor understand. Happiness and joy had briefly been theirs. Now they dwelt in a world of sorrow.

The moor was never truly silent. The wind whistled and moaned, rain hammered and battered, animals snuffled and shrieked, birds sang and chirruped and at this time of year, guns fired shot after shot.

It was too quiet. Even if his mind had been breaking apart in despair, the sound of guns firing should have penetrated his consciousness, heard, as they were, way across the moor when the Duke invited his aristocratic friends to the annual shoot. Something had silenced the guns. It could not last.

Autumn had long been the season of death at Belverdon.

The crying was not in his imagination. It began again. If anything, it grew louder. He felt he was nearer to the source of it now and tried to convince himself it was an animal in distress or a bird, but the sound was too similar to the cries of his newly buried daughter to be mistaken for anything but the bawling of a recently born infant.

He dismounted and walked gingerly around, until he found himself staring down at a basket wedged into place amongst the heather. His mind turned biblical as he thought of Miriam finding Moses in the bullrushes. It was a sight his mind was wary to take in. It made no sense to him. Babies were abandoned, it was a fact of life, left in church doorways where someone might find them and take them in, or outside a cottage door. Never high on the moor, where only wild and hungry animals were likely to find them. On any other day he would not have passed near this place and never known the infant was there.

'The Lord giveth and the Lord taketh away,' he recited. The Lord had given him a daughter and taken her back into his keeping. Now here was another child in desperate need, left to die from the harsh elements or be dragged away to an animal's lair.

There were cart tracks and the easily distinguishable tread of horseshoes, nothing unusual on a dirt road, but how fresh were they? How recently had someone come to this desolate place and left this child alone? Not dead, not buried, but carefully concealed, almost nesting in the heather. A girl child, her fate callously left in the hands of the Lord God.

She was small like his Sally, nought but a few days old, wrapped in a good woollen blanket, alive and warm, but maybe not long for this world, frail as she was. He thought she could not have lain there long. Perhaps she still had a small chance at life.

He would take her home to Letty, whose breasts were full and tender with milk she had no use for, to see if she would let this scrap of humanity suckle.

What, he wondered, would his wife make of it? Would she see this infant as a gift from God, a replacement for her own lost child, or would she reject it, fearing it to be a spectre in her mind? He had no idea, but just as he had carried his own dead baby cradled against his chest, so he held this living one, wrapping his coat around her to provide warmth to her tiny limbs, hushing her crying with soothing words of comfort.

The basket, he strapped securely to his saddle bag, in case someone might recognise it, and in regret claim the child back. Then he shrugged as he realised it was unlikely, for only a heartless person would ride so far into the wilderness and leave a baby to die. He clenched his fists in anger at the unknown perpetrator.

'God's justice be upon whoever sought this child's death,' he murmured, since death had to have been their only intention and might yet be the result of their cruel actions.

Letty did not reject her. Letty was heartsick. She only saw her Sally, come back to life. Sally, who needed her nourishing milk, who they could love and care for together, watching over her as each hour passed, and she lived another day.

Death rode the moor, but this time kept well clear of William and Letty's cottage and the foundling child. They were doubly vigilant. William stayed awake to watch the child whenever Letty slept. He could not bear for Letty to lose this child too. Their own sweet Sally must have had an internal weakness, such that on the tenth day of her life, she had given up the struggle to live, and stopped breathing in her sleep.

Letty remained fearful of this child leaving her too, but she had a strong will, was healthy and began to gain weight, waking regularly with lusty cries, demanding to be fed.

They thought it both a miracle and a blessing. Letty might not have given birth to this Sally and neither of them were blind to the fact, but in their hearts, she was their own beloved daughter, and when the time came, they claimed her as such.

On a fine Sunday morning, six weeks later, with welcome sunshine and clear skies, they rode as a family in the horse and cart, to the Church of the Blessed Virgin at Sawley, where the baby was baptised Sally Mary Foster, the firstborn daughter of William and Letty Foster of Belverhead Cottage, Greater Belverdon. The small congregation rejoiced with them.

There was gossip in the village, there usually was, but nothing was spoken to cause William and Letty any anguish. They had already heard from the Head Gamekeeper how the Marchioness had been prematurely delivered of a son. They knew there had been anxiety for the health of both mother and child in the days following the birth, which had been the reason for the silent guns. Thankfully, the fear had diminished. The new Viscount Rossington, though small, still lived and grew in strength daily.

The Marquess had left Belverdon taking his wife and son to the family seat, Tremar House, to receive tender care in more peaceful surroundings. The Duchess, never having had a fondness for the shoot, had travelled with them, thankful of an excuse to leave the Duke at Belverdon, allowing him to celebrate in raucous fashion with his rowdy friends, in recognition of a new heir in the family.

The shoot went on. Noblemen challenged each other daily for the most kills. They dined on their shooting prowess, drank late into the night, and lustfully indulged their senses.

In the village, those of a pious nature spoke in hushed tones of lewd semi-naked women, foul mouthed drunken men, and scenes of licentiousness. They might inwardly disapprove of the Duke's behaviour and abhor his friends, they might speak softly of the devil's work at hand, but they never thought to openly dispute his unquestionable right to behave in whatever manner he saw fit.

One day, he would have to answer to Almighty God for his crimes.

Chapter One

London England 1814

Bella knew she had not adjusted well to the strict uncompromising rules of high society. In her other life as a vicar's daughter, if she saw someone at a gathering standing alone, she would approach them, offer a warm smile, and make polite conversation to put them at their ease. In the small community in which she had been raised it would be considered a kindness, a precursor to friendship or simply a comfortable passing of time together.

In this ballroom, according to her aunt, she must not put herself forward in any way, but wait on the side lines until a gentleman approached and asked her if she cared to dance, to which her answer would be yes, since it was considered bad ton to decline, leaving you without partners for the rest of the evening.

So far there had been no opportunity to either acquiesce or decline, since no one had approached her.

Why would they? They didn't know her, and never would if this state of affairs continued. Her aunt had promised to introduce her to suitable gentleman, by which she meant dull, old, widowed, or desperate, having earlier informed her that little in the way of a dowry, and no worthy connections, would exclude her from a marriage to anyone else. Instead, she too often left her to her own devices as she gossiped with her chaperoning friends.

So why was she even here? Why had her aunt descended on the family unexpectedly and whisked her off to London for a season, squashing any objections made by her parents, upsetting and harrying everyone until they agreed it was for the best?'

'It might amuse me,' she'd said on the way to the capital in her well sprung coach. 'I should have had a daughter to launch, a diamond of the first water. You will have to do instead. Just aim to sound less provincial.'

Why should she care if she sounded provincial? Fate had decreed she would live a provincial life, a happy one, cherished within a loving family, a busy and fulfilling life. She had not desired to leave.

She did care, quite desperately, if she was bored out of her mind. It made her restless and agitated, pushing her towards some action, some activity.

Across the ballroom she saw a young man who stood alone, glancing casually around, maybe seeking out an acquaintance. She set off in his direction and came upon him in a manner which was not only highly irregular, but quite startling to the said gentleman.

He tried to ignore her. She failed to take the hint.

'What may I do for you miss?' he reluctantly asked, in an abrupt tone, meant to imply he had no intention of doing whatever it was she imagined he would do, so she might as well take herself off.

'You mistake me sir,' she answered with a warm smile, noting that he was even more handsome than had at first been apparent from his profile. 'I've come to aid you, to offer some conversation, so you won't appear to be alone, friendless perhaps.'

He glanced down at her then, with an air of aloofness she failed to notice, him being somewhat taller than her diminutive height.

Friendless! How dare she suggest such a thing. He had a coterie of remarkably close friends, and numerous esteemed acquaintances. He had no need of pushy women like her who tried to force their unwanted presence upon him. He thought to dismiss her with ease.

'I assure you miss, I am not without friends, so you may happily leave me to myself.'

'In that case,' she persisted, 'perhaps you will assist me, by passing a few moments in conversation, as if I were someone of interest to you, so I won't appear friendless.'

An original stance, he'd grant her that, as he looked her over more thoroughly. He had no idea who she was and was certain he'd never seen her before. She wasn't without looks. He might even consider her pretty if she wasn't being so disrespectful to his rank. She was well enough dressed, he had to admit, in a fashionable figure becoming frock, with an abundance of shiny brown hair wound around with ribbons, the rich colour reminding him of one of his more favoured horses.

He contemplated his options. He could just walk off leaving her standing there as if she were beneath his notice, but even to someone as lofty as himself, it felt cruel. Besides, she had attractions he did notice, he could hardly help it, when there was so little bodice to her dress and so much soft creamy flesh to admire. Maybe he could spare her a moment of his time and enjoy the view, since Rossington was tardy in arriving.

'What conversation do you have then?' he asked, 'because if it's about the weather, I ain't interested.'

'Well, no, I agree that would be tedious. However, you must concede it is fairly solid ground on which to begin a conversation, without delivering any offence.'

'How so?'

'Well upon approaching someone who might become a new acquaintance, it would not do to ask questions of a personal nature, nor comment on their appearance, which would be impertinent and draw censure, so the weather is usually a sound opening salvo.'

'You think so?' he scoffed, 'yet you chose to imply I'm standing here alone because I'm friendless. Is that not impertinent Miss ….?'

'Wrighton. Miss Bella Wrighton of Stillford.'

Stillford! Where was that?

'Never heard of the place,' he said dismissively.

'Few have, I'm afraid,' she said ruefully. 'It's rather a backwater.'

'Why live there then?'

'I have little choice, since it's where my parents live,' she replied with artless honesty.

'How come you to be here then?' he asked, glancing down at her animated face, the inference being she didn't belong and would be wise to go back where she came from as soon as possible.

'I'm staying with my aunt, Lady Bellingham. She's set on me having a season.'

He pondered the notion. Lady Bellingham was a popular matron with adult sons, well versed in the etiquette of social functions amongst the ton. Why then was this niece of hers lacking in both caution and respect?

'Hasn't she told you not to go walking up to strangers and begin talking to them as if you had known them forever?' he asked curtly, his head turned away, his eyes searching for Rossington amongst the gathered throng.

'I expect she did,' Bella confessed, 'but it doesn't seem sensible to me. How will I ever get to meet anyone?'

'In the polite world,' he said with emphasis, as if explaining to a small child, 'you only get to meet people who want to meet you. In other words, Miss Wrighton, you wait for a gentleman to ask to be introduced to you. Now if you will excuse me, I see my friend approaching.'

He gave her the shallowest of bows then walked with purpose towards a gentleman advancing from across the room, hooking an arm in his, and swiftly turning him in the opposite direction.

'I say John,' Rossington said, slightly bemused by his friend's unusual behaviour, 'I was just coming over to join you, to get an introduction to that taking young lady you were engrossed with.'

'She is not taking, and I was not engrossed,' he said in a surprisingly firm tone. 'She was forcing a conversation on me, and I was trying to depress her pretensions, but she was too brazen to notice.'

'Brazen? I say that's a bit harsh. Can't say as she looked brazen to me. Who is she anyway?'

'She's a country protégé of Lady Bellingham's, her niece I recall, not up to snuff. Doesn't know not to go accosting men she hasn't been introduced to, in a ballroom, or anywhere else for that matter.'

'She must have some pedigree though,' Rossington persisted, 'Lady Bellingham is an Earl's daughter as well as being married to the Viscount.'

'Is she? Which Earl?'

'Earl Wrighton.'

John shrugged, not impressed.

'Miss Bella Wrighton must be a very poor relation then since she lives in Deadwater.'

'Not Deadwater surely?' Rossington said wryly, sensing his friend's continued irritation, which in itself was a bit strange.

'Somewhere like that. A backwater she said.'

'She's relying on her looks then to find a husband,' Rossington assumed. 'I suppose you did notice she was pretty.'

'I suppose I did,' he was forced to admit. 'I haven't suddenly gone blind.'

Oh no, he'd noticed everything there was to notice about the irritating Miss Bella Wrighton and wasn't thrilled to find himself having visions of slowly undressing her and rolling her in the sheets naked, with her mass of luscious glossy brown hair fanned in disarray across his pillows. Catching a glimpse of her soft creamy skin and low revealing neckline must have encouraged sensual thoughts he ought not to have for such an innocent. Whatever the cause, he had no intention of becoming involved with her, when she had little, or no social standing.

'If you're not staking a claim, I might pay her a call and see if she'd like to come driving with me,' Rossington declared.

'Be sure you have plenty of conversation planned then, my friend. Miss Wrighton is an aficionado of conversation. You should begin with the weather and avoid being impertinent.'

'Seriously?' Rossington laughed. 'Who introduced you to her?'

'No one. As I said, she's not up to snuff. She came up to me as bold as brass, having made the incorrect assumption that I was lacking in friends, since you were behind times in arriving.'

'My apologies,' Rossington said, with a nod of his head to hide his continued amusement.

'Be warned my friend. She's naïve, untutored in social etiquette and lacking in all caution. Let's circulate and forget the encroaching chit. Mark my words, she'll come to grief in no time at all.'

Bella, hauled ungraciously into the ladies' retiring room by her aunt, felt as if she'd already come to grief.

'What are you about child?'

'What do you mean aunt?'

'Walking up to Walborough as if you were an acquaintance of his, without an introduction and you far below his notice anyway. You're lucky he didn't cut you dead and walk away as if you didn't exist.'

'Wouldn't that have been rude of him?'

'You were the one being rude, my girl.'

'Why? He was on his own. I was just making polite conversation with him to pass a little time and relieve the tedium. Then his friend arrived. He excused himself and walked away.'

'You've heard of Icarus haven't you?' her aunt said sharply, 'who flew too high to the sun and crashed back down to earth. Set your sights on Walborough or Rossington and you'll crash to earth in a hurry. You will do well to remember you have very modest expectations, very modest indeed.'

'I don't have any expectations at all Aunt Susannah,' Bella said, close to tears at her aunt's censure. 'If you recall, I never wanted to come to London. I told you I was ill prepared. I've learnt all the wrong things. I can't pretend I now want to learn to behave as if I'm a dimwit, happy to stand around until I die of boredom. I just want to go home. I'm sure Owen was about to propose before you dragged me away, without giving him the chance.'

'Ungrateful girl,' her aunt said, raising her voice and looking as if her greatest wish was to shake some sense into her. 'I try to rescue you from that God forsaken backwater your father insists you live in and what do I get in return, a bluestocking with a mind full of useless knowledge about heavens knows what, without a clue how to go on in society. Do you want to spend the rest of your life as a farmer's drudge?'

'I don't want to be anyone's drudge, be he a farmer, plain mister, or peer of the realm. I just want to be happy, but how will I find any happiness here? I know you've been kind to me, but I wasn't raised to simper meekly and waft a fan around in an unspoken language I don't understand. I'm not good at sitting or standing doing nothing, waiting for someone to notice I exist. I like to be busy, and helpful, and as you rightly pointed out, no one I'm likely to have a rapport with, will consider me worthy of their notice. You've ruined my only chance of marrying. I'll likely be a spinster forever.'

Her aunt relented a bit seeing her downcast expression and sensing how close she was to tears.

'You have more to offer than you know, dear girl, and as for being busy, you can make use of your excellent memory to learn the rules, until they are second nature to you, unless you want to go home in disgrace and have Owen Lawton say I told you so. Now, hold your head up, try and look pleased to be here and let me see who I might introduce you to. At least you can show off your skill at dancing. Who taught you?'

'Mama taught me,' she said, which was a slight stretching of the truth.

Her aunt sniffed and led her back to the ballroom.

She danced with Mr Henry Boyle, elderly gentleman and Mr Isaac Wallace, widowed gentleman and Mr Rufus McAllister, single Scottish gentleman, whose rather rapid mode of speech and strong dialect meant she had little, if any understanding of his few choice words, generally spoken in an untimely manner as they drifted apart in the dance. None of the said gentlemen, all being indifferent dancers, gave her the opportunity to show she could excel at something society did admire.

When Lord Rossington approached her aunt and asked for an introduction, there was a strange silence and stillness all around her, an aura of disbelief. Surely, he couldn't be serious. Then he was leading her out onto the dance floor, and they were playing a waltz. Was she even allowed to waltz? Rossington seemed unperturbed either way.

'I hope I haven't been too presumptuous,' he said by way of an explanation, 'but I saw you were acquainted with my friend Walborough.'

'Walborough! Oh, I wouldn't say we were acquainted,' she freely admitted. 'We haven't even been introduced. I sort of accosted him, thinking him in need of a friend to talk to, but my aunt assures me my efforts were neither needed nor welcome. Quite the wrong thing altogether in fact, so you might want to reconsider dancing with me.'

Rossington was amused by how candid she was, and unabashed.

'I have no wish to reconsider, Miss Wrighton. There isn't a young lady in the room I'd prefer to be dancing with.'

'You don't think you should know a bit more about me before you are so bold with your statements?'

'It isn't necessary to know a young lady well in order to enjoy dancing with her. There are other ways to get to know someone better.'

'I shan't go out into the garden with you, if that is what you had in mind.'

Rossington laughed at her presumption as Walborough stood watching them with a group of friends.

'I had in mind calling on you tomorrow to take you for a drive. Would that meet with your approval?'

'If my aunt will allow it. She said I was to stay away from you lest I crash to the ground like Icarus.'

'Really! That's too bad of her, but fear not, I'll persuade her she need not concern herself.'

Bella was concerned for her own sake. She was becoming increasingly aware of having homed in on two of the most eligible bachelors of the ton, without knowing anything about them beyond their pleasurable appearance. She'd been a bit slow to notice how perfectly turned out Walborough was, which might have given his valet an apoplexy had he known of it, considering the effort he'd gone to, to ensure his gentleman was immaculate in all respects.

Rossington was also dressed immaculately in the stylish manner her eldest brother Roderick aspired to, emulating Mr Brummell's preference for simple elegance over the flamboyance of the fops. He also danced the waltz superbly and made her feel as light as a feather as he whirled her around the dance floor in a level of intimacy she'd never experienced before and wasn't certain was proper. Her cheeks bloomed and she longed to open her fan.

When the whirling stopped, he escorted her back to her aunt with a promise to collect her the next afternoon for a drive in the park, leaving Lady Bellingham with no time to object and uncertain whether she wanted to. What a coup that would be if she could bring Rossington up to scratch.

She redefined her motives for having Bella to stay. Getting one over on her sister-in-law, suddenly seemed of little consequence, when she might propel Bella towards the marriage of the season.

'What are you about?' Walborough asked Rossington as he returned to his friend's side. 'Much more of that and you'll find yourself in parson's mousetrap.'

'These affairs are generally terminally dull. Miss Wrighton's candid conversation amuses me and she's no hardship to twirl around the dance floor, but there is something else. Have you ever had the feeling you already know someone, even though you're certain you don't?'

'Can't say as I have. Why do you ask? Does Miss Bella Wrighton of Stillford remind you of someone?'

'There lies the mystery, John. I have absolutely no idea who she reminds me of.'

'Probably some doxy from your past,' John said drily. 'Forget about the irritating Miss Bella Wrighton from nowhere, and let's get out of here.'

Although Rossington went with him willingly, his mind wasn't on the hands of cards he played later, nor the sum of money he lost, which in itself was unusual.

His mind insisted instead on recalling the strange feeling of familiarity he encountered when thinking of Miss Bella Wrighton, as if when looking at her, he saw the shadow of someone else, too indistinct to recognise.

Bella, alone in her bedroom, found herself thinking not of Rossington but of Walborough, recalling his high collar points and intricately tied cravat, his curly fair hair, slightly unruly, his short sideburns and his compelling light blue eyes, eyes frequently turned in her direction as she danced with Rossington. She knew neither of them were for her, but with so many men of indifferent looks and foppish appearance on display, they were always likely to catch her eye.

Walborough, taller than most, handsome and wholly masculine, easily impressed in his black tailcoat and silk knee breeches, the figure-hugging fit of which all men might envy, and ladies admire. He seemed always to be there when she looked up or glanced around the ballroom, although he was never alone again, and when he left with Rossington she found the evening had swiftly turned dull and didn't quibble when her aunt called for their carriage, to take them home.

Chapter Two

After an indifferent night's sleep, Bella was wearing a very becoming white muslin dress, enhanced with green embroidery around the neck, sleeves and hem, chosen by her aunt, so she said, to set off her sparkling green eyes.

Thankfully, the bodice was more discreet than those her aunt considered appropriate for the evening, when it seemed to Bella, she hardly had any bodice at all, an open invitation she felt for men's eyes to settle on her bosom with lustful intent, which she had no wish to encourage.

It was a pleasantly warm day and having brought down a recently published novel to read, she planned to sit for a while in the garden, convinced she would be sadly lacking in callers. Instead, she found herself alarmingly popular with the gentlemen she'd danced with the evening before, all vying for her attention.

When Walborough strolled in as casual as you please, elegantly attired in a blue superfine coat over snug white pantaloons tucked into black hessians, all heads turned in his direction. She politely excused herself from her admirers and went over to him, cutting her aunt out, who had also begun to walk his way.

'What are you doing here?' she asked him boldly.

'I was passing by,' he informed her. 'So, I thought I would look in on your aunt.'

'Passing by on the way to where?' Bella prompted, not believing him for one minute.

'To a variety of places on my day's schedule, too tedious to list. I see you have become popular.'

'I have no wish to become popular, at least not with gentlemen of little conversation, little physical appeal and a false notion of my social aspirations.'

'A little harsh my dear Miss Wrighton, considering I held you in conversation for some considerable time yester' evening.'

She almost laughed at his rueful tone.

'And escaped at the very first opportunity.'

'I had promised my company to Rossington for the evening if you recall. Have you heard from your beau in Stillford since you came to London?'

Bella blinked, confused by his question.

'How do you know about him?' she asked, unsure of how he could have heard of Owen and her hopes for a future with him.

'I overheard you talking to your aunt as I passed the ladies' retiring room. The door had been left ajar.'

'So, you eavesdropped,' she said accusingly.

'Not as such, no. Sounds carried from beyond the door and caught my attention. I merely recognised your voice and your aunt's agitation and lingered a moment to remove a speck of dust from my coat. So, has he written to ascertain how you go on in the city?'

'He has not. He has much to keep him busy.'

'A poor correspondent then. What of conversation, is he more adept in his mode of speech?'

'We have not been alone sufficiently to have any in depth conversations,' she was forced to admit.

'He has no longing to spend time alone with you then Miss Wrighton,' he whispered, his breath soft against her cheek, before he smiled, bowed respectfully, and prepared to take his leave.

'Enjoy your drive with Rossington this afternoon,' he added as an afterthought, loud enough for the gentlemen close by to hear and sigh with disappointment. If either Walborough or Rossington was after her, what chance did they have? Only she knew Walborough was playing some kind of game, paying her back for her impertinence in approaching him without first being introduced, implying by his presence, he might be interested in her when she knew he couldn't be.

She wished he'd stayed longer. She wished he hadn't come at all. He made her feel on edge, standing so close, leaning down to speak to her so no one else could hear. What was he doing other than ruining her chances with her prospective suitors and implying Owen had no affection for her, which had made her think perhaps she had exaggerated his interest in her? How did he know Owen had no longing to be on his own with her? Surely, he wasn't suggesting he did, when he'd given her the impression the evening before, he'd like to swat her away like an annoying insect.

'What did Walborough have to say?' her aunt asked eagerly when at last they were alone.

'He said he was passing by and decided to call in on you.'

'Fustian! He's never called on me once in his life. Nor would I expect him to. He's up to no good, my girl, and he won't offer for you, whatever he implies, unless it's a backhanded offer, so don't be taken in by his good looks and charm. His family wouldn't allow it. His mama and sisters will demand an Earl's daughter at the least. At a push they might settle a little lower, but a plain miss simply won't do.'

'Why not? Won't he have a say in his choice of wife?'

'His wife will also be his duchess,' she said with emphasis.

'The lady he marries must have the right pedigree and meet society's rigid requirements to be seen as a fitting mate for his Grace the Duke of Walborough.'

'He's a Duke!' How had she not realised?

'Of course, John Selwyn Charlton Becket, sixth Duke of Walborough, to be precise, twenty-six years old and still unmarried.'

'And Rossington?'

'Randal Ivor Rossington, Viscount Rossington, twenty-five years old, eldest son of the Marquess of Deane who is heir to the Duke of Aven, although little is seen of the Duke and Duchess nowadays. They have both lived a secluded life at Tremar House these past ten years.'

Since she'd had no acquaintance with either Walborough or Rossington before her arrival in London and no one had introduced her to them, how was she supposed to know they were at the top of the tree she was more like the roots of? How could she easily identify who was a viscount, who was an earl, who was a marquess and who was a duke, when they were frequently addressed by a single word - their surname or title?

If she'd grown up in their world, it would be second nature to her, but she had been in no position to recognise either the man or his title, when she'd first approached Walborough, in itself a social sin of mighty proportions, let alone holding him in an unasked-for conversation.

What now then was his intent? To amuse himself at her expense. To dally with her and then humiliate her with a swift rejection. She would have to devise a plan to outwit him. She might realistically have few social aspirations, but her father had made certain she was nobody's fool. He was an Earl's son after all, even if his father had rejected him, the day he'd married her mother.

Thaddeus Ignacious Wrighton, her beloved father, was the youngest son of Jeremiah Arthur Wylde Wrighton, the eighth Earl Wrighton. In defiance of his father's edict, he had married his sister Susannah's personal maid, losing all entitlement when he was ignominiously cast off from the family in disgrace. Oxford educated and newly ordained as a Clerk in Holy Orders, a timely and generous offer of the living in the rural parish of Stillford had kept them from disaster. Devotion to parish affairs, published works of religious or academic significance, careful investments, and the support of his loving wife, had over the years moved them to a position of greater security. Love and education had always been the mainstay of their family life, worldly aspirations, less so.

Due to the lasting estrangement, Bella had never met her paternal grandparents, both now deceased, nor the current Earl Wrighton, her father's eldest brother; nor her uncles George and Thomas, three of her aunts, numerous female cousins, and the heir, Hunter Harding Wrighton. Her father's only remaining connection to his family over the years had been through a regular correspondence with his sister Susannah, the eldest of the eighth Earl Wrighton's children, married at twenty-three to Viscount Bellingham, who had been her own mistress at the time of her brother's inauspicious marriage. She had refused to distance herself from him completely, although she'd kept their continued contact a secret from her father, for as long as she could.

Her husband Alexander Hyde, Lord Bellingham, a man of refinement and compassion, had seen fit to discreetly offer what help and support he could to his brother-in-law in those early years, when life was more difficult, such that he and Thaddeus had remained firm friends ever since. Bella would have been surprised to learn that her uncle had been the one to promote the idea of his wife sponsoring her for the season, feeling Susannah at sixty needed something meaningful to occupy her time, now their three boys were married and living independent lives.

They had left the nest rather spectacularly. Ralph the eldest to live in Scotland, Matthew, until very recently, away with Lord Wellington's army, and Jonathan in Italy. She had seven grandchildren, but she only had any regular acquaintance with three of them and that, very infrequently.

Susannah might have reached out to her brother after his marriage because she preferred him to any of her other siblings but allowing herself to approve his choice of wife was something else entirely. She had always considered her to be socially inferior and held her responsible for his dramatic fall from grace. Beauty such as hers drove men to make rash decisions, and she had expected him to weary of her in time. Now, she would have to admit her brother had never for one moment regretted his decision and was as much in love with his wife as he had ever been.

She had also been fortunate in her marriage to Bellingham who was devoted to her, and she to him, but such devotion to one another was uncommon. Affection and tolerance were the passionless aspirations of too many couples. She hoped now for better for her niece.

Bella donned her favourite carriage dress for her outing with Lord Rossington, deep blue velvet, decorated with military inspired cord appliqué on the bodice and sleeves, matched with a cheeky little hat crowning her curled brown hair. She couldn't deny the generosity of her aunt in kitting her out in the very latest fashion and providing her with a maid who knew just how to send her out into the world looking her best. She'd always had her own modish style, encouraged by her mother, but never the resources to have the extensive wardrobe she now possessed. Her clothes had been practical, suited to her country lifestyle. Granted she'd had pretty dresses for local balls and assemblies, but they were limited occurrences and less formal. Jollier sprung to mind. More gathering around and chatting and less waiting around, hopelessly hopeful of being noticed.

On this pleasant afternoon, she didn't have to wait around for Lord Rossington. He was punctual and she was ready in the hall to receive him when he knocked for admittance. As usual he looked every bit the wealthy man about town wearing a green superfine tailcoat, cut away high at the front to reveal a pink and white striped silk waistcoat and white form fitting kerseymere breeches tied and buttoned at the knees. His black leather top-boots with the buff-coloured cuff had been polished to a perfect shine. His high crowned hat he carried in one hand, hidden behind his back. Bella gave him a warm smile of welcome and curtsied to his formal bow. What lady would not be impressed by such an elegantly attired and charming escort.

'I've brought my greys,' he said cheerfully, as he helped her up into his curricle and nonchalantly placed his hat on his windswept dark hair.

'Are they newly acquired?' Bella asked with genuine interest. To her untutored eye, they looked magnificent beasts.

'Got them just last week. Uncle Frederick tipped me the wink. Perfectly matched. Envy of Walborough who didn't know they were available, having found out too late. Had to go out of town to visit his mother on one of her fool's errands. Hopping mad, I can tell you when he got back home. Likes to be seen with the best horses, you know.'

'Does he visit his mother often?'

'Not if he can help it. Harassed, he is, by the women in his family, his widowed mother and five older sisters, all except the eldest Esther, plaguing him to go to this ball or that house party to check out yet another potential bride. He don't like it above half. Won't get pushed into marriage against his better judgement.'

'And you? Do you have the same problem?'

'Thankfully, no. My family are pretty easy going. Parents were a love match. Don't believe in arranged marriages. My great grandparents were an example of the worst kind of arranged marriage, hardly spent any time together, used to cut up rough when they had to spend any time in the same building. The Duke and Duchess, my grandparents, fell in love and that's been the pattern ever since. Grandpa is seventy next year which will involve a large celebration at Tremar where they mainly live now. I have two healthy younger brothers too so there ain't any pressure on me to marry in a hurry.'

'I have three brothers, Roderick, Lawrence and William.'

'And sisters do you have any sisters?'

'No, do you?'

'Eliza and Annabelle. Eliza is engaged to Lord Ancaster and will marry at Christmas, but Annabelle is just sixteen, and papa is not eager for her to fully enter society yet.'

'Is she the youngest in the family?'

'No that would be Thomas, recently turned thirteen. Rather a keen scholar is Thomas, always got his nose in a book, spends the bulk of his day with his tutor.'

He sounded like Roderick had been as a boy, soaking up any knowledge he might acquire, rarely seen without a book in his hand, except papa had of necessity been his tutor.

'Walborough came to call earlier,' she told him. 'Have you any idea why?'

Rossington was surprised to hear of it and wondered what his friend was about.

'Did he ask for your company on an outing?'

'No. He didn't stay long. He said he was on his way to a list of appointments.'

'He does have a great many responsibilities which he takes seriously. When he's in town, he will have a diary full of engagements and as you might imagine, is selective as to where he chooses to spend his evenings.'

'Are you warning me away from him because I should tell you there is no need? I know my place in society and am comfortable with it. Stillford has more to offer me than might be imagined, honesty, integrity, fellowship, beautiful countryside, and tranquillity of mind. Here I feel unsettled and on edge. I don't know who I'm supposed to be, who I'm supposed to talk to. Aunt Susannah wants me to find a husband, but like yours, my parents love each other, and I would prefer not to marry if I cannot have a relationship like theirs.'

'I understand that sentiment. An arranged marriage would not do for me either. I might be wrong, but I would advise you to be yourself if you want to meet someone worthy of you. Can't spend your whole life pretending to be someone you're not. Now shall we see what these greys of mine can do and offer the gossips something to get their teeth into.'

After a breathless exciting ride, they slowed to join the procession of vehicles in the park where acquaintance, after acquaintance of Rossington's hailed them and he made the introductions. The Wrighton name was well known to them, but Miss Bella Wrighton was not, being something of an enigma they couldn't quite place. Of course, she must be someone, they assured themselves, if Rossington was squiring her about.

'Ah, here is Lady Goldsborough approaching on foot,' Rossington told her with genuine warmth in his voice. 'She might be someone you can befriend. Married to Lord Goldsborough last season, Augusta is a spirited lady, not afraid to voice her own opinions on matters she deems important, like the care of orphaned infants and schooling for the poor.'

Bella's eyes lit up and she directed a warm smile towards him.

'She sounds like a lady I would have much in common with. I was used to help out with the teaching of young children in the parish. I miss it and their eagerness to learn.'

'Might I ask what position your father holds in the parish?'

'He's the Vicar of St Jude's, but Aunt Susannah said I was to keep it a secret.'

'Why? Surely that is an honourable occupation, not to be held in any disdain.'

'No one in Stillford holds papa in disdain,' Bella said with assurance.

Further conversation on the subject was halted when Lady Goldsborough came close enough for introductions to be made. After some brief social exchanges, Bella found herself warmly invited to Lady Goldsborough's house on the upcoming Thursday afternoon.

Rossington realised a smiling, animated Miss Wrighton was something genuinely to be admired, but the spectre in the back of his mind became no clearer.

As he handed the reins to his groom to stable the horses and put the curricle away, he pondered on those few choice words of hers.

No one in Stillford holds papa in disdain.

So, who did?

When Walborough joined him for dinner later in the evening at White's, Rossington contemplated how long it would take him to bring Miss Wrighton's name into the conversation, convinced his friend was not as indifferent to her as he chose to imply.

Not long, it seemed once they were relaxed and enjoying a glass of the finest port.

'How went your afternoon drive?' he asked. 'Did you take the greys out to impress Miss Wrighton?'

'I took them out to give them a run and yes, Miss Wrighton was indeed impressed. She is not afraid of a turn of speed either. I introduced her to Lady Goldsborough in the park. It seems the prospect of helping orphans and being busy holds great appeal. You should allow yourself the privilege of seeing her when her eyes light up and her face is animated with a smile.'

He could have told Rossington he'd already had the privilege.

'Who is she though? I made discreet enquiries, but for all that there are a number of Wrighton females of a similar age, no one referred to a Miss Bella Wrighton.'

'Her papa is the Vicar of St Jude's at Stillford, which is a small parish in the gift of Miss Wrighton's uncle, Viscount Bellingham. Apparently, her aunt told her to keep it a secret, but why?'

'Do you sense a scandal or some kind of family falling out?' Walborough asked concerned.

'Possibly the latter. She did say no one in Stillford holds her father in disdain, so who, you might ask, does?'

'I cannot say. It seems improbable that Lord Bellingham would have countenanced his wife sponsoring a girl for the season if there was a family scandal involved, so it must be another issue.'

'Do we know anything about her mother?'

'More importantly, I think, do we know anything about her father? If Lady Bellingham, a Wrighton before her marriage, is Miss Bella Wrighton's aunt, doesn't that make her father, Lady Bellingham's brother?'

'It ought to, but if the family don't recognise him, can we be certain he's of legitimate birth? Maybe acknowledged by his father and given his name, but not welcomed into their midst.'

'It is a possibility,' Walborough had to agree, 'but would Lady Bellingham try to foist the daughter of an illegitimate brother on society?'

They both agreed it was unlikely. Bellingham was highly regarded amongst the ton. He would not wish to tarnish his reputation in such a way when alternative sources of help could more easily be offered.

'I have an idea how we might find out more about Miss Wrighton's father,' Walborough said thoughtfully. 'Did you get an invite to Hunter Wrighton's coming of age party?'

'I did, but I have no inclination to go. His cronies' views of how to behave around ladies, innocent or otherwise, are not those I aspire to, so I don't make a habit of associating with him or his friends.'

'Same here, but now I think we might consider attending, since he is the heir to the current Earl Wrighton, who is Lady Bellingham's brother. There is only a year between them in age, but whilst Lady Susannah was married young, he played the field until he was in his thirties. His children are consequently still in their twenties.'

'Hold on a minute,' Rossington said feeling a sense of panic. 'If we put in an appearance, the Countess will likely see us as prospective husbands for any number of awful Wrighton chits, four at least, two of them her daughters if I recall, and two her nieces.'

'We'll keep clear of them. Bound to be a card room,' Walborough said shrugging off Rossington's concerns.

'What if Lady Bellingham is there with Miss Bella?'

'Somehow, I think it highly unlikely, don't you? In the meantime, what do you have planned?'

'I'm going out of town for the whole of next week. Father wants me to go to Belverdon with him.'

'Are the repairs finished at last?' Walborough asked.

'It would seem so. Father is talking about putting the place up for sale. It's barely staffed these days and he hasn't been near for years. Something about Belverdon always unsettles him so he chooses not to go there if he can avoid it. He's only going now at mama's instigation as she feels I should have a say in whether the lodge is kept within the family or sold. I'm not certain I have a view either way, or would choose to contradict father's intentions, whatever they are.'

'Does Miss Wrighton know you will be unavailable to entertain her?'

'I have sent her a note. If you find yourself at the same functions, will you converse with her or ask her to dance?'

Walborough became very formal and disinclined to oblige his closest friend.

'I doubt I will be at the same functions. It would be unfair on my part to give any impression of a singular interest in her. She should be dancing with men who might be interested in marriage.'

'She isn't though. Is she?'

'Have you wondered why? You should ask yourself what young lady fresh from the country wouldn't jump at the chance of making the match of the season with a duke or a prospective duke. Was her approach to me merely artless or by clever design?'

Neither had occurred to Rossington.

'If you view her as a schemer, why then did you pay her a call the next morning?'

'She told you of that?'

'She mentioned it and wondered what your intent was.'

'I overheard a conversation by misfortune of being in the wrong place when it occurred. It seems she has a beau in Stillford. I merely went to point out how unlikely he was to propose, as she imagined he would, if he had made no contact with her since she left home.'

'Why John? What concern is it of yours, if as you say, you have no interest in advancing your acquaintance with her?'

'No concern at all,' he said sharply, whilst knowing it to be an outright lie.

He wasn't certain what had possessed him. He should have no interest whatsoever in Miss Bella Wrighton's marriage prospects. He had never, since becoming the Duke, paid a morning call to any debutante, lest her aspirational mother should think it a precursor to a marriage contract. What had Miss Wrighton's aunt made of his brief visit? Nothing good, he imagined. What worried him most was his concern for how Miss Wrighton might now view him, when he shouldn't care. She had no right to invade his thoughts. He would not seek her out again, even for Rossington's sake.

Chapter Three

Belverdon had never played a huge part in Rossington's life. The storm, ten years since, which had torn a large part of the roof off and damaged rooms on the western side of the lodge had meant it had been uninhabitable for years. Long before then the family's association with the place had dwindled to almost nothing.

The old Duke, his great grandpapa, had suffered a fall whilst riding to hounds and the deep wound to his leg, which had never fully healed, had put paid to the majority of his sporting activities. Belverdon had then begun to slowly drift off their horizon.

Neither his father nor his grandfather had any interest in shooting. Servants had mainly been dispersed elsewhere, some to Tremar and some to Deane Castle, or had simply departed of their own accord, to work elsewhere. The moor had been left to itself, to flourish or die without interference, according to the vagaries of the weather, and nature's cycle of life.

The roof had been repaired in a timely fashion making the building watertight once again, whilst the wind and water damaged rooms had been merely cleared, cleaned, and closed off, until two years ago, when a restoration programme had finally been set in motion. This work, entering its final stage of completion, was what they were now going to view.

Rossington was fortunate to have an affectionate relationship with all of his family yet the occasions when he could spend time alone with his father were few, and the more precious because of their infrequency. Travelling to Yorkshire together provided them with a quiet time of easy companionship, with questions asked and answered, advice given and received and the bond between father and son strengthened.

'I was born here,' the Marquess of Deane informed his son as they wandered through the restored rooms with only each other for company. 'It was a worrying time for my mother. She should never have left London being within a month of her confinement, but your great grandfather was not a reasonable man. A defiant stance to his strictures was pointless. Father's choice was to bring her with him or leave her behind with only the servants to care for her, which he would never have countenanced. It might have been different if her mother had still been alive. Smallpox earlier in the year had sadly left her parentless.

'After I was born, mama was ill, and my father feared for her life. He took her, on the doctor's advice, to Tremar where she could rest quietly with all the care she needed. Gradually she made an excellent recovery and was able to give father four more children in subsequent years without the anxiety attached to my birth. I doubt you will understand it, but my father was not the first to know he had a son.'

'How so?'

'His father failed to send anyone out onto the moor to inform him his wife had begun her birth pains. He sat through a prolonged dinner, assuming his wife was resting and dining in her room and was not told she was in labour until the early hours when the shooting party retired to bed. When he tried to see her, he was given the assurance that everything was being done for the Marchioness and he had no need to concern himself with women's matters.

'When he challenged his father's right to keep the news from him for so long, the Duke apparently coldly pointed out that had he known earlier, he would have become anxious and unsettled, spoiling the evening for their guests.

'He also kept him from my mother's side until well into the following day with one excuse or another, although perhaps it was reasonable for my mother to be allowed time to be made presentable, before receiving him.'

'A lot of pacing around the room then, in a state of unrelieved agitation.'

'Father readily recalls it being the worst time of his life as he had no real idea what was going on and no one would go against the Duke's orders to enlighten him. Around midday he was finally told he had a son and heir, news the Duke had been given a few minutes after midnight but kept to himself.

'When he did choose to pass on the news, he told father his wife and premature son might not survive the birthing, in a voice so matter of fact, papa said he was hard pressed not to hit him.'

'Why did he behave in such a cruel way? Did he have no concern for your parents' feelings?'

'He was a ruthless tyrant Randal and insisted he must always be the first to be informed of any news or events within the family, after which he would decide who should be told as he saw fit.

'He also made it known he would choose his grandson's name and he would decide the date of the christening with my parents having no say in the matter.'

'He named you Ivor after himself, adding your mother's maiden name of Reid.'

'The Reid name was important to him. Lady Elizabeth brought considerable wealth to the family, although she was not the woman he had chosen to be his son's bride.'

'Did he object to the match then?'

'It seems so, but my father stood his ground, and being of age made it plain he would marry Elizabeth or no one. There was no social impediment to them being married and they were deeply in love, so he raised no objection, but there was always a price to pay if you defied him. He didn't want his son making decisions for himself. He liked to control everyone around him. He was the strict patriarch, and everyone knew it. My father said giving him hours of unnecessary worry when I was born, was his way of making him pay for having a will of his own.'

'How cruel. You never liked him, did you? You don't like it here either? What makes you feel so uncomfortable?'

'I wish I knew Randal. I never liked him because he used to stare at me when I was a small boy, which unnerved me. As to this place, there has always been something strange here, something ethereal, mystical, not quite of this world or maybe just a long-forgotten memory from childhood, a memory I feel I should recall but can't.'

'You think there are ghosts?'

'Maybe a ghost in my mind, nothing tangible, nothing real.'

'Will you sell the lodge now it's back to a habitable state?'

'I don't know. Will you ride the moor with me before I decide? I'd like to be reminded of its beauty. The heather will still be blooming.'

They rode at a leisurely pace to the head of the moor and across towards the village of Sawley, passing empty and dishevelled cottages where once gamekeepers had lived a lonely life managing the moor, protecting the birds from predators, burning the heather to produce new growth, and witnessing the slaughter of the red grouse in the latter months of the year, when the old Duke invited groups of favoured guests to his shooting parties.

There had been no shooting parties at Belverdon in Rossington's lifetime. He was a keen sportsman, but shooting was not amongst his favoured pursuits nor that of his friends, neither was the popular pursuit of chasing a fox through the countryside with a pack of baying hounds.

Curricle racing, horse racing, pugilism and fencing were more likely to occupy his spare time, where his combatants had a reasonable sporting chance, as was the tender pursuit of feminine company, a practical exchange of money or gifts for a lady's favour.

Neither he nor Walborough kept a mistress, but might visit a favoured lady for a time, while the passion burned brightly. Inevitably, they would move on. They owed it to their family and their name to marry well and produce heirs.

Rossington wondered if Walborough had seen Bella whilst he was absent from the scene. She was lovely, engaging and the perfect foil for his friend who ought to keep his distance from her but probably wouldn't. It couldn't end well.

His Grace the Duke of Walborough would not, he thought, choose to marry a woman of such inferior social standing, however lovely she was, and he doubted Bella would accept any other kind of offer.

Even if that was the truth of the matter, his Grace was not at that particular moment of time concerned with anything other than holding Bella in his arms as he waltzed her around the dance floor at Lady Arnley's ball. Bella felt overwhelmed.

He was too strong, too close, a little pressure from his hand on her back and their bodies would touch briefly, breast to breast, thigh to thigh.

No wonder it was considered indecent and risqué.

When the dance ended, she felt hot and breathless. He led her towards the open casement window for a breath of fresh air. She opened her fan and tried to cool herself down.

'Don't go outside,' he warned, 'if you have a care for your reputation.'

'Have you no care for how others will have watched and questioned how closely you held me?'

'Should I beg your pardon?' he asked, his eyes on her flushed face.

'Have you a mind to?'

'No.'

'Is it your intention to ruin me?'

'Not my intention, but if we continue to be seen in each other's company, speculation will arise as to the nature of our relationship.'

'Then you should keep away from me as you have the choice of where to spend your evenings and I must go where my aunt dictates.'

'What if I go where my heart dictates?' he said, standing too close and looking more directly into her eyes.'

'Your heart might then be broken, since you know there is no future for us.'

'You have no room in your heart for me?' he asked speculatively.

'I must safeguard my heart from men of excess charm and experience. I am prepared to go home unmarried, but not compromised.'

'Then I will bid you goodnight fair lady and resign myself to not seeing you again.'

He left her standing by the doorway.

Of all the infuriating men! He'd set her body on fire and walked away cool as you like. He didn't spell it out in words, but the inference was there. He wanted her, but only on his own terms. There might be speculation as to their relationship, but no one would imagine it to be one likely to lead to a marriage proposal. When she'd professed herself unwilling to be compromised, his goodnight had been a final goodbye. She only wished her heart didn't haggle so much with her head.

Mr Rufus McAllister came to claim his dance, thankfully a more sedate series of movements allowing her heart rate to return to normal and her common sense to re-engage itself. Then perhaps not. It seemed she had agreed to go for a drive with Rufus and she still found it difficult to make sense of what he was saying. She only found out the following morning she had inadvertently given him permission to speak to her father.

'On what pretext Aunt Susannah?'

'About his prospects as a suitor for your hand. He is a Laird and finds you very comely, very comely indeed.'

'Oh no. What am I going to do?'

'I have no idea but here is a letter arrived for you.'

The script was not familiar, so she knew at once it was not from her parents or brothers.

'It's Owen's hand,' she told her aunt as she unfolded and scanned the page.

'Does he say he misses you?'

'No. He says he hopes I'm taking advantage of all the wonderful places I have the opportunity of visiting in the capital. He suggests the Royal Asylum for Female Orphans on Westminster Bridge Road where I might see how they are educated and supported, until they are old enough to enter service. I might look upon Bartholomew's Hospital which he deems from an illustration might be a building of note. I should visit the King's Mews to view the royal horses and watch the Horse Guards troop off as the band plays. Then he mentions Covent Garden Theatre, Drury Lane Theatre and the Picture Gallery in Pall Mall. Westminster Abbey has wonderful monuments; St Paul's Cathedral is very grand, and I must be sure to go to Exeter Exchange to see the collection of fine beasts.'

'Is there more?' her aunt asked growing bored.

'More in the same vein, I'm afraid.'

'Has he swallowed a guidebook do you think, or does he believe those of us who live here have no notion of what to enjoy and where to go for an outing? I perceive Rossington promised to take you out and about to view the sites when he returns from Yorkshire. He talked of putting together a party to Ranelagh or Vauxhall. Did he mention it?'

'He did and he intends to ask for your permission to take me to a masquerade.'

'Does he indeed? I might need to have a quiet word with him as to what constitutes a suitable outing.'

'I think I should like to attend one though aunt, for the experience, to see all the costumes and masks on display.'

Lady Bellingham was not convinced about the masquerade, but she was convinced Owen Lawton was something of a dull dog who might just as well have sent her a guidebook to peruse if he could not muster up the courage to write even the simplest of endearments, to a lady he professed to have an affection for. She would not encourage Bella in his direction and felt she had been timely in the removal of her niece from his vicinity.

Now she had the problem of Rufus McAllister. How was she going to manage him?

She need not have concerned herself.

If there was anything guaranteed to infuriate Walborough it was Rufus McAllister telling him at White's exclusive gentlemen's club on St James's Street that he had been granted permission to court Miss Bella Wrighton.

'I would be gratified Sir,' he said pompously, whilst failing to address him in the proper manner, 'if in future, you would keep your distance from her.'

Walborough would have been gratified, if no one had seen the need to sponsor the rough and ready Rufus McAllister, Laird or not, as a member of his club. The nerve of the man was astounding, his request, quite astonishing. Having previously decided to keep his distance from the enticing Miss Bella Wrighton, he now did an about turn and made up his mind to seek her out at the next available opportunity, thus spiking the Scotsman's guns.

Two nights later, he bowed before her at the ball Lady Granville was hosting to celebrate her daughter Iphigenia's engagement to Lord Shields and asked if she had any dances left.

'Good evening your Grace,' she said curtseying formally whilst trying to avoid giving him the impression she was pleased to see him, a challenging task when the very sight of him, looking so handsome and tailored to perfection, set her heart racing. 'I think I might be able to accommodate you. I have a waltz, the supper dance, or a cotillion.'

'Not the cotillion. Keep me the other two. Who else have you agreed to dance with?'

'Laird McAllister, Mr Charles Bishop, Viscount Chelston, and Mr Dante Culpepper, so far.'

'Laird McAllister! You did not offer him the waltz or the supper dance?' he asked sceptically, unsure of how she viewed the wealthy McAllister in terms of a suitable marriage partner.

'There are two waltzes, so I had to concede one to him. I told him the supper dance was already taken.'

'And how Miss Bella Wrighton were you going to explain the lack of a supper partner later?' he asked with a quizzical smile.

'I was hopeful of some handsome and charming gentlemen requesting a dance before supper arrived.'

'And did they?'

'It appears so, your Grace,' she informed him, too easily succumbing to his charm and offering him her warmest smile.

'Might I ask which waltz I should collect you for?' he said without taking his eyes from her face.

'The last one, your Grace.'

'Minx,' he said laughing as he walked away, knowing he would have to stay until the early hours if he was to claim his second dance.

He headed for the card room until the supper dance was announced. Torn between excitement and alarm, Bella watched him wend his way around the dance floor, ignoring all efforts to catch his attention. Had he come with the sole purpose of dancing with her then?

She was probably foolish to think so.

Chapter Four

Rossington, having been away for almost two weeks in the company of his esteemed father, arrived back in town in a timely fashion to attend the party at Belcourt, Earl Wrighton's country seat, an hour's drive from the capital. No expense appeared to have been spared in the lavish decoration of the ballroom, the open doorways of which led out into the garden where lamps lit secluded walkways, an invitation to lovers, or those with lecherous intent, of which Hunter Wrighton was one. It was his birthday after all and not all his guests could call themselves ladies. He had made certain to invite his latest amour, as well as actresses and cyprians to entertain his friends.

There was an excess of Wrightons on display; the Earl and his Countess, his brothers George and Thomas, his sisters in law, four nieces, his three daughters, and his son Hunter Harding Wrighton, Viscount Wylde.

If the Viscount was surprised to greet Walborough and Rossington in the receiving line, he made a good fist of not showing it, knowing they rarely moved in the same social circles.

His mother, on the other hand, felt it was quite a coup to have two such eligible gentlemen in her ballroom when her two unmarried daughters were also present and she grew visibly excited when Rossington asked Annelise to dance and Walborough chose Sybella, dressed in a froth of pale pink organza over deep rose silk, dark haired and the youngest of the four unmarried Wrighton ladies.

'How fortunate it is for your mama to be able to rely on gathering together so many family members in one place,' Walborough said to Lady Sybella Wrighton, for want of anything better to say, before the steps mercifully sent them in different directions.

'I don't find it fortunate at all to have to compete with Annalise, Charlotte and Ann Marie at every function I attend,' she said, leaning into him, and batting her eyelashes in a futile attempt to look coy. 'I suppose you will feel obligated to dance with them all.'

After another short parting of the ways, he continued the conversation.

'Not obligated to, no. What of your cousin Bella, is she here with your Aunt Susannah?'

'Bella and Aunt Susannah!' she spat with undisguised venom. 'One would hope not since they weren't invited, and had they the gall to appear, would have been speedily sent on their way.'

Definitely not a happy family then.

'Do I sense some family falling out?' he asked, with an air of not caring one way or the other, which invited Sybella to indulge him with a more detailed explanation, thereby, she thought, holding his interest for longer.

'It's an old scandal, your Grace,' she whispered, taking the advantage of being able to lean up close to him and entice him with a view of her generous breasts down her gaping bodice. 'Bella's father, Papa's youngest brother Thaddeus, is dead to us all since he chose to marry Aunt Susannah's maid. A servant! Can you imagine it? We have absolutely no communication with him, or his low-class wife, or his misbegotten offspring.

'Aunt Susannah, who used to be close with the family, seems to have completely taken leave of her senses as well, having been persuaded, obviously against her better judgement, to have Bella to stay for the season. Such nonsense when the bumpkin will easily be caught out for what she is. I hope if you come across her, your Grace, you will give her the cut direct and not be taken in by her coming behaviour, but then, what can you expect when her mother was a lowly servant in my aunt's household?'

'I'm rarely taken in by anyone Lady Sybella,' he said as if to reassure her. 'After all, true character is difficult to disguise.'

'I thought you would see it our way,' she stated enthusiastically. 'Do you know my brother well?'

'Not so well as perhaps I might, but my time is fully occupied with my many responsibilities, so often a brief raising of my hat in passing, is the most I can manage.'

'I hope then you will find time to pay a little attention to me when I come to town next week your Grace,' she simpered. 'Our start to the season has been delayed of necessity, by the preparations for this celebration.'

'I must commend whoever was in charge of creating the decorations. They are quite magnificent,' he said without committing himself to any further contact with her.

He bowed as the dance ended and led her back to her sisters, offering his hand for subsequent dances to Annelise, Charlotte and Ann Marie before moving swiftly away to find Rossington.

'I have it,' he said in hushed tones.

'So do I,' Rossington informed him. 'Lady Bellingham's youngest brother, Thaddeus Ignacious Wrighton, gifted with a fine brain, educated at Oxford, and ordained into the clergy, was destined for a lucrative living in one of his father's parishes, until he ruined himself socially by marrying well beneath the family's expectations for him.'

'He married his sister's maid,' Walborough added. 'Did you by any chance discover her maiden name or who her parents were?'

'Lady Ann-Marie said the father was a gamekeeper on the estate who was summarily dismissed when the marriage was revealed to have taken place and booted out of his home. At least that was her understanding of it. Funny ain't it how compassion and refinement is more about character than birth.'

'Are you speaking of Miss Bella Wrighton?'

'Wouldn't you rather spend time with her, than any of these Wrightons?'

'Most definitely. I'm not inclined to spend any more time here than is necessary for our purpose, but we will have to investigate her mother and her maternal grandparents.'

'Will we John?'

'Of course, or how will we discover what makes Bella superior in every way to her estranged relatives?'

Oh, my dear friend, you are in deep trouble, Rossington thought to himself and sighed. Wherever this led, they were in it now until the finish and what could come of it but unrequited love, broken hearts, and despair.

The scion of the house of Becket with its long history of service to the crown could not have a lady's maid for his mother-in-law, even if there might be the odd precedent for it. As for the Dukedom, he would not wish to tarnish its position of prestige amongst his peers, with a marriage unworthy of his lofty status.

Rossington vowed to find Bella a husband more suited to her station in life and keep Walborough well out of her vicinity.

Fate, however, would prove to have an entirely different view of future events.

As the evening progressed, the two friends mingled, danced, and relieved incautious gentlemen of substantial sums of money in the card room, prior to enjoying the generous supper provided. Later everyone gathered on the large terrace in the moonlight to watch the estate workers dance around a large bonfire, devour spit roasted sides of beef and imbibe too much of the free ale on offer, although in reality, little could be seen in the dark against the bright sparks from the bonfire.

When the midnight hour arrived, a shout went up and everyone raised their glasses to toast Hunter Harding Wrighton as he began his first day as an adult on his twenty first birthday. Military friends of his, in dress uniform, tossed him in the air - some thought too enthusiastically - accompanied by three raucous huzzahs, leaving him horribly dishevelled and moody. *No love lost there then.*

With the strong self-preservation instincts of the hunted, Walborough and Rossington made certain, as the hours ticked by, to resist any frolicking in the gardens with intoxicated females and Walborough turned down an unsolicited offer from Hunter's sister Melinda, married young to the much older Viscount Moreson, to meet him in the library for a pleasurable interlude, as she put it. Affairs with married ladies were one thing when the husband had become bored with his wife and uncaring of what she did or who she slept with. Cuckolding a man who loved his wife, however flighty she was, could only be seen as dishonourable and he would not comply. Not that he had any inclination to meet her anyway. Adultery in any disguise was something he hoped he would never aspire to.

Around three in the morning, in a timely escape from the advancing debauchery, they slipped away, disappearing into the night to find their coachman and groom patiently awaiting them.

'Good man, Oswald. Take us home,' Walborough urged.

'As you wish your Grace,' he answered as the groom closed the carriage door, sprang up onto the seat behind and indicated they could be on their way. The carriage lamps had been lit, but the first hint of dawn would not be too many hours away.

'Have you ought in place for tomorrow?' Rossington enquired, when in a timely fashion, the carriage came to a halt in sight of his front door.

'Nought but the demands of my correspondence, which even with Harry Keats filtering out what he can deal with without me, will keep me tied to my desk for most of the day.'

'Shall you come round for dinner then?'

'If it's not too early.'

Bella knew her place and had accepted the likelihood of both Walborough and Rossington not always being at the events she attended, but she would look for them at the more prestigious gatherings of the ton, to which she had been invited.

When they were away on business or chose to spend their evenings elsewhere, she found herself too often in the company of Rufus McAllister, who was becoming annoyingly persistent in his regard for her. At the end of a waltz, she found herself manoeuvred into a small, secluded alcove with him. He was a tall, solidly built Scotsman. She had little armour against his greater physical strength.

'I must speak with your father,' he said earnestly, breathing heavily over her. 'You will give me his direction.'

'On what matter must you speak with my father, Mr McAllister?'

'I wish us to be married,' he announced boldly.

Bella tried not to cringe at the prospect.

'I am sorry Mr McAllister, but I do not. That is, I do not wish us to be married, so there is no point in you seeking out my father.'

'Fathers know best,' he continued, determined to have his say. 'He will persuade you it's the right course to take.'

'He will not, I assure you,' Bella snapped back, resisting the desire to stamp her foot in her thinly soled slippers. 'He will take my feelings into consideration, and I don't have those kinds of feelings for you.'

'Feelings can grow, given time.'

'I don't think so.'

He pulled her closer to him and she resisted the best she could, pushing both hands against his solid chest.

'If you let me kiss you lass, I could prove you wrong.'

'Let go of me,' she cried, trying to push him away and turning her head to one side. 'I don't want you to kiss me.'

'You heard the lady,' Walborough said from behind her. 'Get out, or I'll see you ostracised from every ballroom in the land.'

'You think you could do that, do you?' he challenged, fronting up to Walborough with his brawny strength, but he'd let go of Bella and Walborough had placed her out of harm's way behind him.

'Do not let me see you hanging around her again,' he threatened. 'Miss Wrighton was clear enough in her intentions.'

McAllister strode off in a temper, whilst a frightened Bella stood in the shelter of Walborough's arms.

'Did he hurt you?'

'No. He tried to kiss me.'

'Any red-blooded man finding you alone would wish to kiss you, Miss Wrighton. You must be more circumspect. Now, find your aunt and stay by her side.'

Bella, thinking he had been about to kiss her as he stared at her lips, left him in a huff of disappointment. Wretched men. The ones she didn't want, wanted her, the one she did want was out of reach.

'I think I should go home aunt,' she said wearily.

'You have been having consistently late nights. Perhaps a more restful day tomorrow will have you feeling more the thing.'

'No, I mean I should go home to Mama and Papa. I don't belong here. All my future holds for me are shattered dreams.'

'Nonsense girl. You are only tired, and you have so much to look forward to, outings with Rossington, tea with Lady Goldsborough, Mrs Hepworth's soiree, our visit to Drury Lane.'

'And what of Walborough?'

'You know you can have no aspirations there. This is only the pre-season. When parliament sits, he will be invited to balls and parties where you can never go. His mother will come to town. He will have debutantes left right and centre thrown at him. He has to marry, and he has to marry well. You know I'm telling you the truth.'

'And Rossington?'

'Likewise.'

'In that case Aunt, if I stay, when the time comes, I must be too busy to see either of them.'

'That is the kind of fighting spirit I like my girl. It's surprising how men's attitudes change when faced with a little difficulty.'

Keeping busy had become easier for Bella in the weeks since she had become acquainted with the philanthropic Lady Augusta Goldsborough. She was now a regular at her Thursday afternoon meetings where lively discussions took place, and her views were listened to with interest. She was learning for herself at the same time, particularly about the setting up of Augusta's, *Families for Orphans* charity, which matched orphans with childless couples, or parents willing to accommodate another child within their existing family.

It was not without difficulties and a deal of time went into vetting families to ensure they were not looking for a child they could set to work at little cost to themselves. Unannounced visits were frequently made to ensure the child had all the new parents had signed up for and promised. In most cases this was true but occasionally they had concerns. If these concerns were worrying enough, the child would be returned to the orphanage until a new placement might be found.

One such small boy was Cuddy Willis, Cuddy being short for Cuthbert. He had dark curly hair, was sad and adorable, with the most compelling deep blue eyes Bella had ever seen on a boy. On her visits to the orphanage, she would seek him out, read to him or tell him stories and walk with him in the gardens, holding his small hand.

'Why didn't the lady like me, Miss Bella? I was a good boy and did everything she asked.'

'You did everything she asked Cuddy, but the lady didn't do what she promised. She didn't see you got your schooling. She didn't feed you regular meals and she made you work all day at tasks a servant should have been doing.'

'I didn't mind doing the work, but she still didn't like me.'

'I don't think she ever wanted to like you, which makes her a very foolish woman. She wanted a free servant. We don't mind our children keeping busy and helping out, but we didn't let you go to live with her to become a drudge. You were supposed to become part of a family.'

Sight of her husband since the initial interview had been sadly lacking which in itself was suspicious. Cuddy testified to having never seen him at the house and had been told he was away on business. The placement had ended abruptly.

'Lady Goldsborough believes you must be happy and have chances in life. If they are withheld from you, it is better you stay here where you are cared for and can learn to read and write and perhaps acquire a trade.'

'Couldn't I stay with you, Miss Bella? I wouldn't be any trouble and I can work hard.'

'I wish you could Cuddy, but we're only allowed to place the children with married couples.'

Then she had an idea.

'What would you think Cuddy, of living in the countryside? I think I might know of a couple who would love to have you as their little boy. It would mean quite a long journey to get there.'

'Don't they have their own little boy?'

'I'm afraid not. God hasn't granted them the blessing of a child of their own. You could go for a visit first and see if you would like to move to the country.'

'Can I come back if I don't like it?'

'Of course, you can. Do you want me to ask Lady Goldsborough if it might be arranged?'

'Yes please,' Cuddy said with the excitement and optimism of a small child about to go on a new adventure. He was five years old and had never known his parents. It was thought his soldier father had ruined a young girl and left her when she became pregnant. She'd died in childbirth and the baby boy had been left in a doorway to live or die as God saw fit when he was but a few days old. Cuddy had fortuitously let out a loud wail of hunger as Augusta Mallory, as she was then, and her friend Hannah Stuart, had walked past.

He wasn't the first orphan she'd saved, and he wouldn't be the last. Neither of his parent's names were known so he'd been baptised Cuthbert Willis, Cuthbert after the vicar and Willis, a surname picked at random.

'You can vouch for this couple Bella?' Augusta asked her later in the day, after she had suggested offering Cuddy to Adam Foster and his wife Jane.

'They are cousins on my mother's side. Good Christian country folk. They have lost three children in late pregnancy and despair of having a child of their own. I think Cuddy would be good for them and I know they'd be kind to him.'

'We'll make enquiries if you give the details to Mabel. Is it all right to mention your name as Cuddy's sponsor?'

'Of course. I wish I could keep him myself.'

'You'll have your own children. How old are you?'

'Nineteen.'

'There you are then, plenty of time.'

'At least if he goes to live with Adam and Jane, I'll be able to see him from time to time as they don't live too far away from my grandparents.'

'I'm so pleased Lord Rossington introduced you to me. You have an affinity for this work with the children's interests at heart. I know there are far too many orphans for all of them to receive the care we give, but more are off the streets now, and being properly fed and clothed, even if their prospects are to go into a life of servitude.'

'Cuddy will likely grow up with a love of horses. Adam works in Viscount Bellingham's stables at Oakley.'

'You have some interesting connections,' Augusta observed.

Chapter Five

Bella did have interesting connections, but she also had too many London society looked down upon, despite them being better people than some of the aristocrats she'd met. For her they were family and she loved them all. Even so, she was intelligent enough to understand what her father had given up, to spend his life with her mother. He didn't regret it. He'd made his choice. He'd lived quietly in the country where his wife was loved and respected, shelving any ambitions he'd had to rise to prominence in the church.

He'd seen in Sally Foster something unique, something he couldn't put into words beyond knowing she was extraordinary for one of the servant classes. She never struggled to learn anything; it came easy to her. She was gifted with more grace, more compassion and more elegance than any of the women he'd known in his social life as the youngest son of Earl Wrighton. Falling in love with her had been the easiest thing he'd ever done.

Persuading her to marry him had been much harder.

She'd known all too well what he'd have to give up, to be with her. She'd resisted, but he'd eventually worn her down with his words of love, and his honest devotion.

Bella had no real idea how much like her mother she was, blessed with the same inner strength, the same gift of learning easily, of making sound judgements, of being compassionate, of admiring people more for their worldly actions than their inherited birth right. She wanted what was best for everyone and was thwarted too often by her inability to provide it. Thwarted by a world where women's views were valued less than men's and options beyond marrying well and raising a family were almost unheard of.

At least she had Lady Augusta's discussion group where like-minded ladies could get heated over topics considered beyond their understanding.

Philanthropy and charity were ways forward but so much needed to be done and progress was painfully slow.

As Bella became more involved with Lady Goldsborough's ladies and their charitable works, so Rossington and Walborough seemed to distance themselves, only rarely appearing at events where she was present. Walborough, so she heard, had been seen at Almack's dancing with Lady Edith Moreton, the seventeen-year-old daughter of the Marquess of Ridsley, said to be the cream of the new debutantes. Rumours of a forthcoming engagement had abounded for weeks, but nothing was announced and the panic inside her subsided. Like her aunt had told her, Walborough could go anywhere he wanted to, including the exclusive ballroom at Almack's, where only those with vouchers could attend. Vouchers she was never likely to receive from the patronesses due to her parents' marriage.

Still, her social life was busy enough since Augusta Goldsborough had introduced her to new acquaintances within the world of the arts and music, and her Aunt Susannah had friends enough to keep them in demand for balls, parties, outings to Vauxhall, visits to museums and soirees, particularly Mrs Hepworth's soiree, where music of the highest standard might be heard and appreciated.

In early August, when she had seen little of him for over a week, Rossington invited her and her aunt to the Haymarket Theatre to see Oliver Goldsmith's play *She Stoops to Conquer*, which kept the audience 'laughingly amused' but made her wonder if he was once again warning her away from Walborough, implying some unlikely stooping on his friend's part would have to take place in order to secure her love, as if she wasn't aware of that already.

In the interval he told her Walborough was out of town visiting his estates and he didn't have a firm date for his arrival back in town. She told herself she didn't miss him and didn't care where he was. She didn't ask Lord Rossington for any more details. What was the point? He introduced her to David Carlisle, the second son of Viscount Trench, which perhaps had always been the point of the outing. You can't have Walborough, but here is someone you could have.

Unfortunately, love didn't work that way and as amiable and attentive as David Carlisle was, Bella couldn't see him as anything other than a good kind friend. However foolish she was, she had fallen in love with the Duke of Walborough and that was all there was to it.

Walborough, having taken himself out of harm's way, or so he thought, was glad to be homeward bound with only one more stop on his tour, at Hopston Chase, a rural country house built late in the reign of Elizabeth I, one of the substantial properties he'd inherited along with the Dukedom and where his thoroughbred racehorses were stabled. A chance glance from his carriage window to ascertain how close they were to their destination, revealed nothing of interest but a signpost with the words Stillford, one mile, burnt into the wooden upright. He tapped on the roof and the carriage drew to a halt. The groom climbed down from his perch amid the luggage and opened the door.

'What is it, your Grace?'

'Walk back about fifty yards and read the words on the signpost. Then come back here and tell me what you think they say.'

Jacob thought it was a strange instruction but wasn't about to argue, almost missing the sign, since it had nothing obvious to commend it. There was one short arm pointing along the road to Hopston, where they were headed, and a word burnt into the post, probably by a hot poker at the local forge.'

'I judge it to say Stillford, one mile and Hopston, five miles, your Grace.'

'Just as I thought. In that case, tomorrow I intend to explore Stillford.'

'Stillford, your Grace?' Jacob answered with undisguised astonishment. 'I don't think there is much to explore excepting a fine church.'

'Then I shall visit the fine church. Now let us be on our way.'

When Walborough was safely inside the house, the luggage unloaded and the horses and carriage dealt with, Oswald, the coachman and Jacob the groom went upstairs to the loft accommodation above the stables.

'I thought we were only here overnight and off home tomorrow after his meetings with the stable yard manager, the trainer and the steward,' Jacob recalled, as he stretched out on one of the low beds.

'Seems to me all this racketing about is just to escape all those eager women who want a piece of him.'

'You could be right. Don't repeat this but his valet, Mr Ryder, told me he is not only avoiding all the ladies he has no interest in, but also one he's fascinated with, but can't have.'

'Can't have? Why not, is she married?'

'Skeletons in her closet. Her family pedigree won't pass muster.'

'Fancy having everything he's got and not being able to have the woman he wants. Don't seem right, do it?'

'Seems to me he could have her if he made up his mind to it. Who'll gainsay him? Might just have to put up with nasty jealous people being rude about her for a while. Could go abroad to Italy or somewhere warm or live for a spell in the country until everyone has forgot her past.'

'You going to tell him that?'

'Course not. You don't get work like this any day of the week. It ain't no hardship being in his Grace's household. Can't say as I've ever before come across a fairer man to work for. Shall we wander over to the kitchen and see what cook has got for us. See if we can find out what the attraction of Stillford is?'

'I'm sure it ain't got one,' Oswald said dryly. 'If you came across it by chance, you'd no doubt drive through it before you realised you was there.'

'Waste of time then,' Jacob said ruefully.

Walborough didn't think so and woke the next morning to a heightened sense of anticipation. He was eager to go to Stillford but had no wish to actually appear to be so. He went out early to the stables to watch his young horses show their paces, breakfasted late, met with his steward, signed off the accounts, agreed to a new schedule of essential works, ate a light repast, and asked for his horse to be brought around at two o'clock.

His valet, William Ryder. who had travelled on ahead so everything was as it should be when the Duke arrived, dressed him for his outing to Stillford in clothes suitable for a country gentleman, quality but understated. The expensive cloth and perfect fit of his jacket, the complicated arrangement of his cravat, the stylish cut of his riding breeches and the mirror like shine on his boots hinted at a country gentleman of considerable wealth, if not some higher status. As for his stallion *Tulpar*, such a magnificent beast was a rare sight anywhere in the country, let alone in the backwater village of Stillford.

'You'll enjoy the ride and the fresh air if nothing else,' his valet said encouragingly as he gave him his hat and gloves.

'And the splendid church, Will, don't forget that.'

Will wasn't likely to forget, being privileged to have some understanding of the significance of Stillford to his employer, but he couldn't imagine what he might find there to give him any peace.

Stillford was a country village where country folks lived, nothing more.

Walborough easily recalled Rossington telling him about the living at St Jude's, Stillford, it being in the gift of Viscount Bellingham, yet his steward was unaware of Bellingham having any substantial amount of land nearby.

'Most of the Hyde family's land has been quietly sold to your own family over the years,' he was subsequently informed, a map being readily produced revealing the current boundaries of the estate.

'They still retain ownership of the village and farmland over to the east but you will travel within the boundaries of your own estate for all but the last ten minutes or so of your journey.'

He had not, in the past, paid much attention to the extremities of his estate or the countryside beyond, so

Stillford had never been on his horizon. His visits to Hopston Chase in recent years had all been short and efficient. He was telling the truth when he'd denied any knowledge of the place to Bella, but now he sought to discover if it held any attraction worth his time and effort.

It was a pleasant enough ride. As it had been explained to him, there wasn't anything obvious to indicate you had arrived at Stillford, no ford, still or otherwise, just a road leading to a raised market cross in the centre of a village green, a rickety wooden seat, cottages on four sides, and a drinking trough on a wayside verge, where he let his horse refresh himself.

A young boy ran out of one of the cottages.

'Are you looking for someone mister?' he asked with cheeky eagerness.

'I had a mind to visit the church,' Walborough informed him in a kindly fashion.

'It might be open if the vicar or his missus are inside. If not, you must needs go to his house for the key. It's that grand one behind the gates,' he said, pointing to a substantial building amongst the trees. 'Shall I watch your horse for you? You'll not have need of him in the village.'

'If you would then. He'll graze quite happily on the green if you don't alarm him. What's your name boy?'

'Arthur Briggs, sir.'

'Here Arthur is a shilling for your trouble. Take good care of him.'

Arthur promised he would and stared at the shilling as if it shone like gold. He thought he should provide more information for such a generous payment as a list of all his mother might now be able to buy for the family danced in his head, and all because for once his eagerness to be helpful had paid off.

'The church is up yonder past those cottages, mister - sir. If you be lucky, you might catch Mr Lawrence still there, practising the organ for the concert later.'

'Here at the church?'

'Yes. There is to be organ music, singing, readings and poems and a supper to follow, a proper supper with pies and the like,' Arthur announced with undisguised enthusiasm, his mind on the juicy meat pies he would eat later.

'Do I need a ticket?'

'Just turn up if you want to hear it. There be a collection after for the aid of the poorest folks in the village.'

He thought the concert might be an unexpected treat but realised it might also be very amateurish and offensive to his ear drums.

The church, a fine-looking building with a Norman square tower to which a clock had been added at some point, was a five-minute walk down a leafy lane. It stood surrounded by a churchyard, with both simple graves and impressively fine monuments, testament to there having been wealth in the village at some point in the past.

He heard the organ being played as he pushed open the heavy door to the porch, the inner, lighter door having been left ajar. He might have expected to see a modest chamber organ but here was a double manual pipe organ, being played he had to admit, with considerable skill.

'More air William,' the organist shouted, at which point a youth ran out from behind, claiming he was too fatigued to continue pumping the bellows.

'Might I be of help?' Walborough asked, astonishing both the organist and his assistant.

'Can you work the bellows?' Lawrence asked.

'Perhaps if you show me.'

'Who are you? I mean you're not local. Are you visiting in the area?'

'Passing through really, but I was advised to view the church before I moved on. John Becket,' he said by way of introducing himself.

'Lawrence Wrighton, and this is my brother William who is filling in for the Blacksmith who won't be available until this evening. Thank you for the offer but I won't impose on you. I've done enough practice, and I should let William get back home to his studies. I can show you around if you like.'

'If you don't mind, I'd appreciate your local knowledge. I'll probably miss anything important otherwise.'

Those who knew Lawrence well, were used to his fast-paced recollection of facts which he recited with barely a breath in between. He was only truly calm when he was playing the piano or the organ. Walborough listened with interest to his speedy potted history.

'The church is medieval in origin with additions through the centuries, side chapels, new aisles, the bell tower, the clock, and the porch you came through. The main door is arched with elaborate carving dating from the early ninth century. The floor was replaced last year due to it rotting and these new, less enclosed pews, were installed. The organ dates from around 1750 and is a two manual pipe organ with wind pumped by the bellows. I am the current organist and choirmaster, and my father is the vicar.

'The tombs in the Hyde Chapel, off the south aisle have some historical significance being of prominent figures from the fifteenth and sixteenth centuries, ancestors of Alexander Hyde, the current Viscount Bellingham. A project is underway to replace the plain glass in a number of the larger windows with stained glass depicting scenes of religious significance, although what those might be, has caused a great deal of discussion amongst the parishioners. The village of Stillford and the land for several miles around belong to the noble Hyde family, retained because of the significance of the church when most of the estate was sold in 1790 to fund enhancements to Oakley Park, including an extensive landscaped garden and internal renovations.'

Silence followed.

'I understand there is to be a concert this evening,' Walborough stated, to reignite the conversation.

'At six thirty. We start early as many of the families need to bring their children and if we finish at eight thirty, they can have some supper before taking them home to bed. Would you like to come?'

'I would if I can find somewhere to stable my horse.'

'Why don't you come back to the house with me? I'm sure mama and papa will be delighted to have a visitor. We don't get too many around here. You'll stay for dinner I expect. Mama will no doubt insist upon it.'

'Won't it put her out?'

'Nothing puts mama out. Not much anyway. Will you come?'

'Very well. I should like to hear you play. What little I heard was most pleasing to listen to.'

'Thank you. I hope you won't be disappointed. Where is your horse?'

'Young Arthur is watching it in the square.'

'It's called *The Round*. You don't need to tell me it's not round but square. A long time ago there used to be a round pond. Arthur will have taken diligent care of your horse. I'll ask him to take it to the stables for you.'

Arthur had indeed taken diligent care of his horse and was at that moment singing him a folk song about a keeper hunting a doe, the words of which might seem innocent to a child but sung by an adult with the right vocal inflection had a much bawdier meaning.

'He's young yet,' Lawrence said laughing. 'He'll learn in time.'

'Not too soon I would hope,' Walborough said equally amused. 'The lad is enterprising enough already and looks set to be in looks as he grows.'

Arthur led the calm, subdued horse away as Lawrence led Walborough towards the house, more of a mansion in truth, behind tall ornate gates.

'Papa,' Lawrence shouted in a loud agitated voice, immediately after opening the front door.

'Is it a disaster Lawrence or an emergency of some kind?' a male voice asked from a room beyond.

'No papa.'

'Then, calmly if you please, in the manner of a gentleman. Come through and tell me what it is you wish me to know.'

'Shall I wait here?' Walborough suggested.

'No come through to the library with me and I'll introduce you.'

'Papa this is Mr John Becket, who whilst visiting in the neighbourhood has come to see the church. He plans to stay for the concert. I've brought him to meet you. Mr Becket this is my papa, Mr Thaddeus Ignacious Wrighton, Vicar of St Jude's.'

Walborough shook hands with Mr Wrighton and apologised if he was disturbing his peace.

'My peace is regularly disturbed Mr Becket, and if by a visitor to the area then it will be a welcome disturbance. Lawrence, go and seek out your mama and tell her we have a guest. If she is in the garden, tell her she has time to set herself to rights and Lawrence, go steadily and quietly.'

'Yes papa,' he said and dashed off to a loud sigh from his father and a wry smile from Walborough.

'Have a seat, Mr Becket,' Thaddeus urged.

'John is fine.'

'John then. Welcome to Stillford Manor House. I hope my son has not harried you into coming here when you wish to be elsewhere.'

'I think it might be more that he has offered your hospitality without first ascertaining if you were prepared to give it.'

'You may rest assured on that score. My wife and I offer a welcome to all travellers in good Christian faith. As to the concert, is it truly your wish to attend?'

'It would be my pleasure. I heard your son play. I'd like to hear more. I believe him to be gifted musically.'

'He is. He gets it from his mama, although she was late in discovering her own talent. Lawrence, you will have noticed is not as other boys.

'He's as intelligent as his brothers but also impulsive and disinclined to observe many of the social niceties, not because he has no knowledge of them and their purpose but rather because they hold him up from what he wishes to do, which will always take precedence in his mind. I've kept him at home when I might have sent him to Oxford.

'He has grand passions – to travel to Germany and Austria, to play great organs in great cathedrals, to compose on a grander scale than he does at present, but I have reined him in for his own safety. In a matter of months, he will be of age. I have decisions to make, and I hope I will make them wisely.'

'Does he have a music tutor or mentor?'

'He hasn't had either for a while. He needs one more skilled than he is himself and I don't have the connections or resources to find him one.

'William, the reluctant bellows blower, is myself as a boy, studious - thinker, speaker, and philosopher. I don't want him to enter the church. I think he might use his natural speaking talents in Parliament. The usual bellows blower, I might add has gone to Hopston Chase, to shoe the Duke's fine horses.'

'Has he?' Walborough said wryly, feeling a little guilty.

The tea tray with what looked like generous slices of plum cake on a large plate was brought in then by a maid and set down on a side table.

'Thank you, Meg,' the lady of the house said as she entered the room with grace and charm, reminding him of Bella, but reminding him more startlingly of someone else entirely.

How astonishing. How could it be? He kept silent but his mind whirred with unanswerable questions. This mystery grew even more mysterious and made little sense to him.

He needed to speak to Rossington as soon as he got back to London. Until then he would enjoy the hospitality of gracious hosts.

Chapter Six

Thaddeus Ignacious Wrighton, introduced his beloved wife to his visitor.

'Mr John Becket, my lady wife, Sally.'

Walborough, who had risen from his seat as she entered the room, bowed respectfully.

'My pleasure, Mrs Wrighton. I hope my presence here will not upset your household routine.'

'We don't hold to rigid routines, Mr Becket. My husband might be called out at any time by a parishioner in need, so we are adaptable to events. Equally we do not have the pleasure of company so often that we are ever likely to tire of it. You are most welcome here and I hope you will be our guest for dinner. Are you in any hurry to depart on your travels?'

'I hope to hear tonight's concert before I head back to my lodging. I was privileged earlier to hear your son playing the organ.'

She smiled at his praise for her son's skill. A smile so reminiscent of Bella.

'Our music society is well rehearsed for this evening's event. We aim to please without overreaching ourselves. Lawrence will reveal his skill on the pianoforte as well as the organ. Our daughter Bella was used to duet with him or sing to his accompaniment, but she is gone to London with her aunt for an extended visit. I'm sorry you will not have the advantage of hearing her.'

So was he.

'I shall be content then with what has been rehearsed.'

Lawrence came back into the room and encouraged by his mother, gave out the cups of tea and offered the cake.

She whispered in his ear.

'I beg your pardon; would you like a plate?'

Lawrence duly handed the plates around, his active mind questioning at the same time.

'Are you staying at the Horse and Hounds in Hopston or maybe the Boar's Head out on the London Road?' he asked Walborough, after the delicious cake had been eaten with relish.

'At Hopston,' Walborough told him, which was the truth, if not quite the whole truth. 'I suppose you get supplies from Hopston, do you?' he said thoughtfully, as it was the nearest town to Stillford as far as he could tell.

'There and from the farm. Owen Lawton delivers milk and fresh produce daily. Not him personally,' Lawrence added, 'but his carters.'

'Is it a large farm?'

'Substantial – lots of cows and pigs, chickens, and plenty of crops. He's opened a dairy, a butcher's shop, and a bakery over beyond the vicarage. He's done well for himself has Owen.'

'Is there a large enough community to keep him in business?'

'He sends a lot of produce to the market in Hopston as well, which is where he makes most of his money,' Lawrence supplied, 'and …'

'Why don't you take Mr Becket for a stroll around the village?' his father suggested, 'maybe walk along the stream to the mill, work up an appetite before dinner.'

'Should you like to Mr Becket?' Lawrence asked and practically rushed him out of the door when he agreed he would.

They settled to a steady walking pace, going behind the church, past the vicarage where the curate and his family lived, past the previously mentioned premises of Owen Lawton and some other small shops deemed a necessity in any village, and around behind the forge where the Blacksmith provided several useful services besides shoeing horses. Adjacent to the footpath they trod, was the aforementioned, gently flowing stream, lined with light foliage. Beyond into the distance, Lawrence pointed out the large open fields, some with the ground ploughed, some fallow, which were farmed by Owen Lawton. Walborough thought again of Bella.

'Your father told me you would regularly duet with your sister.'

'I did until Aunt Susannah appeared one day and insisted Bella should go to London with her for the season. There was an almighty row and mama got upset, then papa got angry because mama was upset and then Bella refused to go. I don't know what was said in the end, but our aunt got her own way.'

'Do you miss her?'

'I don't see how you could not miss her. She's very pretty like mama, and clever, but won't let on about that too much. When she was at home, she was always busy about the house or the village. I had someone to talk to and she would keep me calm, sit at the piano with me and play something soothing. When people said I was strange, she said I was different, when they said I was useless, she said I was hugely gifted.

'When I get an idea for something, I feel tight inside, as if I must do it straight away or I'll burst, even if it's the middle of the night. When Bella was here, I could go to her room and wake her up and tell her about my idea and she would ask me questions until I either fell asleep or no longer felt the urgency. I want to do so much, experience so many things. I could be more peaceful if Bella were here.'

Walborough understood the sentiment all too well, except thoughts of Bella constantly disturbed his peace.

'You, say she is clever. In what way?'

'Papa has been our tutor from when we were small children and he taught us all the same. Like Roderick, my eldest brother, Bella has studied Latin and Greek and can also read French. She has a love of history and literature. We have in more recent years been encouraged to discover a fact, question its veracity and at times argue our own point of view, rather than accept with absolute faith what we are told. Bella now holds her own views on many important matters which are seen by some as radical, and others as reforming. She has studied the stars and is interested in science. She helped papa with organising the Sunday School. She would find topics to interest us all, in the magazines Aunt Susannah sent on, even if they were a few months out of date, instigating lively discussions, particularly when Roderick was still at home.'

'What about?'

'War, poverty, philosophy, literature, women's lives, orphans, crimes, punishments, and fashion of course. Ladies like fashion plates to admire.'

'Does she speak out on any of these weightier matters?'

'Not publicly, except on the proper provision of education and care of orphans which are considered safe enough topics for an educated woman. Privately she will have views on more contentious matters, but she will say there is little point in launching a boat you cannot sail.'

Wise in the current climate but sad in so many other ways.

How little you learnt of someone in the ballrooms of grand houses. He despised the superficiality of society, the parade of women with the right pedigree and nothing in the way of informed views beyond the latest fashion, mainly taught to plead ignorance and not sully their pretty heads with worldly matters. Bella had everything he wanted in a wife. Be dammed to society. If he could, he would find a way to make her his, and have those lively conversations with her. In the meantime, he sat down to dinner with the Wrighton family.

It was easy to see Thaddeus's heritage in the way he spoke, in the way he held himself and through his extensive knowledge of both religious and secular matters. He was neither stuffy nor overbearing, offering opinions of his own but willing to listen to what everyone else had to say including his wife and children, who found no censure when putting forward alternative viewpoints to his, backing up what Lawrence had told him earlier.

Whatever Sally Wrighton's heritage was, she had more presence and charm than many of the noble ladies of the ton. When he sat beside her at the concert in the church, she amused him with anecdotes about some of the participants and past disasters; when words had been forgotten, music was left at home and necessary improvisations made to cover these events, frequently proving to be hilarious, although too much laughter had to be restrained to avoid embarrassment and the disdain of the most pious parishioners.

'You don't mind then if some of the performances are less than perfect?'

'We have the concerts to entertain ourselves and draw the community together. Organising a programme, practising together, then performing, are all occasions on which young and old can mingle, as well as allowing our single sons and daughters to get to know each other better under the watchful eyes of their elders. Lawrence will excel and thrill us with his music, the rest, as you will see are not on the same level but not a hardship to listen to either.'

Later as they ate the homely supper, Walborough agreed with her judgement on the performances. Lawrence was the delight of everyone in the audience, perhaps not a virtuoso yet but quite exceptional for his age considering the limitations to his study of the instrument.

Mrs Wrighton, who had been remiss in telling him she was also a talented performer, sang a popular ballad about a valiant lady who follows her press-ganged young man to sea, rescues him when injured and returns home with him to marry and live happily ever after. She also joined in some mixed voice madrigals which were taxing musically and mainly on more mournful topics of unrequited love or tragic death, secular works being allowed providing they were not frivolous nor bawdy since they were gathered together in the Lord's house.

A fiddle player added a little light-heartedness to the proceedings when he played some country dance tunes and tapping feet could be heard around the church. Even the readings and poems were well received, if not always well expressed. There was much to be said for the happy state in which the community of Stillford and its environs went home to bed.

Walborough pondered on several matters as he rode home. Owen Lawton had introduced himself during the supper. Granted he was a canny businessman, but his enterprises concerned him, particularly those at Hopston village which came under the jurisdiction of his steward. He would be interested to know what terms had been set for Lawton to trade so freely in competition with his own farmers, and why he as the landowner, had hitherto been unaware of it.

Lawrence, he knew, needed help and guidance to move forward with his music but it would have to be done with care since he had no wish to offer offence to Bella's father nor appear to be interfering with his fine upbringing of his extraordinary boy. He would need to think about it and make some discreet enquiries.

Sally Wrighton was a mystery he would like to solve but what might he uncover of a hurtful nature to those she loved, those she cared for, those whose lives might be changed forever by actions carried forward without proper consideration?

He would not trample on her life of contentment nor destroy that of her husband and family but there was a truth waiting to be uncovered and he wanted to find it to ensure his own happiness.

Daniel Cunningham, a clerk in the service of Ivor Reid Rossington, The Most Honourable, the Marquess of Deane, having taken advice from both religious and legal gentlemen, was on his way to Yorkshire to complete a task of an unusual and sensitive nature. A task he had little appetite for but would carry out with all due care.

Above Belverdon Lodge, at the head of the moor was a walled area of hallowed ground, used to legally bury those who had lived, worked, and died in the isolated moorland cottages over the years. He was to go to the Church of the Blessed Virgin at Sawley and establish who had been buried at the site, record their names, and if possible establish their burial positions in the graveyard. He would make a note of how many bodies they would have to exhume and later reinter in the churchyard, besides ensuring all the necessary official steps had been taken for the exhumations to take place.

'You will supervise Daniel,' Lord Deane explained, 'but the church will supply you with experienced grave diggers. The site must be guarded at all times and any remains treated with respect. The bodies will most likely have been wrapped in wool rather than placed in a coffin. You will be searching for bones, not corpses.'

Even so, it seemed a gruesome task to Daniel. Out on a lonely moor, removing bodies from what should have been their final resting place.

'I would have this task completed efficiently and the site left with no indication that it had ever been a burial ground. There is a distinct possibility that the Belverdon Estate, intact, will be sold, if not immediately, within a few years. I must know the remains of our faithful workers will not be disturbed again in future years, or their graves desecrated.'

'I'll see it done, my Lord.'

As Daniel made his way to Yorkshire, Walborough left Hopston Chase to travel home to London, two days later than had been his original intention, having spent longer with his steward than was previously planned.

In the matter of Owen Lawton, he was relieved to find no deceitful practices. Fees were applied to the market stalls allocated to Lawton, which only enabled him to sell produce not already being supplied by farmers living and working on the Hopston Estate.

Where a need for extra supplies had been identified, Lawton had strict quotas and was subject to fixed pricing so he couldn't undercut his rivals. Walborough wanted this matter addressing immediately, pointing out his desire for his own farmers to be providing more efficiently for the villagers needs and making the profits.

Owen Lawton was not a crook but an enterprising man, wisely taking advantage of an available opportunity. Even so Walborough hadn't taken to him. He seemed more pleased with himself than he had a right to be. His intimation that he had an understanding with the daughter of the vicar, who would be home soon having found London society not to her liking, made him want to hit him. He'd almost hoped he could take some action against him in regard to the markets but there was nothing amiss to act upon.

When he thought about it, there was little chance Bella would have found Owen Lawton appealing if he had been some kind of a criminal. More than anything he hoped she no longer saw him in the role of a prospective husband.

Having met Bella's mother, he was eager to speak to Rossington as he felt he might have found the answer to his friend's imperfect understanding of who Bella reminded him of. It wasn't going to be an easy conversation, however carefully he stated the facts as he knew them. Causing Rossington or his family any heartache was never going to be his intention.

When he arrived home mid-afternoon, he immediately sent a footman round to Rossington's house to invite him to dinner. He came back some twenty minutes later with unwelcome news.

'Lord Rossington is not at home your Grace. He left yesterday for Tremar House and is not expected back until next week.'

'Bring me the invitations for this evening then, the ones I've replied to.'

'Very good your Grace.'

He looked through them and tried to imagine which parties or balls Lady Bellingham might have deemed suitable for Bella to attend. Mrs Hepworth's soiree seemed a reasonable possibility and was a regular event Lady Bellingham chose to patronise. Mrs Hepworth always provided a high-quality musical entertainment and if nothing else it would be a relaxing way to spend the evening.

Disappointingly, neither Lady Bellingham, nor Bella were there but a few of his regular acquaintances were, including Lord and Lady Goldsborough. He managed to have a few quiet words with Augusta when refreshments were served.

'I thought to find Lady Bellingham and Miss Wrighton here this evening,' he said trying to sound unconcerned because they weren't and failing miserably.

'They left last week to travel to Oakley where Lord Bellingham is currently in residence. Miss Wrighton has some cousins, I think, who are going to give a home to one of our orphans and they have taken him with them to see him settled.'

'I see. Is it usual for your orphans to travel so far from London to find a new home?'

'No, but Miss Wrighton felt this might be a situation where both parties would benefit. The young couple are eager to welcome a child into their home and Cuddy is a sweet natured boy who hopefully will find happiness with them.'

'Do you know when she plans to return?'

'I'm sorry I don't.'

Walborough rarely found himself at a loose end, but he had no particular wish to go to White's nor to sit gambling well into the early hours. Instead, he went home, selected a book from his extensive library, and sat down to read it with a large brandy to hand. Weary in the morning having read too long into the early hours, he made a leisurely start to the day, planning a peaceful afternoon going through matters needing his urgent attention, with his secretary, Harry Keats.

It wasn't long before their peace and concentration were disturbed.

'Your Grace; Lady Sophia, Lady Lydia and some young person, have called to see you,' Harry told him, passing on a message delivered a moment before by a footman at the library door.

'Can't you send them away? Tell them I have work to do.'

'It seems not. They are most insistent upon seeing you.'

They would be, wouldn't they. People with time to waste always seemed to think they had a right to waste yours.

Sophia and Lydia were his twin sisters, born eight years before him and a huge disappointment to his father when he realised once again that he had not been granted the son he desired.

'Surely if two were to come at once,' he'd complained, 'one of them might reasonably have been born a boy.'

He'd calmed down later apparently and apologised to his beloved wife who had laboured hard to deliver twin girls and eventually resigned himself to never having a son and heir. Seven barren years later, when it seemed unlikely his mother would ever carry another child, she had unexpectedly found herself to be enceinte again. His father had philosophically taken it for granted another daughter would arrive in timely fashion. To then be told his wife had been safely delivered of a strong and healthy boy had been a delight he had never dared to imagine.

They'd been close, father and son, kindred spirits, but a weak heart had taken his father at the age of sixty-five and at twenty-one, in deep mourning, he had laid him to rest in the family mausoleum at Bascombe Hall and become the sixth Duke of Walborough.

How he missed him, and how he wished his sisters miles away, one of them would have been bad enough, two of them, identical in looks and equally irritating, was too much to bear. He hardly dared to think who the young person was who accompanied them.

'Shall you meet them in the drawing room, your Grace?' his secretary enquired.

'No Harry, I will not do the sociable. Tell George to bring them in here and ask him to arrange refreshments, will you?'

'As you wish, your Grace.'

'Show them in, then excuse yourself for half an hour at which time you may return. We will continue where we left off. Imply a sense of urgency in matters relating to parliament and the King. You would think two women in their thirties, married with children would have enough to keep them occupied without the need to keep plaguing their only brother, as if I had nothing of importance to do.'

'I'm sorry to say your youngest sisters take little interest in matters beyond fashion and entertaining unlike ....'

'Do not say her name Harry. I would not put it past them to overhear.'

Lady Sophia, being the eldest, was the most outspoken of the two.

'This will not do Walborough,' she said indignantly, 'we should retire to the drawing room.'

'As you please Sophia but do not expect me to join you. You have interrupted my time with Mr Keats, and I must ask you to state your purpose in coming here and then leave us to complete our lengthy list of tasks.'

'We have brought Lady Selina Grant with us. We have taken this opportunity for you to make her acquaintance.'

'Have you,' he said standing and making a formal bow. 'Good afternoon, Lady Grant, a pleasure.'

Then he sat down again behind his desk.

'Come Walborough, you can spare us a little of your time,' Lady Lydia piped up. 'Selina is new to town. It would be of benefit to her to have become acquainted with you before she makes her debut.'

And no benefit to him, whatsoever.

'Be assured Lydia, if I am in attendance at any functions Lady Grant attends, I will make the effort to give the impression we are acquainted.'

When tea and cakes arrived, he invited his guests to take a seat in the chairs positioned around the fireplace, temporarily joining them. Sophia took charge of pouring the tea and Walborough indulged in polite discourse with the shy Lady Grant.

She hailed from Winchester, he discovered, the only daughter of Walter Henry Grant, Earl of Wessington. She was in London with her mama, one of Sophia's friends, who had fallen ill, and Sophia had seen it as her duty to take Lady Selina under her wing until her mama was better.

Walborough looked her over, without appearing too obvious. Whilst not beautiful, she was pleasing enough to look upon. She did not, however, have the power to stir his loins nor cause him to have lustful thoughts, nor even romantic ones.

She seemed, to him, little more than a child. He could hear in his mind, Rossington's earthy Uncle Frederick assessing Lady Grant as if she were a filly and dismissing her as not well proportioned for breeding. Walborough feared he would be right. He could be kind to her on occasion, but nothing would come of any interaction between them, whatever hopes his sisters harboured, he could not summon up any enthusiasm for women who looked as if they were so frail, they were likely to faint at any moment.

Harry came back in and bowed respectfully to Walborough and the ladies.

'I have no wish to rush your guests away, your Grace, but we have time restricted matters requiring your personal attention before the end of the day.'

His sisters reluctantly took the hint.

'I shall leave some intimation of where we might be in the evenings for you to seek us out,' Lady Sophia informed him as they reluctantly left.

'How kind of her,' Walborough said laughing. 'Now I know which events I would be wise to avoid.'

Chapter Seven

He could not, of course, avoid aspiring ladies of the ton entirely since he had already made clear his intention to attend a selection of the upcoming social functions to which he had invitations. He had promised to attend the Duchess of Claremont's ball and seeing Lady Grant without a partner, reluctantly offered to dance the cotillion with her.

At the precise moment when the music began, Rossington and Bella walked into the ballroom together, each of them avidly watching his progress in the dance for quite differing reasons. Rossington noted his friend's discomfort with amusement whilst Bella eyed Lady Grant with envy. As Walborough escorted Lady Grant off the dance floor, so Rossington escorted Bella onto it, frustrating his efforts to seek her out.

Rossington felt encouraged by the glare Walborough sent his way, which told him more of his friend's feelings than any questions he might have asked.

He also knew Walborough was wary of making his interest in Bella too obvious to his sisters. It would not do for them to suspect she was the one woman he wanted to share all his dances and all his evenings with.

After weeks of not seeing her, of telling himself she was not for him, of denying his inner most feelings, Walborough finally admitted to himself, resistance was pointless. He ached to hold Bella in his arms.

'Please tell me you don't have partners for all the dances,' he said hopefully when he finally had a chance to cross the room to where she stood with Rossington.

'Which would you like, your Grace?'

'What have you left?'

'Apart from the one Lord Rossington has, all of them. We have but recently arrived. Shall I save you the supper dance and a waltz, or have you promised them to another?'

'I have not so far promised any, Miss Wrighton. I have but danced a cotillion with Lady Grant for whom my sisters are hoping I will have a degree of admiration.'

Rossington chuckled beside Bella.

'Which of course you won't,' he said, knowing his friend's tastes when it came to feminine company.

Bella was not so sure, but she had little time to contemplate the matter either way as being in the presence of both Rossington and Walborough seemed to inspire more gentlemen to seek her company on the dance floor.

'I must talk to you,' Walborough said to his friend. 'I have an interesting tale to tell but we must be private.'

'Come to dinner then tomorrow evening. I shan't have any company besides you.'

'Very well. How went your visit to Tremar House? Are your grandparents well?'

'Fine, but grandpa has become obsessed with finding the old family Bible, which is so enormous, with brass corner plates and a heavy brass lock, you would imagine it being difficult to misplace. Even if they find it, will anyone recall what happened to the key after great grandpa died? Papa certainly has no idea where he might have kept it.'

'Have you any idea why he wants it?'

'An Oxford historian fellow wrote to him, asking to view it. Seems it might be a rare hand scribed and illuminated edition of considerable interest. Grandpa consequently told papa it was astonishing that no one knew of its whereabouts, and he has decreed that it must be located immediately and placed where it should be, in the library at Tremar.

'Papa has no idea where he might even begin to start looking for it, so I suppose I will have to instigate a search, as he is not inclined to. A lot of fuss, if you ask me, over a Bible none of us can read, it's so ancient.'

'You might have to pay another visit to Belverdon and go to Deane Castle at least.'

'I expect so. Deane Castle I can muster enthusiasm for. Belverdon, less so.'

'Have you talked to Miss Wrighton since she returned from Oakley?' Walborough asked him.

'Only briefly. She was eager to tell me about the boy Cuddy who has gone to live with relatives of hers on the estate. It looks to be the perfect match up, delighted new parents and a happy little boy.'

Rossington might have said more but Walborough grew agitated.

'Hold up a moment Randal, my sister is heading this way. Let's go to the card room until the supper dance is due.'

'You go, I'll join you after the next dance which I am fortunate enough to have with Miss Wrighton.'

'Mind you don't get dragged into dancing with Lady Grant.'

'Not my type. Too young and too fragile.'

Walborough had to admit Rossington's impression of Lady Selina Grant was spot on.

'Have you missed me?' Walborough asked Bella later in the evening as he led her towards the supper room.

'I have, but that is neither here, nor there, as I have no right to such emotions as well you know. You have been busy and so have I.'

'I have not been busy with Lady Grant, if that is what concerns you.'

It did but she would deny it. If his family pushed enough eligible women his way, one of them might be successful in gaining his interest. She didn't want him to know how anxious it made her. She aimed to sound matter of fact as they found a quiet corner to sit in.

'You have responsibilities. I understand how seriously you take them. I hope all is well with your estates.'

'It is, and is all well with you? Was your trip to Shropshire successful?'

'Far more so than I could have hoped for,' she told him, growing animated and failing to remember which topics were not considered appropriate for ladies to discuss in male company, in ballrooms, or anywhere else much for that matter.

'Cuddy Willis is the sweetest little boy. Adam's wife Jane has miscarried three babies late in the seventh month and the doctor fears she will never carry one to term. Cuddy has never known his own parents and spent his first five years in the orphanage. A recent, hopeful placement put him with a woman who promised much, but instead, worked him all hours of the day, hardly fed him and showed him no affection, so he was taken away from her and returned to the orphanage.

'Jane, in contrast, has decorated a bedroom for him with a bright coverlet she made herself and put toys in a box for him to play with. He could not believe the whole room was his and he would not have to fetch coal or wash floors. He cried with happiness when Jane showed him his new clothes and the little shelf with the books she would read to him at night, before he went to sleep. Later Adam took him to the stables to see the horses and introduced him to a placid pony he had searched out, so Cuddy can learn to ride.

'I promised him he could come back to London if he found the countryside not to his liking, but I cannot see him asking to when his little face was a picture of happiness as I left. I am so happy for them all.'

'And your grandparents, did you get time to spend with them?'

'I stayed with them. Aunt Susannah has not seen my uncle for over a month due to the many commitments he has, so I felt they should have some time alone together. He returned to town with us and now we will all see more of him.

'Grandmama and grandpapa are both well. They wanted to know all about my time in London, who I had met, where I have been.'

'Did you tell them about me?'

'I told them how I met you and what bad ton it was. They said I was just like mama when she was young, bold, and daring. I never thought I was being bold or daring when I walked up to you. I thought you were uncertain of what to do and maybe felt out of place like I did. How wrong I was.'

'Not entirely. I was uncertain, but only because Rossington was unusually late arriving. I was concerned lest something had happened to him.'

'You didn't really want to talk to me, did you?'

'Not at first, no, but something about you caught my interest.'

'What was it?'

'You'll want to slap my face if I tell you?'

'Were you looking down my bodice?'

'As I recall, there was little of you actually in the bodice, it was so shallow, and I am taller than you.'

'Aunt Susannah says it is the height of fashion to be so revealing.'

'I wasn't complaining,' he whispered, his warm breath touching her face. 'Come let us return to the ballroom. I will envy every man who dances with you until it is my turn to hold you in my arms and waltz you around the floor. Then we must part company. Will you let me take you driving tomorrow?'

'Yes, if it pleases you.'

'Walborough is taking you driving, not Rossington?' her aunt asked the next morning at breakfast.

'He asked me last night. I saw no reason to refuse.'

'You need have no fear for Bella, my dear. Walborough will behave with impeccable manners,' Bellingham said, glancing from behind his newspaper.

'But what are his intentions?' her aunt asked bemused.

'What are the intentions of any single honourable and titled gentleman but to court a lady with a view to marriage?'

'You can't think a marriage between Bella and Walborough is a possibility?'

'I see no impediment my dear. Bella is the granddaughter of an Earl after all and who could deny she has many other charms.'

Bella blushed at her uncle's kind words.

'Just remember to be very circumspect, my girl,' her aunt warned.

'Just remember to be yourself,' her uncle said, smiling warmly at her. 'Walborough is no fool.'

Walborough was certainly no fool, and neither was Rossington.

'You went to Stillford?'

'Not intentionally. I had no idea where it was. I was on my way to Hopston Chase, my last stop before returning home. Tired of the carriage and hoping we were not too far from our destination, I looked out of the window, and there in front of me was a signpost with Stillford written down the upright post. It seemed propitious.'

'So, you went to have a look around?'

'The church was recommended to me as a building worthy of a visit and indeed it was, not solely for the architecture, I might add. Young Lawrence Wrighton was playing the organ with considerable skill and there was to be a concert in the evening. I said I would enjoy hearing him play more, so Lawrence took me home to meet his parents.'

'And?'

'And……. Mrs Wrighton is the image of your grandmother in the portrait on the stairs at Deane Castle and Bella is very like her mother, which is no doubt why you felt you knew her from somewhere.'

'Mrs Sally Wrighton, who was Lady Bellingham's maid?'

'I know it makes no sense and I have no idea how she came to be Lady Bellingham's maid but there is something else.'

'You better tell me then.'

'I spent some time with the family and after a while whenever I looked at Mrs Wrighton, your father's image sprang to mind.'

'How could it John? Do not ask me to believe my grandpapa was unfaithful. I will not countenance it.'

'Neither will I,' John agreed. 'It makes no sense. Your papa was their first child and Mrs Wrighton must be about the same age as him. Your grandparents were virtually inseparable at the time, weren't they?'

'They still are. If she is not grandpa's by-blow. Who is she?'

'Therein, I think, lies a mystery. Of course, it could be entirely a coincidence, the similarity of looks,' Walborough suggested, but he was not inclined to think so. Mrs Sally Wrighton had mannerisms he recognised too.

'What is she like?'

'Beautiful without a doubt, gracious, kind, loving and now very well educated if she wasn't when Thaddeus married her.'

'Did you tell them who you are?'

'I said I was John Becket, which I am. Bella's father may have suspected I was the Duke staying at Hopston, but he kept it to himself if he did.'

'What is he like?'

'A wonderful man, educated, refined, loved I would say by his parishioners. I suspect he has been the main tutor to his whole family, his wife, and his children. They all feel the loss of Bella from their lives and never wanted her to leave Stillford. Lawrence, her middle brother sang her praises very easily. He has some kind of impulsive personality and told me she helped keep him calm. I would like to help Lawrence with his musical education, but I have no desire to give offence to his father. I don't suppose you know any wonderful organists do you who would love a very apt pupil?'

'Well, yes, in fact, I do, and I know where there is a very splendid organ imported from Germany. They replace them so often over there with something grander, purchasing one is not difficult if you know what you are looking for. It even has a pedal board which isn't common here.'

'A pedal board?'

'It might be called something else, but you play some notes with pedals beneath your feet. It has lots of stops too.'

'Stops?'

'Knobs you pull out and push in. Don't ask me to be technical. Listening to it is my thing, not playing it.'

'Where is it, at Tremar?'

'No, it's at Deane Castle, or rather in the church which if you recall is a building of substantial proportions.'

'So, we have a fine German organ and a brilliant organist at Deane Church. How do we connect them up with Lawrence Wrighton at Stillford?'

'I don't know. We'll need to ponder the possibilities.'

'There must be a way which won't appear contrived,' Walborough said thoughtfully.

'If there is, it must wait,' Rossington informed him. 'I can't be going off anywhere in the next few weeks. My mother is organising a splendid party for father's birthday.'

'When is his birthday?'

'The seventh of September. You'll come down won't you, to Tremar? We should invite Bella and the Bellinghams too.'

'Do you really want to set the cat among the pigeons?'

'Who is to say there is a cat?'

Daniel Cunningham was on his way back from Yorkshire. He had hoped this sombre task the Marquess had trusted him with would be straightforward. He had not, however, found it to be the case.

The death records for the parish of Sawley recorded nine burials at Belverhead in the walled graveyard. The tenth grave was unexpected, discovered by chance, the remains of a baby, the fragile bones almost missed except for the discovery of the small skull and the details of her short life carved neatly into a wooden cross, hard to read until it had been carefully cleaned when the words and numbers had become remarkably clear.

Sally Mary Foster 7 - 17 Sep. 1768.

Who then was Sally Mary Foster, also born on the seventh of September 1768 and baptised on the twenty-third of

October in the parish church almost six weeks later? Had her mother delivered twins with only one of them surviving?

Unlikely, the elderly retired vicar he'd been directed to had told him, as the baby's death would still have been recorded and they would have been given different names.

'I was here forty-six years ago, newly ordained. I remember William and Letty Foster and their daughter, a pretty fair-haired child like her mother. They left the district when Sally was about ten years old. Belverdon was rarely visited by the family then and most of the servants and estate workers had reluctantly left to find other work.'

'Do you know where the family went?'

'I'm sorry, I have no idea. William was a gamekeeper as I recall so I imagine he found work on another estate.'

'Just one more question if you don't mind.'

'Of course not.'

'Did anyone at that time report a lost child or believe their child to have been stolen?'

'No. The records will show there were only four baptisms in September and October that year and the other three were all boys. All the births were expected as all the women in question attended the church. Maybe not every week as the weather could be treacherous but often enough to be aware of them nearing their time. The Marchioness of Deane also gave birth to a son at Belverdon in early September, but he was baptised at Tremar House on their country estate.'

'So, we have a mystery.'

'It would seem so. I will say one thing if I may. William and Letty Foster were good devout Christians. I cannot imagine they would ever have behaved in an unchristian manner.'

'All I can do is put the facts before the Marquess. If he wishes me to investigate further, I will.'

Daniel's journey south should have taken no more than four days, but the devil seemed to be after him and he encountered delay after delay.

The first was a flooded river and a damaged bridge causing him to take a wide detour.

The second, an accident between the stagecoach and a private carriage up ahead of them, where shattered vehicles blocked the road and several battered passengers lay by the wayside requiring attention. They could not in all conscience do anything other than offer assistance, and ferry some of the passengers to safety and the care of a doctor at the next town, a mile down the road, but the day was gone with only three miles travelled.

The third was a jam of sheep wedged in the road who stubbornly refused to return through the gap in the hedge they had escaped from. Finding the farmer and clearing the road wasted most of another day. Thunder and lightning shortened another day's travelling time and so it went on.

'This is what you get when you go about lifting bones from their graves. Someone has put a curse on us,' Daniel's weary coachman, Peter Brock said, honestly believing it to be true.

'We will rest up for a day and begin again. We should be on better roads from now on, perhaps we can make up some lost time.'

'The Lord be praised if we do,' Peter said sceptically.

Of course, they did not. The carriage wheels slid on a wet muddy corner, and they landed in a ditch, thankfully unharmed but without transport for another three days.

Even the ever-practical Daniel, began to wonder if they were cursed.

Chapter Eight

Rossington having promised to take Bella to a masquerade had found the perfect occasion when his Uncle Frederick, thirty-eight, unmarried and a bit on the wild side, informed him and Walborough of his intention to hold such an event at his London mansion, by invitation only, in the week prior to Lord Deane's birthday bash. Frederick thought nought of stealing his elder brother's thunder. Getting an extra invitation for Bella proved easy enough and he went shopping to purchase a mask for her, both becoming and concealing, whilst Lady Bellingham lent her a silk domino, to disguise the classical robe she had carefully chosen for her to wear.

Whilst her aunt thought it just a little daring, Bella, on first seeing herself wearing it, was not certain it was appropriate for a vicar's daughter. It was made in a soft white semi-transparent fabric, held with gold clasps at her shoulders which draped loosely over her breasts to her waist where a tie drew it in and formed a full pleated skirt. No stays could be worn beneath it, and although the volume of the fabric was all concealing, Bella felt very naked wearing it.

Her aunt, seemingly unperturbed by the flimsiness of the dress, deemed the solution to be a narrow-shouldered cotton petticoat with a little support under her bosom which would provide the right degree of modesty without spoiling the fall of the Grecian gown. She had gold laced sandals for her feet and a little gold headdress for her hair which was styled for once with some of it falling softly onto her shoulders. Her domino was black, and her mask, gold with a spray of black feathers.

'Are you sure aunt?' Bella asked when she was ready and waiting for her carriage.

'Of course, child. You are better concealed than those ladies who damp themselves down to reveal all in the ballroom - brazen hussies the lot of them. A masquerade is for pleasure. Disguise offers opportunities to be a little bolder. Go and enjoy yourself. Rossington will take good care of you.'

Once she was amongst the other female guests, Bella realised her costume was not so daring after all. Some wore short tunics revealing stockinged legs below the knee, whilst provocative silk breeches left little to the imagination and Arabian pantaloons with a high degree of transparency, were plain scandalous.

Rossington, dressed as a Pirate, stayed with her for the first hour, enjoying dancing with her himself, or nodding approval to other gentlemen who approached her for the privilege. Rakes and chancers, he hinted away. She had no idea who they were behind their masks and found it strange to have an unknown man's hands around her waist pressing firmly against her soft flesh. Feeling she had been mauled once too often, she headed towards the terrace door to let the night air cool her down.

'Walk casually out through the door,' a familiar voice said from behind her, and she saw no reason not to. Walborough took hold of her hand and led her down the steps into the garden to where a fountain played with stone seats spaced at intervals around it. They were alone with the music from the ballroom in the background and the occasional dog barking somewhere in the distance. The sky was dark behind a curtain of stars but for once Bella's attention was not on the glittering night sky. Walborough held her in his arms. His lips were so near. She wanted him to kiss her.

'Do you remember when I told you any red-blooded man would want to be alone with you and hold you close and kiss your sweet lips?'

'I do and when I thought you were going to kiss me, you walked away,' she reminded him.

'I walked away from temptation because kissing you then and there would not have been appropriate, but I don't want to walk away now, so may I kiss you?'

She knew she was not being sensible. She knew it was just the starry night and a rare sense of freedom from the stifling rules society liked to enforce. She knew she was only adding to her own future heartache, but she wanted what she could have now, even if it was only fleeting.

'Yes please, your Grace,' she answered on a breathless whisper.

'John. My name is John, and might I call you Bella?'

'Yes please, John,' she said a little more firmly as she melted against him.

His lips were soft against hers, his hands warm on her back as he held her in his embrace, the softness of her body undisguised by the loose folds of her costume. Bella thought she might swoon as his lips moved tenderly over hers, setting off strange new feelings deep inside her. He drew her down onto a seat and sat her on his knee so their mouths were close, and he could kiss her until they were both breathless. His hands wandered unhindered, outlining her curves, cupping beneath her breasts, stroking her bare arms.

She ran her fingers through his hair and down his firm back towards his waist.

His intention was not to seduce her, although his body's reaction to her nearness and Bella's innocent response to his kisses gave the prospect greater appeal. Reluctantly he drew the sweet interlude to a close.

'Come,' he said helping her to stand. 'We will walk through the garden and talk. I know so little about you. I want to know you better.'

'What do you want to know?' she asked as they walked arm in arm along the footpath, a Greek goddess, and her bold Cavalier.

'Tell me about your childhood.'

'Where do you want me to start?'

'At the beginning,' he said encouragingly.

'As you must have suspected, I was born in the vicarage at Stillford, the third child and only daughter of my parents Thaddeus and Sally Wrighton. Roderick is my eldest brother, then Lawrence and after me came William. There was no school in the village. Papa gave us all lessons from when we were quite small and encouraged us to be inquisitive as we grew older and ask questions.

'Mama would join in too. She asked papa about the stars in the sky and why they moved, so he took us all out to see the night sky and taught us what he knew. Later he bought a telescope and told us of astronomers, of planets, of how the earth was round and rotated once a day on its axis and travelled around the sun over the course of a year; of those who denounced this knowledge and of accusations of heresy by the catholic church.

'He spoke of Galileo, who discovered so much, who was tried by the inquisition and forced to deny what he knew to be true because it contradicted the scriptures, having to live out the rest of his life under house arrest.

'Lawrence got terribly upset about the injustice of this. Then he was in a frenzy to know if the earth was a sphere in the sky like the full moon, how was it we never fell off? So, we learnt about Isaac Newton and apples falling from trees and even the lightest feather falling to the ground if there was no wind to keep it aloft and how if we should jump in the air we will always land back on the ground. Thus, our interest in science grew, though in truth we remain novices when there is so much more we might appreciate and understand.'

'You have been very fortunate Bella to have a father who is willing to see beyond the narrow teaching of the church and accept the conclusions of learned men of science. What else did he teach you?'

'We learnt about animals and plants, about history and literature, about mathematics. We each had our favourite subjects and papa did his best to teach us all we needed to know but sometimes a tutor would come, to teach Lawrence more about music, to teach us dance steps and to encourage us to draw and paint.'

She hesitated so he encouraged her to go on.

'About five years ago we moved into the Manor House, where mama has a large garden and grows fruit and vegetables, much of which she gives to the villagers. Before Roderick went to Oxford, the boys used to go into the woods and collect firewood for those unable to get out themselves.

'When I could I helped with the children in large families, reading to them or telling them stories. The community grew closer like a large family. It was a happy childhood. I was happy at Stillford. I never asked to leave. Aunt Susannah came and insisted I went to London with her. She wasn't kind to mama and made her cry. Papa was angry but I still had to say goodbye to all I knew and valued.'

'What about your grandparents, do you see them very often?'

'I only see mama's parents. They live in Shropshire now but were both born in Yorkshire. Grandpa's father and grandfather were gamekeepers for the Dukes of Aven at Belverdon Lodge, and he began his own working life there as an apprenticed gamekeeper which is where mama and two of my uncles were born, but now he's a steward.'

'Do you know why they left Yorkshire?'

'There were no prospects for advancement. Belverdon was closed up for longer periods every passing year and servants were let go until there was hardly anyone left. They ultimately made the decision to leave and moved to Lincolnshire when mama was ten. Grandpapa became Head Gamekeeper for Lord de Laurent at Follcliffe, and grandmama worked in the house. They stayed there until a few years after mama married papa, when they took up new positions at Oakley Park.'

'Isn't Oakley Park the seat of Lord Bellingham, your aunt's husband?'

'It is but Aunt Susannah rarely goes there, preferring Bel Manor as a retreat which is closer to London. She misses him when he goes to Shropshire but prefers the bustle of city life to the quiet of the countryside.'

'And what do you make of the city?'

'I'll allow that it has much to offer in the way of new experiences, some educational, some entertaining, some challenging.'

'What do you find challenging?'

'Rules and expectations. Marriages of convenience when neither party has more than a casual regard for the other, but status is seen to have been maintained or enhanced. The ruthless casting off of children for marrying against their parent's wishes. Society's condemning attitude towards those who appear to have married beneath them and an equal condemnation of those who seek to marry above themselves or for financial gain.'

'Does none of this apply in the countryside?'

'I suppose it does. Opportunities are fewer so might be grasped without love, to obtain a home and security.'

'If Owen had asked you to marry him, would you have accepted him?'

'Back then I might have, but now I wouldn't consider him.'

'Why Bella?'

'Because I know now that I have no strong feelings for him, and I doubt he had any for me.'

'And how do you know this?'

'Because I love you, John. I cannot help it.'

Bella's honest confession was music to his soul.

'My sweet Bella. I want you to know you have my heart and I intend for us to be together, but I have something I must try to resolve first, and I must resolve it without harm to good kind people. Even if I fail to resolve it, we will be married.'

'Will we? Aren't you supposed to ask me if I want to marry you first?' she said shyly, having no wish to be taken for granted.

He took her slender hand in his and held her gaze.

'Dearest Bella,' he said, his voice full of emotion. 'Will you do me the great honour of becoming my wife, assuming the consent of your papa and with the proviso that initially it will be our secret.'

Bella thought him sincere, yet her anxieties lingered.

'Will you be long in resolving whatever it is that troubles you?' she asked, uncertain as to why he felt there was a need for secrecy.

'I cannot say at this point, but I vow that if in six months' time, I have not found a resolution, we will be married regardless.'

'Your family will not approve of our marriage,' she warned him.

'I'm the head of my family. They have no right to disapprove. I will marry as I choose.'

'But I don't want to be held responsible for ruining your life.'

'How could you be, my love, when you will make me the happiest man alive?'

'Then yes, my dearest John, I will marry you. Kiss me some more.'

'Let us go deeper into the garden then, where we can be truly alone.'

A week after the masquerade, Hubert Lang, organist and choirmaster at Holy Trinity Church, Deane, received a strange letter from the young Viscount Rossington, grandson of his patron the Duke of Aven.

My dear Hubert,

I congratulate you on your recent approbation in respect of the recital you gave at Holy Trinity. I only wish I might have been there to hear it. Respect for my honoured parent took me to Belverdon instead and now I have a proposition for you which I hope you will find to your liking.

I wish for you to go to Stillford in the county of Hertfordshire where there is a fine church with a quality pipe organ. You will present yourself as a scholar preparing a treatise on the pipe organs to be found in country churches, noting their condition, the quality of sound they are capable of and their origin, if known. Under this guise you will ask for the opportunity to play the organ yourself and make certain to listen to the playing of Mr Lawrence Wrighton, the vicar's son. You should find an opportunity to speak of the wonderful organ at Deane and offer Lawrence the chance to visit you and play it, with a view to providing him with further tuition if you assess him as having a talent worth developing.

You should not underestimate the intelligence of his father and will have to appear very plausible to avoid giving any notion of contrivance in this matter. Sponsorship and financial assistance will be provided by his Grace the Duke of Walborough, but no hint of this is to be revealed.

I trust in your ability to achieve the Duke's ambition of providing Lawrence with a greater opportunity to excel than is currently available to him, without giving offence to, or worrying, his father. I will not prejudice your view of Lawrence, only tell you that you will appreciate his father's concern when you meet him.

Address all correspondence in regard to your progress in this matter and requests for remuneration of expenses to Mr Henry Keats at Walborough House, Mayfair, London. I enclose an initial bursary.

Sincerely yours
Rossington.

Hubert might have asked numerous questions in relation to the Duke's interest and Rossington's part in the plan, but he had no time for such concerns when he had a task in hand which required detailed planning. He took out his satchel from his student days, a bound notebook from his desk and began to make a list of known organs in churches he had visited in the past.

He outlined a route he might have followed which encompassed notable churches and their organs on the way to Stillford, such that his journey would be seen as authentic, and his process of assessment, easily apparent to an intelligent observer.

A week later, he set off, leaving his sub organist, Dieter Meyer, in charge of the church's music, handing over several scores for him to learn and practice, expecting him to be able to demonstrate his newly acquired skills when he returned. He would look upon this time away as a holiday and hoped this Lawrence Wrighton did have an exceptional talent.

Bella had always written regularly to her family and received plenty of correspondence in return. It was her habit to write freely and honestly, but now she felt she was hiding something of significant importance from them, and it was not in her nature to keep secrets.

John had proposed and she had accepted him as her future husband with a feeling of euphoria. It was hard to believe and hard to truly accept. Sometimes she was not certain if she did believe it. She was not seen out in his company with any greater frequency then before, neither could she dance more than two dances with him without questions being asked. Rossington remained her primary escort and her friend. When she was in John's company, she had to retain the formality between them and soak up the tender smiles he sent her way when no one was looking. She longed for more of his kisses and to experience the way he made her feel when she waltzed in his arms.

He still danced with other women, with other debutantes, with her cousin Sybella.

How could he when Sybella was determined to set others against her with cruel words about her mother? She felt cross and irritable.

She should have gone to Dorothy Wynter's coming out ball but knowing her cousins would be there, she chose to stay at home instead. Her aunt grew concerned and John sent round a message asking her to go driving with him.

'Why Sybella of all people?' Bella asked as he took her out into the countryside for a picnic, his tiger as their chaperone.
'If I dance with you and ignore her, she will be even more offensive. It's a few minutes of my time for your sake.'
'Should I be jealous of every lady you dance with, every lady you speak to?'
'Why not when it's the same for me? Do you imagine I want to see you in another man's arms, dancing the waltz? I even find myself jealous of Rossington who is the best friend a man could have.'
'Am I being foolish?'
'No. I have put you in a difficult position. Perhaps I should have delayed asking you to marry me, but I couldn't bear the thought of some other man winning your hand because you believed I was not available.'
'You should not be available. You know that. The Sybellas of this world will continue to spout their poison about my mother if we go through with this marriage.'
'Possibly, but as the Duchess of Walborough, you will be able to cut them dead and organise lavish balls and parties to which they will find themselves uninvited.'
'It is not in my nature to be offensive. I like to be kind and forgiving.'
'I know my sweet Bella which is why I love you. Have you heard from Shropshire how Cuddy goes on?'
The thoughtful change of subject lightened her mood.

'Jane wrote to tell me he is putting on weight, beginning to be more competent with his letters, loves his pony and likes to follow Adam around, although he has made strict rules for his safety in the vicinity of the horses.

'He's been collecting apples in the orchard and eggs from the chickens which Jane says makes him feel he is helping them, but he is also learning to play, and they are hoping to get him a puppy soon as well. She says their only concern is Cuddy's fear that someone will come and take him away.'

'That's not likely, is it?'

'No. Adam and Jane want to legally adopt him which Augusta is organising. He will soon have a mama and papa of his own and lots of other relatives to love him.'

'He's very lucky you thought of Adam and Jane.'

'I wanted to keep him myself, but I couldn't.'

'You have a fondness for children then?' John inferred from her words.

'I do. Shall we have lots when we're married?'

'If God grants us them,' he replied with more hope than certainty.

Bella thought of how you got them and went pink, which pleased John more than she knew.

He drew the horses to a halt.

'This place should do nicely for our picnic, a shady tree, soft grass and the sun shining upon us.'

He helped her down, unloaded the picnic basket and spread out a thick rug to sit on. The curricle moved off at a steady pace.

'Where is he going?' Bella asked concerned.

'He'll do some circuits with the horses and come back for us later. He won't go far. I need you to myself for a little while. I need to kiss you and tell you about Lord Deane's birthday bash.'

'Oh! I wonder which part I'll like best?' she teased.

'Food first and then you'll find out.'

Someone had gone to a great deal of trouble over their picnic. There were cold meats, pork pies, sandwiches cut into bite size squares filled with minced chicken in a lightly spiced sauce, cheese, and fresh fruit. There were tiny tartlets filled with almond paste and vanilla cream, flaky fruit filled puffs - blackberry and apple flavoured, sugar biscuits, plum cake, and sweet wine.

'This is delicious, John. Who prepared it for you?'

'My chef. He is greatly sought after, but promises never to leave me, probably because he is very well rewarded for his skills and is not currently overburdened with parties or balls.'

'Would he leave if he were?'

'I doubt it. He would likely relish the challenge.'

'No wonder Rossington likes to dine at your house.'

'Has he said so?'

'He remarked that you were an excellent host and the dinners put before him at your house were of the best.'

'I could say the same of him. He is a very comfortable friend and dinner companion to have, which reminds me of what I wished to speak to you about.

'Your aunt, uncle and yourself will have received an invitation to Tremar House to join in the celebrations for Lord Deane's birthday on the seventh.'

'On the seventh, but that is mama's birthday too. What a coincidence!'

'It would seem so. Now, the invitation is at Rossington's instigation and bearing in mind how often you have been seen together, there are those who will imagine an understanding exists between you. You will meet Rossington's parents and grandparents as well as his uncles and aunts. It might be a challenging time for you as I cannot openly proclaim you as mine, but I will be there and will hopefully have the opportunity to enjoy your company.'

John had no realistic idea how the evening would evolve. He just hoped Bella would not be hurt in any way.

Time was passing, so keeping an eye out for his curricle returning, he put all thoughts of Lord Deane's party from his mind, manoeuvred them into a relaxed and comfortable position and set about kissing his fair lady.

'Oh, how disappointing,' she said when the curricle drew near, and they had to leave the picnic site. John smiled to himself and thought of days in the future when he would not have to limit his caresses to her lips, and they could share more of love's delights.

Bella hoped it would be soon.

Chapter Nine

Lady Bellingham was in a frenzy of activity.

'Look sharp girl or we will never be away in time,' she ordered as what seemed like a mountain of clothes disappeared into a large dressing case.

Bella stood by bemused.

'I thought we were only staying one night at Tremar.'

'We are, but we must have stand by outfits, should a disaster occur when we are away from home, and travelling clothes for the next day. It would not do for us to travel shabbily.'

'Of course, not aunt. Is there anything I can do to help?'

'No, be off with you. Have some discourse with your uncle on a matter of import. He will enjoy a good argument.'

'I would, but he went out about an hour ago. I will find a book and read for a while.'

'Very well. I hope you understand the honour being bestowed on you and will be more restrained in your speech when being addressed by those of superior rank. Do not give me cause to regret inviting you to stay with me.'

'I'll do my best,' Bella promised.

It was all she could say when she had no idea at all what to expect as a guest of their hostess, Lady Deane.

'How old is Rossington's papa?' she asked.

'Six and forty, though why it should be of import to you I have no idea.'

'I was curious. Lord Deane shares the same birth date as mama and now you say he is the same age as well.'

'Is he? A coincidence no doubt shared by more than just your mama. You will not of course raise your mama's name or speak of your grandparents at the party since they were once servants to the Duke at Belverdon and below the notice of the guests at Tremar. Inviting you to accompany us is to my mind a folly, but we must make the best of it.'

Bella mused that her aunt would not appear quite so pleased with herself if she discovered they had only received an invitation to make it possible for her to attend. It would be unwise to suggest such a thing, so she kept quiet.

She had not thought of Tremar, nor imagined it in her mind. It was the seat of the Rossington family and the Dukes of Aven, set in a vast parkland within a vast estate. They entered the main gates in the carriage and Bella sought a glimpse of the house from the window.

'I can only see fields and woodland, Aunt. Where is the house?'

'Some distance yet. When it comes into view it will occupy all of your vision. You need have no fear of missing it.'

They eventually came around a turn in the road and there ahead of them, cradled on three sides by mixed woodland, stood the magnificent frontage of Tremar House.

She could never have imagined the impact of her first sight of the imposing architecture, nor have comprehended the activity in the open forecourt; as guests arrived, luggage was unloaded, and horses and carriages were driven away to the stables.

They were shown to their rooms and had several hours to occupy before the party was due to begin; hours the guests would pass being dressed by maidservant or valet, in the latest fashions from the most exclusive tailors and seamstresses. Bella had her hair styled upwards, à la grecque, entwined with blue ribbons and white lace to match her frock of cerulean blue silk, the bodice and hem similarly adorned. She had modest jewellery lent to her by her aunt and dainty slippers.

'It would not do to go down too early,' her aunt told her, but she caused no fuss when Rossington came to collect her less than fifteen minutes later.'

'John is here,' he whispered to her on the stairs. 'He will seek you out whenever he can.'

'This is so very grand. I feel entirely out of place.'

'You look wonderful. Be happy and enjoy yourself.'

Easy for Rossington to say, who had been born to all this grandeur. Here was his family and his family's close friends. Men and women who moved in the highest circles of society, dukes, earls, marquesses, and viscounts, with their wives, sons, and daughters. And who was she?

Walborough's intended? He made her feel as if he truly held her in great regard, yet he could not have considered the repercussions of a marriage between them. This was his milieu, where he was admired and looked up to, where he had unquestioned status, where hopeful women flirted with him outrageously and he smiled and bowed as he led them onto the dance floor.

Rossington danced with her, then led her to one of his friends who engaged her in conversation as they trod the steps of the cotillion. When the dance ended, he introduced her to another friend and so the evening went on. When at last John came to dance with her, she was feeling out of spirits.

'Am I an unwanted parcel to be passed from one gentleman to the next?'

'I have the supper dance with you.'

'Should I flirt with you then, flutter my eyelashes and simper behind my fan?'

'I hope you will not. Rossington has in mind a quiet place where we can enjoy our supper together.'

'Secluded, isn't that dangerous if we are found together?'

'Not secluded but a little apart.'

'Shall we share a waltz later?'

'I would feel myself privileged to have the opportunity. You have attracted interest with your dancing skill. Rossington may have coerced his friends into offering themselves as your dance partners, but none seemed to have found the task arduous. I think you will find yourself even more in demand after supper.'

She did and that was when the whispering began.

'Who is she? Is Rossington enamoured of her? What of Walborough's interest? Wrighton, did you say? Which branch? The youngest son. Wasn't he … cast out of the family? Bad ton. Are you certain? Not the place for her here. Rossington should know better than to foist her on us.'

Bella had no idea what they were whispering about behind hands and fans but guessed it was nothing good about her. Her evening was too much a contrast of highs and lows for her to say she genuinely enjoyed it.

In the morning, when she was dressed and ready to go down for breakfast, a footman knocked on her door and asked her to accompany him.

'Where to?' she asked concerned.

'If you will just follow me Miss.'

Who wanted to see her, Rossington, Walborough, her aunt and uncle? None of them it seemed.

She was shown instead into the presence of the Marquess of Deane, to whom she had curtsied the evening before.

At first, he stared at her, as if uncertain of what to say.

She waited for an inkling of why she had been brought to see him. Ominously, he did not offer her a seat and Bella began to worry.

'I understand you are Miss Bella Wrighton,' Lord Deane stated.

'I am, my Lord.'

'Why are you here?'

'I thought you asked to see me.'

'Why are you here at Tremar?' he clarified.

'I came with my aunt and uncle, Lord, and Lady Bellingham. Your son invited us to your birthday celebrations.'

'That much I understand but why did he invite you?'

'Shouldn't he have?'

'I'm not well acquainted with Bellingham; my wife is not well acquainted with his wife, and until today I had never heard of you. You lack the pedigree to be considered an equal partner for either my son or Walborough, so what are you to them?'

'I do have pedigree,' Bella pointed out. 'My grandfather was an Earl.'

'As you say but he never recognised you, did he? Who are your grandparents on your mother's side?'

'William and Letty Foster.'

'And where were they born?' he asked, failing to disguise the disrespectful sneer in his voice.

'Grandpa was born at Belverhead in a cottage high on the moor above Belverdon, the son of a gamekeeper in service to your family. Grandmama was born at Sawley, the daughter of a stone mason. My mama was born at the same moorland cottage on the seventh of September in the year of our Lord, one thousand seven hundred and sixty-eight. She was in the service of my aunt Lady Bellingham when she met and married my father, Thaddeus Ignacious Wrighton.'

'So, whose amour are you, my son's or Walborough's?'

Bella might have wanted to scream inside but externally she was calm and composed.

'I suppose you think you have the right to belittle me and be disrespectful to my family. I may not have titles nor wealth, but I have so much more than can be viewed in a few hours or even a few days.

'By amour, I assume you mean lover or kept woman. Quite an insult to my aunt and uncle who have cared for me since I came to London. More so to myself brought up in a vicar's household by a man of irrefutable integrity and a mother whose loving kindness is an example to all, and worse still, a poor view of both Rossington and Walborough who have been my friends when few others chose to be.'

'You find me at fault?' he said angrily.

'If there be fault, acknowledge it. You know nothing of me nor my family, yet you consider you have the right to label me – what exactly – a loose woman, an opportunist, a schemer? Bluestocking is more appropriate, or reformer, the latter of course not easily within the scope of a woman. I shall not cross your path again and if I must part company with Rossington, I will for his own sake.'

'What would it take for you to do so immediately?'

'I beg of you, do not add insult to injury. You have nothing I want, nor need.'

She turned then and left the room, running into Rossington down the corridor as tears flowed freely from her eyes and she tried to dab them away.

'What is it, Bella? What has happened?' he asked with genuine concern.

'You should ask your father. I must get ready to leave. Do you know where John is?'

'I was coming to find you to tell you some grave news. John's nephew, Lowen Trelawney has died suddenly, and he has left for Cornwall to offer support to his sister and brother-in-law. Lowen was eighteen and Trelawney's heir. He seems to have had some kind of brain fever and died within twenty-four hours of its onset. His family are devastated.

'He asked me to tell you he will write to you and return to London as soon as he can. In the meantime, he remains your devoted friend.'

For how long? she wondered, when the ton's malicious gossiping would continue to sully her reputation beyond repair, however unfairly.

'You have been a dear friend to me Randal, and I hope you will always look kindly on your memories of the times we have spent together. I must go now. You should speak to your father.'

'Bella, wait,' he called but she had scurried off down the corridor and did not look back.

Daniel Cunningham's belief in a curse having fallen upon him, increased when he finally arrived in London only to be told Lord Deane was at Tremar. If he had thought about it rather than setting out straight away to meet up with him there, he might have expected to receive the news upon arriving at Tremar that the Marquess had already left for his townhouse.

At Tremar, he also learned that Lord Rossington and his father had fallen out over a woman, and neither was prepared to apologise or offer further explanation, leading to raised voices and an eventual stalemate, the like of which had never been known before, between father and son.

Hardly surprising then, when Daniel did eventually get to report to his employer, his initial reception was not only tepid, but testy.

'You took your time,' Lord Deane accused.

'I do beg your pardon my Lord. I have had an accursed journey from Yorkshire with one mishap after another.'

'Do not plague me with your excuses. What do you have to report?'

'Something of a mystery, my Lord. Facts which will not add up.'

'Sit down then and tell me what you know.'

'I did all that you asked, discreetly and with due reverence to the remains, but the church records and the number of bodies buried did not correspond. We found the nine adult skeletons and set about removing the wall and turning the ground when we came across a small human skull, that of a baby in fact.'

'Infants are often born, but never live. The parents may have been too distraught to go and notify the vicar. Why make a mystery of it?'

'The infant lay buried with a wooden cross, on which someone had carved:

Sally Mary Foster 7-17 Sept 1768.

'Despite the years the cross had been in the ground it remained remarkably intact. The inscription could be clearly read when the dirt had been cleaned off. Who then, we asked ourselves, was Sally Mary Foster, also born on the seventh of September in the year of our Lord, 1768 and baptised on the twenty-third of October in the parish church, almost six weeks later?'

'Who were her parents?'

'William and Letty Foster. William Foster was a gamekeeper at Belverdon. His parents and grandparents were four of the bodies buried at Belverdon Head graveyard.'

'Did you question if Letty Foster had twin daughters?'

'According to the elderly vicar I was directed to, it was most unlikely. He said twins would each have had their own names and if one had died and been buried, the birth and death would have been recorded in the parish record on the same day as the surviving child was baptised. He would have then ridden up to the head of the moor, to say prayers over the grave. This service was never requested of him. The birth and death date of the child buried in the moorland grave, were never officially recorded.'

'Who then gave birth to the second child?'

'Nobody knows. There was never any reason to suspect there was a second child. The only other child born on that date in September was yourself, born at Belverdon.'

'Then the only person who knows the details of the birth of the Sally Mary Foster who survived, is the father who had her baptised.'

'It would seem so my Lord, but I have not been able to discover yet where he is living, assuming he still lives as he must be approaching seventy.'

'Would you believe I might have had the answer to this mystery in my own hands but a few days ago? A young friend of my son's was at Tremar, a young woman whose family background I questioned, whose mother was born on the same day as I was in the same year, whose parents were William and Letty Foster.'

'Then you know how to find him?'

'I might, if I can find the young lady and she will deign to speak to me.'

Not an easy task, he told himself, when he had no idea of where he might begin to look for her, let alone find her.

'I could follow this lead for you,' Daniel offered.

'No. I think not. This is something I must do myself. I thank you for your conscientious efforts on my behalf. Now perhaps we should have some refreshments and you can tell me of your perilous journey from Yorkshire.'

Daniel breathed a heavy sigh of relief and began his tale of misadventure.

Lord Deane went first to his son's house to try and re-establish their previously convivial relationship only to find him away from home.

'He's gone to Cornwall, my Lord, for the funeral of young Lowen Trelawney, to be of support to Walborough who is deeply cut up by his nephew's sudden demise.'

'A sad business Jameson, a very sad business indeed.'

Since it was obvious Walborough was also away, he made for Lord Bellingham's address, where he hoped he might be favourably received.

Only Lady Bellingham was at home, so he felt himself to be truly fortunate when she made him welcome and offered tea or something stronger. He accepted the tea.

'Bella ain't here if that's who you intended to see,' she told him, before he'd formulated a sentence he felt was appropriate in the circumstances.

'Do you know where she is?'

'Probably at Stillford, but I have no certain knowledge of the fact.'

'Couldn't you have persuaded her to stay?'

'I used up my powers of persuasion the first time I asked her to stay. She never wanted to come to London, never saw the point of having a season. I own I did it more for my own entertainment than for her benefit. She was ill prepared, like a fish out of water until she walked up to Walborough as bold as brass and began talking to him because she saw he was standing on his own and thought him in need of a friend. Rossington was amused by Walborough's reaction to Bella and seemed to take to her, and they became friends, nothing more. If there is a spark, it's between Bella and Walborough, but nought will come of that. It's even more inappropriate than Thaddeus marrying Sally Foster.'

'How did Thaddeus and Sally come to meet?'

'By a strange chance, I suppose. Sally had been in London since she was seventeen, in service as a maid. She was talented, could do wonderful hair and had a way of refreshing frocks to give them a second life. I poached her from Lady Spiers by asking her to be my exclusive maid, which she accepted. At the end of seventeen-eighty I had Jonathan, and I was slow to recover so Bellingham sent me to Bel Manor to recuperate and Sally went with me. Thaddeus came to visit whilst I was there and since I was often resting or sleeping, and Sally was not overtaxed with work, they would sit and talk.

'He was at Oxford then and at the end of the week he had to return to his studies. I suspect that was when they began to correspond with each other. I know he would seek her out in the holidays as soon as he came to stay with us here. Sally was beautiful with a sweet nature, the kind of woman men made fools of themselves over. Thaddeus fell heavily for her, proposing for the first time after he was ordained.

'She turned him down knowing his father would be wholly against such a marriage and his brilliant future would be in jeopardy, but he stayed steadfast to her and wore down her resistance. They were married quietly by an ordained friend of his from Oxford when Thaddeus was twenty-three and Sally, twenty-one.

'Father disowned him that day and said he never wanted to set eyes on him again, nor would he recognise his wife or any of his children even if he died and left them destitute. He sent men to throw them out of the vicarage with nothing but the clothes on their backs. Friends took them in, and Bellingham offered Thaddeus the Parish of Stillford with the intent of doing more for him when he could. It was Thaddeus who chose not to move from there. He was happy in his hideaway with the woman he loved and the children she bore him. He's still happy and as much in love with Sally now as he ever was, and she with him. He educated her over the years at her request and has always considered himself fortunate to have been able to live his life with her beside him. Bella is so much like her. I miss having her around.'

'So, you think I should go to Stillford to look for her.'

'If she cannot be found there at least they should know where she is. She writes to her parents regularly.'

'Just one more thing. You say Sally wrote to Thaddeus. Had she received some level of education as a child?'

'I suppose she must have. She could already read and write well when she came to work for me.'

The Marquess went away with a great deal to think about. The connection of Sally Foster to the Belverdon estate intrigued him. Then there was the Hunting Lodge itself where he'd always felt strange and uncomfortable. It bothered him still to walk around the empty rooms burdened by the mystical shadow on his mind, which was why, out of choice, he kept away.

He fervently hoped he might discover all he needed to know by finding and questioning Miss Bella Wrighton, though why she would wish to speak to him in the wake of their last meeting, he couldn't imagine.

Chapter Ten

Whilst Lord Deane was contemplating going in search of Bella, his son was trying to console his best friend, whose grief at the loss of his nephew was profound.

'Why him, Randal? He was such a good-natured boy, an excellent scholar, and a talented sportsman. Esther has worn herself out crying and Tristan is not much better and Madern is out in the fields somewhere bearing his grief alone.'

'I cannot think there is any why John. There are many ways we can die if we survive being born - accidents, sickness, fever, war, pestilence, injuries we can see, and diseases hidden inside the body, of which we have no understanding. I do not suppose it helps to hear the words of Ben Jonson, written upon the loss of his son.'

For why will man lament the state he should envy? To have so soon 'scap'd world's and flesh's rage. And if no other misery, yet age.

'Not really Randal, John confessed, though I appreciate the thought. He has been spared the misery of old age and he will never suffer to die a young man's death in agony on the battlefield but there was so much life in him. I will miss his happy smiling face, his energy and enthusiasm, his delight in winning a game, his thirst for knowledge, his tender emotions towards his family and his many acts of kindness. It seems cruel to lose him before he grew to be a man when he promised so much with his intellect. Yet perhaps it is some brief solace to know the unbearable pain he suffered in his head was at least of short duration. Should we find Madern? He will not easily get over losing the brother he idolised.'

In the early hours of the morning by the light of a single candle, John wrote to Bella, a sad emotional letter of grieving laced with a few loving words to tell her how much he was missing her. He had no idea she had left her aunt's house and knew nothing of her confrontation with Rossington's father. His compassionate friend had not wished to burden him further when his heart was already bruised. Neither could he have known when he sealed his letter for posting that Bella's movements would delay the receipt of it for over two weeks and upon receiving no reply, he grew increasingly concerned.

Bella had gone home to Stillford. It was the obvious place to be, where she might regain her equilibrium and not have fanciful thoughts of a loving marriage with her fair-haired charmer. It had been a dream and now she had woken from it. She did not doubt John had been sincere in his feelings but many a woman had been promised marriage, allowed her fiancé more intimacy than was wise and then been abandoned. They had not gone beyond kissing but the temptation had been there none the less. Love had blinded her to reality.

Perhaps Lord Deane had done her a favour, making her realise how impossible it was for her to become the Duchess of Walborough. The lowly beginnings of her beloved mother and grandparents would always be a barrier she could not get over. In the eyes of the ton, she was unworthy, not a fit mate for their most eligible bachelor, not when someone of their own still had a chance to win the coveted prize. Even so, she chose to spend as little time as possible with Owen who called regularly and was hard to avoid, no longer in her mind a man she could marry and grow old with. It was hard to accept how swiftly her life had changed. Nothing was the same as it was before. She had seen more and felt more.

Her eyes had been opened to the world beyond Stillford, to a more exciting world, to newfound pleasures and wider opportunities. Now the village seemed small and almost stifling. This new understanding, this awakening, she kept to herself. Implying she was dissatisfied with life would be hurtful to those she loved. She would not give her parents cause to worry over her, she would find her own way back to contentment.

Life grew a little more interesting when several days later, a traveller, of middling years, arrived in the village unexpectedly. He rode a horse of indifferent lineage and had little baggage save a satchel and a small carpet bag. His clothes were tidy and clean, leaning towards the clerical rather than the fashionable, simply styled and well fitted to his tall, rangy frame. Neither a poor, nor a rich man.

He rode into Stillford unsure if he had reached his destination. There was little to be seen on a damp misty day in September and he prayed he had not been sent on a fool's errand.

Young Arthur Briggs, longing for a little excitement, saw him first, with his perfect view of *The Round*, which looked square, and he was out of his house in a flash.

'Who ye be looking for Mister?' he asked, aiming to be helpful, and hopeful of some small recompense for his local knowledge, a farthing, or a halfpenny or maybe a whole penny if he was lucky.

The shining silver shilling, Mr Becket had given him, had been a rare reward, not many had a shilling to spare. He had liked Mr Becket and his splendid horse. Mr Becket had been a proper gent.

'It's more a question of what I'm looking for,' Hubert Lang stated firmly. 'I wish to make a study of the church organ for a treatise I'm working on.'

Arthur had no idea what a treatise was. It sounded important and if it were to do with the church organ, he thought it might be something to interest Mr Lawrence.

'You best go to the Manor House then,' he said as if for all the world he was the official local guide, which in some respects he was. 'That one behind the gates,' he added pointing in the direction of the substantial house ahead of him. The vicar lives there. Shall I watch your horse for you?'

'If you wouldn't mind,' he said as he fished out a penny from his pocket and gave it to Arthur.

Arthur loved horses and had a unique way with them. One day, when he was older, he wanted to work in a busy stable. He knew it was a wild dream. His prospects in Stillford were to labour all his life on the land, land he would never own.

The shilling he had earned from Mr Becket he'd given to his mother to fill the larder. She had wisely saved some of it and he would save his penny, adding it to his growing collection.

If the time came when his mother needed his pennies, he would give them to her but right now she still had his dad's and his brother's earnings and the leftover from the shilling, so his stack of pennies for his future, grew a little taller.

Hubert Lang, organist and choirmaster at Holy Trinity Church, Deane, a position of some considerable prestige, knocked on the door of Stillford Manor House with little idea of what to expect. He knew exactly what was expected of him. How he might achieve it depended on his reception and the opportunity to fully explain his purpose.

Bella opened the door since she was about to go out walking.

'How might I help you?' she asked looking him over with a curious gaze.

'My name is Hubert Lang. Might I first apologise for disturbing you and if it pleases you, be granted a moment to explain my purpose here.'

Bella, still curious, nodded her approval of his polite request.

'I am currently on a tour of the country, dedicating myself to the study of church organs, searching out the more notable ones and recording where they can be found and if possible, be heard or played.'

Bella's enthusiastic response was all he could have hoped for. She forgot about going out and instead invited Mr Lang inside. She then asked Eliza, the downstairs maid, to show their visitor into the drawing room, prior to asking cook to prepare refreshments for all the family. Peeping around the library door, where her father was occupied teaching Lawrence and William, she encouraged them to follow her to meet an unexpected guest. Once the introductions were made, she sought out her mother in the small parlour.

'Who is it?' her mother whispered.

'A Mr Hubert Lang, a scholar studying church organs for a treatise he is writing.'

'Good heavens! Lawrence will be in alt.'

Lawrence, on hearing who their visitor was and his purpose in Stillford; would, had he been left to his own devices, have ushered Mr Lang off to the church promptly. His father had other ideas.

'Stay in your seat Lawrence and let Mr Lang enjoy a cup of tea and a piece of cook's delicious plum cake. Have you come far, Mr Lang?'

'Not so far today. I have a room at the Horse and Hounds in Hopston. Do you know of it?'

'Most certainly, a good clean hostelry. Then you live further afield,' Thaddeus remarked, thoughtfully.

'I am most fortunate to have my time occupied as the Organist and Choirmaster at Holy Trinity Church, Deane. For the moment I am travelling for leisure and hoping to add to my treatise on the distribution of notable pipe organs within country churches.'

'Deane! You say,' Bella butted in. 'Is your church in any proximity to Deane Castle?'

'Why it is - within walking distance, originally the family church of the Dukes of Aven. Do you know of it?'

'I have not had the pleasure of visiting, but I have recently been living in London with my aunt and had some acquaintance with Viscount Rossington. He made mention of the castle on one social occasion.'

'The Viscount is a most charming young man with a considerable interest in music. We hold recitals and concerts in the church throughout the year and Lord Rossington will endeavour to attend. Our most recent one, he missed due to an office for his father.'

'He went to Belverdon, I think,' Bella commented.

'Yes, as I recall, he did.'

'Did Lord Rossington set you on this path of discovery?' Bella then asked, artlessly.

'No, although he does hold it to be a work of interest and is eager to know of my findings.'

'We have a fine organ,' Lawrence said unable to stay quiet any longer. 'It was built around 1750 at the request of Robert Hyde, eighth Viscount Bellingham, when the family lived here and worshipped at the church. The sound it produces is said to be more in the German style than French or Italian. Perhaps you will know if you hear it.'

'I should like to both hear it and play it. Do you have an assistant for the bellows?'

'That would be me,' William piped up, 'unless the Blacksmith is idle.'

'I think we can manage without the Blacksmith for today,' Thaddeus said firmly.

The men went on ahead leaving Bella and her mother to walk over later. Bella was not surprised to be questioned about Lord Rossington.

'Are you in love with him?' her mother asked, following an explanation as to how they had first met.

'Not him, no.'

'Who then? Do not think I'm too old to recognise the signs.'

'With John, the Duke of Walborough,' she admitted.

'John! You are on first name terms?'

'I am mama. He has asked me to marry him and I've said I will, given papa's blessing, but it is not freely known as yet and I worry he will regret it. In fact, I feel sure he'll regret it and I won't hold him to it if he does. What have I to offer a man who needs a duchess?'

'He doesn't need a duchess. He needs a loving wife and a mother for his children. He needs to be happy and so do you. When your father chose to marry me, he was the youngest son, totally reliant on his father for financial support. The Duke is the head of his family. He can make whatever choice he wants without loss of status or wealth and think of the options you'll have. He has numerous homes where you can live outside the capital. You can travel abroad if you wish, or you can brazen it out in London. The ton will gossip for a while but they never like to be ignored by one of their own or lose opportunities for patronage. He has churches under his discretion with good livings as well as boroughs where younger sons of his friends might begin a political career. He has influence, and he won't heed the tittle-tattle-mongers. He'll find a way to protect you.'

'He might not even come for me.'

'If he loves you, he will. Have faith.'

Bella was right out of faith. She had no idea where John was, and Rossington hadn't contacted her since the night of his father's party.

'Mama, I know Mr Lang denied it, but do you think Lord Rossington had anything to do with him coming here today?'

'No. Why should he have?'

'I don't know. It just seems too much of a coincidence.'

Not Rossington, but someone else, Sally Wrighton thought, remembering the handsome, engaging young man who'd visited a few weeks ago with the splendid horse and the unmistakable demeanour of the aristocracy, and unsurprisingly called John. He would have acted in good faith, she felt sure of it, yet her mind was not wholly confident. Her talented son would be heartbroken if he wasn't given an opportunity to impress a fellow organist with his playing.

Lawrence was standing in the church spellbound, as Mr Lang played a voluntary by Handel from one of the few printed scores Lawrence owned. The tutor he'd had for a few years had lent him sheets of music to copy and one of Roderick's friends had copied out the few Bach pieces he'd learned to play. He hadn't overburdened his father with the cost of expensive musical scores.

Everyone in Stillford knew Lawrence played well but Mr Lang with his wider experience and more effective use of the stops made the organ sound like a different instrument. Lawrence had taught himself so much from the books his papa had obtained for him, transferring his keyboard knowledge from the piano to the organ. To progress further he knew he needed to spend time with someone with the skill of Mr Hubert Lang.

'Play something for me Lawrence,' Hubert said to him. 'Anything you choose.'

He played the Bach Prelude and Fugue No 7 in E flat Major, the piece he was most familiar with, which had been carefully copied for him from Book 1 of the Well-Tempered Clavier, dated 1722 and annotated by Roderick's talented musical friend. Bach was not everyone's favourite, and scores were not easy to come by, but Lawrence liked the challenge of the fingering. The sound rang out and filled the church. Hubert Lang knew at once that his time had not been wasted. The vicar's son had enormous potential and he was thankful for it.

They discussed the organ. Hubert questioned the maker but not the date. It had been built with swell which had become more common around the 1740s. 1750 sounded right. The tall organ case used to house the instrument was attractive in itself with some carving and the remnants of gilding. The pipes were embossed and visually appealing.

The tonality was to Hubert Lang's ear, more in the German style, as Lawrence had suggested, which implied it might have been one of the many organs built by exiles returning from Germany after the civil war.

His suspicions as to the maker could not be verified by any obvious distinguishing plate so he could not name him for certain. The Hyde family might have a record somewhere of its purchase which would no doubt confirm the original builder's name.

Hubert addressed Thaddeus directly.

'I had expected to find the organ. I had not expected to find a young organist with such advanced skills for his age. I should like, if it would meet with your approval, for Lawrence to make a visit to Holy Trinity Church and have the opportunity to try his hand on a larger instrument. I think his potential should be explored further. Perhaps a visit escorted by a family member to begin with, then we might look at him becoming an organ scholar, if that would please you and he felt comfortable in his surroundings.'

'What of lodgings,' Sally Wrighton asked. 'Lawrence is not used to being alone.'

'I would take every care to see him comfortably settled. Lord Rossington might take an interest in him and grant him a scholarship if he was made aware of his talent. He does much to promote the education and welfare of promising musicians.'

'We shall see,' Thaddeus said, his mind contemplating the possibilities, 'although I am not against an initial visit. What would you think Bella of going to Deane with him?'

She wanted to say no, having no wish to come across the Marquess of Deane again. She said yes because Lawrence needed her, and Lawrence's talent was greater than her fear. She might, by chance, see Rossington again and then she could find out where John was and discover if he intended to honour his promise to her.

Hubert Lang made all the travel arrangements for them which led their parents to speculate further on who might be directing from behind the scenes. Argument proved pointless when it came to defraying the cost. Mr Lang insisted his invitation to Deane should not be a charge on them and Lawrence was so eager to go, they finally relented and allowed Mr Lang to have his way.

As they left the Manor House in one direction, the post boy approached on horseback from another with John's letter to Bella, forwarded by her uncle from London, in his bag.

Walborough and Rossington were conveyed to the doors of their respective London mansions, two weeks, and a day after they had left to travel to Tremar, a short journey in comparison to their long and tedious return from Cornwall. Desperate for a bath and a change of clothes, they agreed to meet later at White's where they could dine together and sit up late playing cards.

This plan was speedily cast into doubt, when dressed and refreshed they were each handed messages deemed to be of some urgency.

Rossington duly went round to visit his mother who had sent him an agitated missive which made no sense to him whatsoever. He took tea with her and listened to a tearful explanation.

'Deane has gone off chasing after a young woman. He met her at the party and offered her carte blanche which she refused. He then went looking for you and Walborough and finally spent an hour or more with Lady Bellingham. He left her house, came home, had a bag packed for him and set off to find her.'

'Mama who has told you this nonsense?' he asked, sitting down next to her, and taking her hand in his.

'It isn't nonsense and he never spoke to me about any of it because he wanted to keep it secret from me.'

'He will have kept it secret from you because he doesn't know yet what it is he should be telling you. Neither can I explain it to you as I don't have enough information to speak with any certainty either. I can assure you mama that he has no regard for Miss Bella Wrighton, the lady you are referring to. He spoke to her harshly, convinced she was a woman of dubious morals which is absurd when her father is a vicar.'

His mother's hopes lightened a little at his reassuring words.

'Why has he gone after her then?'

'He might consider she has some information of use to him, but to be honest I don't know. Perhaps he realises his mistake in speaking to her so harshly and wishes to apologise. I'm not up to date with all that is going on. I've been in Cornwall with Walborough.'

'Such sad news Randal. His family must be distraught.'

'They are mama, as is Walborough. Lowen was his eldest nephew and he loved him dearly. I must leave you shortly to meet up with him as he is very melancholy when left to himself. Please believe me when I tell you papa has eyes for no one but you, and Bella has eyes for only one man. What will come of it I can't say. If papa is away for a few days, do not make poor assumptions about his purpose. I might be away myself as well. The old family Bible appears to be missing which has put Grandpa in a fret. I must see if I can establish its whereabouts.'

'Why does he want it?'

'Someone has intimated it may be of great value, being exceedingly rare. He wants it returned to the library at Tremar.'

'It must be somewhere. I doubt it has been stolen. It needs two strong men to carry it.'

'You've seen it then?'

'Not for years, not since I was a young bride at Deane Castle. I never saw it open because your great grandpapa was the only one who knew where the key was kept, and he got angry if anyone asked to look at it. Said it was too fragile.'

'Something is not right, but what exactly that is, I can't fathom and must continue to look for answers.'

'Will you be away long, my darling boy?'

'I'm not certain. What I am certain of is papa's love for you. If he learns he has upset you, he will be angry with himself. It might not do either to give him the impression you doubted his fidelity. Go on as you usually do and when he comes home welcome him with love. I think you will find him willing to show his devotion.'

'Randal!'

He left her then, laughing at her mock outrage, and set off for White's where he hoped to find John.

A note from Lady Bellingham sent Walborough on a detour to discover what she felt was so urgent he must call on her at his earliest convenience.

'It's Bella. She's gone.'

'Gone where?'

'Home to Stillford. On the morning after Deane's party, he sent for her and caused her to be deeply unhappy. She slept a night and then announced she was going home on the stage. Thank goodness Bellingham was here for he took matters in hand. He failed to persuade her to stay but insisted she travel in one of our carriages with a maid and the funds to stay at suitable inns on the way. She has been gone a week now.'

'Then she will not have received my letter.'

'Bellingham has sent on any post which arrived for her so she must receive it in a timely fashion. Will you follow her?'

'Do you doubt it? Rossington wishes me to go to Deane Castle with him. We could go via Hopston Chase and see if we can find Bella at home.'

'There is something else you should be aware of. Deane came here looking for her. He wanted to know how you and his son came to meet Bella and how her father came to marry my maid. I told him what history I knew, and he left, but I think he might head for Stillford.'

'Then it's imperative that Rossington and I set off for Hopston immediately and offer Bella what assistance we can.'

Chapter Eleven

When the party from Stillford arrived safely at Deane, Bella and Lawrence were given a pleasant cottage to live in, facing onto a cobbled area known as The Yard, within sight of both the magnificent church and the imposing castle.

'I could have accommodated Lawrence in my house, Miss Wrighton,' Hubert explained the following morning after breakfast, 'but it would not do for a single lady such as yourself to be frequently exposed to the presence of several gentlemen scholars, so this cottage is a compromise for now and Anna can be trusted to take diligent care of you.

'Lawrence, I think will be eager to go over to the church without delay and I will take him with me now. You may accompany us if you wish or choose to acquaint yourself with the town.

'The castle, as you can see, dominates the view. You might ask Mrs Barker, the housekeeper for a tour since the family are not in residence. She will be most happy to show you around.'

'I should like that, Mr Lang, perhaps when I've have had a few days to settle. For now, I'll be content to familiarise myself with my new surroundings.'

When Lord Deane arrived home from his travels, having been absent for three days, no one in his household was entirely certain where he'd been.

Lady Deane still in bed with her breakfast tray, was taken by surprise when without any warning he walked into her room, looking less than his immaculate self.

'Ivor,' she cried with relief. 'Where have you been my love?'

'On the way to Stillford, until I began to question what I was about.'

'Stillford! Is that one of our properties?'

'No, Martha,' he said prowling around the room in an agitated state. 'You must allow me to explain. I have made a serious error of judgement. I have spoken unkindly to a young friend of Rossington's and must make amends for cruel words, rashly spoken. Now he and I are at odds with each other, which cannot continue, and there is another matter of concern, where I am beginning to think I must believe the unthinkable.'

Martha was grateful to discover she wasn't going to have to believe the unthinkable.

'Ivor, my love, have you had any sleep these last few days?' she asked, less anxious now, but still concerned by his confusing speech and behaviour.

'Not much. My mind has been in a whirl and my head aches.'

'Come to bed then and I will soothe away the pain. We can talk when you are less weary.'

'I'm travel stained Martha.'

'Shall I help you undress, or will you call your valet?'

'I have no desire to call my valet, my love.'

'Then what is your desire, dearest?'

'You Martha Wilhelmina. You have always been my one desire.'

'Then let us not delay. The morning is hastening on.'

Morning drifted into afternoon. Martha left him in her bed, sleeping peacefully, sure of his love, yet uncertain of what still troubled his mind.

She would not press him now for answers, knowing he would take her into his confidence when the time was right.

Visitors to the village of Stillford had never been so frequent. Arthur sat by the window looking out onto *The Round,* studiously copying letters from a book Mrs Wrighton had given his mam, hoping for some excitement when two horses and riders came into view.

He was out of the door faster than his mother could chide him for not concentrating on his lesson.

'Hello Mister, Sir Becket,' he said as the horses slowed to a stop. 'Can I mind your horse again?'

'Can you mind two?' Rossington asked him.

'I can. I'm good with horses,' Arthur replied confidently. 'There ain't nobody much here for you to meet with though. Miss Bella came home but now she's gone again with Mr Lawrence and the organ gent.'

Organ gent!

'Is the vicar at home?' Walborough asked.

'Only Mrs Wrighton. Vicar's gone to see Old Joe, who's dying. Joe's daughter came to fetch him this morning.'

'Who is the organ gent?' Walborough asked Arthur.

'A man came last week. Played the organ and listened to Mr Lawrence play it, then they went off in some carriages together, Miss Bella as well.'

'I see,' Walborough said, hoping Rossington knew what the lad was talking about.

They dismounted and handed the reins to Arthur who began to lead both horses towards the green and a rickety wooden seat which he loosely attached the reins to.

'Catch,' called Rossington, and flipped him a coin which Arthur caught easily.

'Sixpence! 'Tis too much for telling you little.'

'I don't have any pennies on me. You'll have to make do with that,' Rossington said wryly.

Arthur slipped it into his pocket with a smile and a thanks and began to sing a weirdly mesmerising song to the two grazing horses.

'If that lad were a bit older, I'd have him in my stables,' Rossington said, as they walked towards the Manor House.

'I found him first,' Walborough informed him, as he stepped ahead of Rossington to knock on the Manor House door.

'Is the lady of the house available to see us?' he asked the maid who stood before him.

'She's taken flowers from her garden for the church. Betty Blythe and George Wilson are to be married at ten o'clock, by the vicar of he gets back in time, if not by the curate. You can no doubt find her there.'

'We wouldn't wish to intrude.'

'Won't be no intruding. Anyone who wants to go and witness them saying their vows is welcome, but most will be at their work.'

'Tell me about the organ gent,' Walborough encouraged, as they walked towards the church.

'Hubert Lang. The organist I told you about from Deane Church. I charged him with coming to hear Lawrence play in the guise of a scholar writing a treatise on country church organs. He must have been impressed if he has already taken him to Deane. It hadn't occurred to me it that my efforts on Lawrence's behalf would take Bella out of your vicinity.'

'According to Lady Bellingham, your esteemed father was responsible for Bella leaving her aunt's house.'

'He took Bella to be free with her favours. Encouraging all my friends to dance with her, gave cause for some jealousy amongst the female guests and jealous tongues wag with lies. I hope you will not feel the need to call him out.'

'I should hope he will realise his error and apologise.'

'He's a good man, John. I doubt Bella left him in any doubt as to her true character, but the accusation obviously caused her some distress.'

'So, I understand from her aunt. I may have to have some speech with your papa but be assured I shall not challenge him in any way. He's been like a second father to me, these past years. I could not think of offering him any harm.'

Sally Wrighton was sitting in a front pew when the two gentlemen approached her, walking briskly down the aisle.

'Do you think it right or wrong to bring flowers inside the church, rather than strew them along the path?' she asked when they stood before her.

'God makes them grow,' Rossington proclaimed. 'Why should he object to their presence in his house?'

'Why indeed? What can I do for you gentlemen, or should I say my Lords?'

'Have you been speaking to Bella?' Walborough asked.

'I should hope I would have taken the time to speak with my only daughter when she was returned to me after a considerable absence. She spoke of you both kindly. She has hopes. She also expects them to come to nothing. She never aspired to be a bright star in society, yet the world is ever a brighter place when she is near.'

Both men would happily agree with her words, tenderly spoken.

'Where has she gone?' Walborough asked.

'To Deane Church, to keep Lawrence safe whilst he explores his world of music on a grander scale.'

'When did they leave?'

'Two days ago.'

'Then they should have arrived by now.'

Sally was happy with the informal nature of the conversation but she knew Thaddeus would expect more of her so she stood up and faced them.

'Would you, my lords, introduce yourselves formally to me, that I might know whom I'm addressing.'

'John Becket. More formally, John Selwyn Charlton Becket, Duke of Walborough,' Rossington said with a respectful bow to his friend.

'And Randal Ivor Rossington, Viscount Rossington,' Walborough said, returning the favour.

'Your Grace, my Lord,' she said curtseying respectfully, 'would you care to return to the house with me and take some refreshment?'

'We would be delighted, Mrs Wrighton, if you think there will be no impropriety with your husband from home.'

'William and one of the maids may sit with us. Did Arthur tell you where Thaddeus has gone?'

'He did. We left him watching the horses. How old is he?'

'Eight years and a few months. His father and brothers work for Owen Lawton, labouring, or carting produce around. Arthur wants to spend his life working with horses. He has a way with them, which you might have observed, but Owen has no opening for a slightly built child when he has grown men to do the work. His mother has kept him home to help her around the house and garden for now. She will have to find him some work soon.'

'Would she let him go to Hopston Chase to train as a groom?' Walborough asked her. 'It's but half an hour's ride away.'

'We can always ask her. His father might want a say too.'

'I'm sure an amicable agreement can be reached,' Rossington added reassuringly. 'I think young Arthur could also have something to say about it.'

Having been graciously invited to stay for dinner, by Mrs Wrighton, Walborough and Rossington took their horses around to the stable and left them in the capable hands of a groom. Arthur thought that was the last he'd see of the gents for the day, but he couldn't have been more wrong.

'What time does your dad get home, Arthur?' Walborough asked him when they found him sitting on the rickety seat, swinging his legs backwards and forwards.

'Did I do something wrong?'

'No, child. You did everything right. I have an idea, but I must speak with your mam and dad first.'

'To do with horses, is it?'

'Be patient and wait and see.'

Walborough and Rossington sat down to dine with the Wrighton's at five thirty. Thaddeus had returned to the house around an hour before with surprising news. Old Joe, thought to be eighty-five, had not died from the long sleep he'd fallen in to, but rallied, got up from his bed and told Thaddeus he was premature with his prayers.

Thaddeus remained cautious.

'I have unfortunately seen this happen before and death has still taken them within a day or so. If he lives a week, then he may live any number of days more. All we can say at the moment is his judgement day is delayed.'

Walborough still stinging from the sudden death of his nephew was interested in the views Thaddeus held as a Clerk in Holy Orders.

'Do you believe we are more blessed to die young and be spared the harsh rigours of life, or are the aged more blessed, given the opportunity to witness so much more?'

'A profound question John and not one easily answered. Life is a path we step onto the moment we are born. We begin our journey and know nothing of where it will lead us. We often lack any control over our destiny and decisions are made for us, both good and bad. Is how we respond to them, our will or God's will?

'When it comes to wars, plagues, famine, and illnesses of the body, does God decide who lives and who dies or are we born with physical weaknesses to which we will at some time succumb, and mental weaknesses which will cause us at times to make decisions, fatal to ourselves and others?'

'You believe we have some control then.'

'Probably little at the moment over the failure of our bodies to function well, but yes over decisions we are allowed to make. There are those thought to be wise and those thought to be foolish or incompetent. Did God endow us with this wisdom or the lack of it? Did he choose to give great opportunity to some and little to others?

'As to death, it awaits us all and wealth might shield us from some of its causes but not all. Labouring hard is not in itself a reason to die young. Idleness, dissipation, and recklessness can as easily shorten a life, and the hidden illnesses of the body are a danger to us all.

'The path we follow has many crossroads. We cannot say when our end will come, nor know of the cause, but must always endeavour to choose the right way for ourselves and others.'

'With compassion?' Rossington queried.

'Kindness and compassion are gifts we have at our disposal. We must use them wisely.'

'Will it be a kindness then, to offer young Arthur an opportunity he longs for, which will take him from the bosom of his family, or am I taking advantage of him for my own purposes?' Walborough asked.

'We must interact with each other. Arthur has his needs, you have yours. If a decision can be beneficial to both of you and consideration has been given to his continuing welfare, why should you fear it? Weigh it against what will likely happen to Arthur if you fail to offer him the choice.'

'He will labour in the fields and never achieve his aim.'

'Are you then God's instrument in both granting him his dearest wish and advancing his life's opportunities, albeit through a desire of your own?'

'I suppose so.' Walborough agreed.

'Then let us contemplate another case. Was it God's purpose to send my sister here with the intent of taking Bella from us and offering her a new life in London? A life she denied she wanted and was in truth, not well prepared for, in regard to the niceties of etiquette within the ton. Has it opened up her life to greater opportunity of happiness or greater disappointment? How my Lords do you figure in her potential happiness and, I might add, that of my son Lawrence?'

Walborough acknowledged that Thaddeus Wrighton had a razor-sharp mind. He felt the need to explain.

'In the case of Lawrence, I looked for a way to offer him patronage and opportunity without the risk of him being first encouraged and then rejected. I left it to Rossington to come up with an appropriate ploy since he has for some time endeavoured to provide music of the highest quality at Deane Church where he assured me the organist was of the best. His knowledge and the expertise of his organist was therefore hugely relevant. It was never our intention to sideline you. It was essential, however, to know Lawrence was good enough. You'd already intimated he needed more than you could provide. I hope you won't feel we overstepped the mark.'

'When you first came John, you were at Hopston briefly. Why did you come to Stillford?'

'Curiosity I suppose. I'd never heard of it until I met your daughter, despite its proximity to Hopston Chase. I saw the sign quite by chance. When I professed an interest in visiting the place, I was told it wasn't worth the effort, except for the fine church. I found the fine church and the fine organist and was privileged to meet Miss Wrighton's family.'

'Not all, as I'm sure you know, would say it's a privilege.'

'More fools them.'

'And our daughter, what are your intentions towards her?'

'They are entirely honourable Sir,' Rossington piped up. 'We both have the deepest respect for her.'

Walborough felt the need to be more specific.

'I would speak to you privately in that regard, if I may, before I leave?'

'After dinner then, in my library.'

Although Arthur's father and brothers came home at the usual time and dinner was near ready to be put out, Arthur felt like an entire day had passed since Mr Becket had spoken to him on the green. When he told his dad about Mr Becket coming to see him, he said not to talk nonsense and eat his dinner, lest the wind should blow him away one of these blustery days. Arthur took after his mother, inclined to be slender, but wiry and strong as well as being quick witted. His dad, also called Arthur Briggs was heavier built, as were his two older sons, Matthew, and Peter. He could just about read and write but was happy to leave paying their way and keeping the money straight, to his wife, who better understood numbers.

At seven in the evening, there was a knock at the door.

Mr Briggs opened it to find two very well-dressed gentlemen on his doorstep.

Walborough was the first to speak.

'May we take up a little of your time Mr Briggs, to have a word about young Arthur?'

'What's he been up to now?'

'Nothing save revealing how capable he is of working with horses and with that in mind, I should like to put a proposition to you.'

'You better come in then. Move over boys and let the gentlemen sit down.'

There was some scurrying about and eventually everyone was settled.

'Arthur knows me from my last visit as Mr John Becket. I am John Becket. I'm also the Duke of Walborough. I'm here with my friend, Lord Rossington staying at Hopston Chase, some half an hour's ride from here, which is where I keep my racehorses.

'For a horse to run fast in a race, he needs a small, light jockey. I'm offering Arthur the opportunity to come to Hopston and learn to ride, with the hope of him becoming a groom and perhaps a jockey in time.'

'Like an apprentice?' his mother asked.

'I prefer to call it training Mrs Briggs. My Head Groom will then have the opportunity to guide Arthur according to his ability to learn, and not hold him back unnecessarily. He will get some schooling and some remuneration, and I propose at the start he could be at Hopston Chase during the week and come home to be with you at the weekends.'

Mr Briggs was not entirely happy with the arrangements.

'How will he get there and back,' he asked, worried his son was going to be offered all he wanted in life only to have it swiftly snatched away again.

'We won't be having time to do it ourselves.'

'I understand the difficulties, Mr Briggs. Once Arthur has learned to ride, he can borrow a horse to get himself backwards and forwards. Until then someone can transport him in the dogcart.'

'He won't be given all the dirty jobs, will he?' Matthew, his eldest brother asked, being fond of Arthur and not wanting him to be taken advantage of.

'He must like all grooms learn to care for the horses, including grooming them and keeping the stables clean. He won't be bullied into doing anyone else's share of mucking out if that concerns you. I treat my servants fairly. If they don't do the same with others, I don't keep them on.'

'What do you think, Arthur?' Would you like to go and work with the horses at Hopston Chase?' his mother asked him, knowing it was a wonderful opportunity for him whilst knowing how badly she'd miss him around the house.

'Will you be alright without me mam?'

'I can't keep you beside me forever and it seems to me you are a very lucky boy to be offered work you've always wanted to do.'

'Since you are still young Arthur, I propose to put you under the care of Mrs Walton, my Housekeeper at Hopston Chase. If you should like to come over tomorrow with your mam, we can show you around. I can send someone to fetch you.'

It was agreed they would go in the morning. His dad would have liked to have gone too but there was no point asking Owen Lawton for time off unless you wanted it to become permanent.

Walborough and Rossington rode back later to Hopston Chase with much on their minds.

Chapter Twelve

'What would you have offered him Randal?'
'To train as a groom, but then I don't keep racehorses and I can see why you thought of him as a jockey. You expect him as he grows to stay the same slender build as his mother.'
'He might become a remarkable jockey with his natural affinity for horses.'
'We're staying a day longer then.'
'Do you mind?'
'I'd like to see Mrs Wrighton again, for something struck me over dinner.'
'She reminded you of your father.'
'Strange isn't it, the mannerisms, the way she talks. It makes no sense. It's like a puzzle with the last piece missing, or maybe several pieces.'

'If we've discounted grandpapa having been unfaithful to grandmama in those early days when they were so in love, could Sally Wrighton be an illegitimate child of my great grandfather. He was in his mid-forties when my father was born, still sexually active but he never kept a mistress, preferring variety. By rights he should have died a painful death of the pox. Instead, he fell off his horse and injured his leg which never healed right, and eventually festered and killed him. As to who he might have fathered a child on. I have no idea. No one ever mentioned him having sired any illegitimate children. Do we know if Bella's grandmother was ever in service at Belverdon? Might she have been seduced by the Duke?'

'I can't imagine it,' Rossington declared. 'Her grandfather was an apprenticed gamekeeper at Belverdon, but they lived out on the moor at Belverhead. I doubt he ever came into contact with the house servants. He would have reported directly to a more senior gamekeeper. Besides Bella said her grandmother was from Sawley, which is at the opposite side of the moor to Belverdon.'

'We must go at once to Deane Castle and find Bella. Then I think we must speak to her grandparents to see if they know of any mystery surrounding Sally Wrighton's birth.'

'We are treading in dangerous waters, John. Bella is not going to look kindly on either of us if she finds out what we are about. Why does it matter so much anyway?'

'It does and it doesn't. I intend to marry Bella but if there is some buried scandal, I want to know what it is so I can be sure it stays buried.'

'You've decided then. Is Bella willing to marry you?'

'She has said she will, but nothing has been announced and won't be until I have some understanding of why Sally Wrighton is so like your father in manner and the image of your grandmother in looks.'

'There has to be an explanation. We just have to work out what it is.'

'Without offending anyone.'

'What did you say to her father?'

'I asked him for permission to court his daughter with a view to marriage and quite naturally, he said yes.'

'Post for you Miss Wrighton. Seems as if it's been following you around.'

Bella took several letters with her to her room where she could open them without anyone observing her reaction. She thought one might be from John with addresses crossed out and others added such that it had been halfway round the country on its way to her.

It was melancholy, as was only to be expected when he had suffered a family tragedy. The tender words he'd written before he'd signed it John Becket, Walborough, were a comfort to her aching heart. She hoped they still held true as it was now three weeks since she'd last had sight of him and her heart ached to be near him again.

Roderick had written to her as well in his rushed scribble which took some deciphering.

My dearest sister,

Terribly busy Bella. Only a few weeks now before we come up to town. Lots to do before we leave. Heard you are something of a hit with Lord Rossington. Go easy there, dashing, and handsome and worlds apart from us. Sir Henry has promised me time to see the sights and have some leisure so I will endeavour to meet up with you once we are settled. He will no doubt keep me busy at other times. I won't complain as the work is challenging, hugely interesting and thoroughly educational. Papa was wise to send me here if I am to have a political career for myself in the future. At this time, I fully retain my enthusiasm at the prospect. I most fervently hope you are happy and enjoying something of life in town.

Your ever-loving brother,

Rod.

Relief flooded her mind knowing he was unaware of her relationship with John. She wanted it to remain a secret until the time came when they could freely announce it to family, friends, and the world at large. If only she knew when that would be, if ever.

Lawrence, despite being away from home for the first time, was in his element. Nothing could douse his enthusiasm nor diminish his high regard for Hubert Lang.

'Mr Lang has given me all the music for Sunday's service to practice including a voluntary, the accompaniment to the hymns and a wonderful chorale by Johann Sebastian Bach, *Jesus bleibet meine Freude,* which I haven't seen before. It's quite magical and joyful with intricate fingering for the organ and smooth flowing notes for the chorus.'

'Where did it come from?'

'It's part of a cantata which a previous scholar of Mr Lang's has copied and sent him from Germany. Originally scored for wind and stringed instruments with continuo, Mr Lang has arranged it for the organ as an anthem. Dieter, the sub organist is German, and Mr Lang has charged him with teaching the words and music to the choir, whilst I learn to play the arrangement on the organ. Hopefully when it's all put together, it will sound wonderful.'

'I'm sure it will Lawrence. Are you happy here?'

'I miss mama, papa, and William but this is what I want to do. This is the world of music making I want to be involved in. I want to learn as much as I can, play as much as I can and study composition. Here I have the chance. No one here thinks I'm strange or obsessed, just dedicated. Mr Lang says I must be steadier, but he is like you and papa in helping me. He speaks calmly and doesn't shout.'

'I'm so pleased for you Lawrence. Will you be able to stay here though, in the future?'

'Mr Lang has applied to Viscount Rossington for a scholarship for me which will pay for my food and lodging and give me some day-to-day expenses. He says it is only a formality as his lordship trusts his recommendations.'

'That's wonderful.'

'What is he like, Lord Rossington?'

'He's a little older than you, handsome and charming, entertaining too as he knows a great deal, like Roderick.'

'Is he very wealthy?'

'I suppose so. He dresses impeccably, has wonderful horses and the latest carriages, lives in a grand house and will be a duke one day.'

'I hope I get to meet him.'

'He often visits here so I don't see why you shouldn't.'

Rossington and Walborough were at that moment making their way towards Deane Castle, about to stop for the night at a pleasant wayside inn with the expectation of completing their journey with ease the next day. In the morning, they planned to dress early, send their valets ahead of them to warn of their imminent arrival and enjoy a leisurely breakfast before setting off.

Mrs Barker, housekeeper at Deane Castle, thoroughly efficient and universally liked, found herself for once put off her stride. She went in search of either of the impending visitor's valets, finding Will Ryder on his way to the boot room.

'Mr Ryder,' she called, 'if I might have a word.'

Will slowed his step, stopped, and turned to face Rossington's housekeeper with a smile.

'What can I do for you Mrs Barker?'

'There is a young lady and her brother staying at No 1, The Yard. The young man has come to study with Mr Lang and his sister, Miss Wrighton, has come to keep him company whilst he settles in. The thing is, she asked me if she might have a tour of the castle since no one was in residence and I told her to come tomorrow. I think I must now put her off.'

'Miss Wrighton, you say?'

'Yes. A pretty girl with lovely dark brown hair and a cheerful disposition.'

'Do nothing immediately. I'll speak to their lordships when they arrive and make sure you have a decision in plenty of time.'

'Thank you, Mr Ryder. You are most kind.'

He watched her walk away. Daisy Barker, not Mrs Barker since she'd never married, just Daisy. A genuinely good woman. A woman of high moral standards which in some ways was a pity and in others was a blessing. She wouldn't dally with him, neither had he been able to persuade her to marry him some years back, despite the attraction they'd had for one another. Walborough hadn't been to Deane Castle in a while, so neither had he. It felt good to see her after so long. He might hope her view on marriage had changed but reason told him it was unlikely. She wanted a settled life and he travelled wherever Walborough went.

Mr Ryder subsequently gave Mrs Barker a list of rooms through which she could show Miss Wrighton and her brother. She was to be sure to take them to the music room and if possible, encourage Lawrence to play the piano. If Miss Wrighton could be persuaded to sing as well, that would be an added bonus.

Bella had no idea Walborough and Rossington had arrived at the castle, so as arranged she walked up to the high gated castle entrance with Lawrence and explained her purpose to the gatekeeper. He let them in through a smaller gate and gave them directions to the side of the castle, which Bella thought was probably the servant's entrance.

A footman then took them to Mrs Barker's comfortable sitting room where she explained something of the layout of the castle before they began their tour.

Like many homes of the aristocracy, it had undergone structural and decorative changes across the years. There were walls of weaponry from the days when the castle had to be defended and an oubliette which Lawrence thought was both fascinating and horrifying.

'Did they really just push someone down into the hole, put the trapdoor back in place and leave them there?'

'I'm afraid they did but it's useful to remember they were enemies who would happily kill you, given the chance. It was rather barbaric, but methods of dealing with one's enemies in medieval times, were generally very gruesome.'

There were stuffed stag's heads on the walls and paintings depicting dead birds with guns and retrievers.

'The fourth Duke was fond of hunting and killing things. Some of these are his trophies,' Mrs Barker explained. 'The current Duke, his son and grandson have no such interest. Their hunting Lodge at Belverdon has barely been occupied in the last thirty years.' A fact which came as no surprise to Bella and Lawrence.

There was much to see and admire as they moved on to more comfortably furnished rooms reflecting some of the castle's history. Tapestries hung against walls to keep out the cold. Huge fireplaces with wide grates stood floor to ceiling, promising warmth. Wood panelling in corridors, some plain, some decorative gave off the aroma of bee's wax. China cabinets and ornaments became a more common sight and furniture, daintier than the heavy oak of earlier rooms, offered comfort. Colour from padded seats reflected the long curtains in rooms with greater light and space.

In a small room adjacent to the music room, Walborough sat with Rossington.

'Is there a purpose to us being here?' Walborough asked, since the poky room lacked much of the home comforts, he took for granted when visiting Deane Castle.

'When I open these doors,' he said indicating what looked like a high up cupboard on the wall, 'you will see a finely meshed screen. We must then remain silent and not utter a single word.'

'Might one ask why?'

'The music room is beyond. We will be able to hear what is going on in there but if we make a sound, they will hear it too.'

'Just a minute. Who is going to be in there?'

'The housekeeper and two guests.'

'Beware Randal,' John warned, 'you know eavesdroppers rarely hear anything good about themselves.'

'Hopefully then, in this instance, we shall be fortunate and hear something pleasant.'

'This is the music room,' Mrs Barker said, ushering Bella and Lawrence inside. 'It was once a receiving room but was altered for the current Duchess, who is gifted musically, and can play several instruments very proficiently. We have her harp, the pianoforte, a harpsichord, and virginals. The piano is kept tuned should you wish to play it. I understand you are both accomplished musicians.'

'Lawrence is accomplished,' Bella said with her usual honesty. 'I play a little,' which was very short of the truth.

'She plays very well,' Lawrence corrected, 'and sings, but she don't brag about it.'

'There is plenty of music available,' Mrs Barker said pointing to a double doored cabinet with a key in the lock.

'May I look?' Lawrence asked eagerly.

'Help yourself.'

Lawrence tried turning the key in the cabinet door, but it appeared to be ineffective. The door opened anyway without the need for it, so he slipped the key in his waistcoat pocket to avoid losing it.

It was like opening a treasure chest to Lawrence. Gold, silver, and precious jewels would have held little interest in comparison to the printed and handwritten sheets and books of music he discovered.

'Bella, look here. Handel's Largo, handwritten for the pianoforte. Come on we haven't performed this for an age. You used to sing often.'

'Oh no, I couldn't. This isn't our home, Lawrence. I think we should go now.'

'Not yet. I want to look at more of this music and I want to play this piano and you should sing. Will that be allowed Mrs Barker?'

'Of course. What use is music if it isn't performed?'

'Come on Bella. You used to be more adventurous. Has going to London trimmed your cloth?'

'No, well I mean, oh go on then. I just hope my voice isn't rusty. The music is demanding.'

'Where did you learn the piece?' Mrs Barker asked.

'At home. We had a music teacher for a while. His name was Signor Bartolenti. Mama said he was no more Italian than we were and his name was probably his own invention, but he was a good teacher and had travelled in Italy. He introduced us to some interesting music, most of it the devil to sing. He wasn't one to teach us folk songs.'

'The Largo is from Handel's opera Xerxes and is sung to a tree.'

'A tree, not a lover?'

'He admires the shade from a plane tree,' Bella explained, as if that was quite normal.

'*Ombre mai fu,*' Lawrence said as he sat down at the piano and began to play the opening bars, then Bella joined in with the long held first note.

Walborough and Rossington sitting quietly in the small room were spellbound as the notes rose and fell, stretching the voice to heights and depths, but Bella found them all with ease, the quality of her voice and the skill of Lawrence on the piano being quite a revelation.

Mrs Barker thanked them. Bella was ready to move on, but Lawrence wanted to make more of a study of the stack of music in the cupboard.

'Couldn't I borrow some of it to copy?'

'No Lawrence. It would be like stealing.'

'It would not. I would copy the music and bring the original back.'

'But you would then keep back something that does not belong to you.'

'How so? Musicians, do it all the time - copy out scores.'

'I am aware of that but in these circumstances, you will not do it. You must request access to the music from Lord Rossington.'

'I could do something for him in return like cataloguing it. I doubt anyone knows what is actually here.'

'Certainly, you could, but only with permission. We are here as visitors, not guests. We will not take advantage.'

'I thought you said you know Lord Rossington.'

'I do, but that doesn't give me or you the right to take advantage of him. If he were here, I'd ask him for you but since he isn't, you will have to be patient. We should go now. We have taken up enough of Mrs Barker's time.'

'It was a pleasure to hear some music in the house again. I hope you will come back.'

'I cannot say how much longer I'll be staying in the area.' Bella stated.

'Where will you go?'

'Maybe back to my aunt's in London. I don't know. I'm standing at a crossroads and need to choose the right way.'

Walborough decided he needed to help her choose the right way.

'Where is she staying?' he asked Rossington later when they were alone in the house save for the servants.

'No. 1, The Yard. It's the first of a row of cottages we use to house visitors to the church. She's there with Lawrence and a chaperone who also cooks for them and acts as a maid for Bella.'

'I must contrive to see her such that she thinks I have only just arrived.'

'I'll send a message inviting her and Lawrence for dinner.'

'No, because Lawrence will recognise me from my previous visit to Stillford, and she isn't aware of my having met her parents. I need to tell her first why I went there.'

'Rocky ground, my friend.'

'I know but I can't change what happened. I will have to hope she sees it from my point of view.'

'Lawrence spends his mornings at the church, either with Hubert or Dieter, the sub organist, and the choir. He has a lesson then spends an hour or more practising the organ or accompanying the choir for their practice. I need to talk to him about a scholarship. Currently you are defraying his expenses. Hubert sends to Harry Keats for reimbursement of any expenses he accumulates on Lawrence's behalf.'

'Then make what arrangements are necessary for Lawrence's education and comfort. I am content to continue to finance his studies. I told his father I would be his patron.'

Rossington was equally willing to be of assistance.

'I thought to provide him with accommodation here which will give him unlimited access to the music room and the wealth of music available. It would be an advantage to have it catalogued and know which scores are original and which copies. There are rooms a plenty which are empty, and Mrs Barker can keep an eye on him. Matthew Greyson, my Steward is not yet thirty and might be a valuable asset in keeping Lawrence calm, since he is rarely ruffled by anything I pass his way. Knowing Lawrence is comfortable and cared for will I believe release Bella to return to London.'

'You would do that for him?'

'For you, my friend and for Bella whom I have come to admire. Besides Lawrence deserves his chance, just as young Arthur does. Each to his own. You with your thoroughbreds, I with my music.'

'I know you sing. I've heard you drunk and sober, but do you play any instruments?'

'Unfortunately, not well, despite having the best teachers. I lacked the patience to sit indoors practicing. I content myself with having a good ear for a superior performance.'

'Invite Bella for coffee and refreshments then. She will assume she is coming to see you. I will be here instead, and you can hear Lawrence play and discuss his future with him.'

Chapter Thirteen

Bella received the invitation to meet with Rossington as she ate her breakfast.

'It seems Lord Rossington has arrived at the castle. He's invited me to go over at eleven. Will you still be at the church at that time?'

'Don't expect to see much of me today. Later Mr Lang is taking me to be fitted for a cassock which I will wear during services if I'm the organist.'

'I expect papa could have given you one. He has any number of black vestments he grew out of years ago but will not part with.'

'Mr Lang says it must not impede my ability to play, so he will have his say on how it is tailored.'

Bella had no wish to upset Lawrence, but she had concerns about where the money was coming from for their food and lodging and now these specially tailored vestments. Great good fortune had come Lawrence's way, but her mind skipped backwards, and she tried to recall what she'd said to Rossington about Lawrence's musical skill, if anything, which might have led him to send Hubert Lang to see just how competent he was. Apart from telling him she had brothers; she could recall no other reference to them. So, was it all just a fortunate coincidence?

On the third Friday evening of Arthur Brigg's new employment, he rode home in the company of Mr Thomas Henson, the Steward at Hopston Chase, rather than one of the grooms. He didn't understand why this was the case, except that Mr Henson wore his serious face and wanted a word with his father.

'Dad, Mr Henson would like a word,' he said the moment he set eyes on him.

'Bring him in then boy and let him have a seat,' Arthur Briggs senior said, fearing his son had not, after all, proved to be as helpful to the Duke, as hoped.

Thomas smiled at the watchful and wary faces. The Latin phrase, *audentes fortuna iuvat*, sprang to mind - fortune favours the bold.

Young Arthur had been bold, offering his help to passing travellers in the hope of earning a coin in gratitude. Now it was his father's turn to make a bold decision and accept fortune's favour for himself.

'Thank you for your warm welcome Mr Briggs. I hope you will think I have good news to share with you. His Grace has asked me to offer you and your two elder sons, immediate employment at Hopston Chase, if as he hopes, you are free to leave your current employer. It is his intent to expand the market at Hopston and bring in supplies from outside the area as well as encouraging his tenant farmers to provide more produce for sale.

'Your experience as carters will be invaluable in setting up this new venture. There are properties available to rent on the estate or in Hopston itself and I think you will agree, a generous wage,' he said handing over a slip of paper.

'Will you want to leave the village Dad?' Arthur asked hoping he would, which would not only mean he had the best job in the world, but he would have his family close by, whom he'd been missing quite badly, even though he would have denied it to anyone who asked.

'I might be sorry to leave the village Arthur. As for Owen Lawton, he thinks he owns us, and will find out soon enough that he doesn't.'

Arthur jumped up and down with excitement.

Thomas Henson breathed a sigh of relief. He'd sent his positive report to the Duke saying Arthur could calm the testiest of beasts in the stables and was already highly thought of by the head groom, but he was also badly homesick, missing his family and crying himself to sleep at night, which had resulted in the offer the Duke had just made to improve matters for him.

His decision wasn't entirely altruistic as some further research into the expansion of Hopston Market had suggested the likely future profits to be worthy of any initial investment.

His Grace would be pleased. Owen Lawton less so.

He expected at some point to receive a visit from an angry Owen Lawton.

If at all possible, he would avoid receiving him.

Bella was dressed comfortably in a mustard-coloured woollen frock for her visit with Rossington, over which she wore a warm matching pelisse, edged with brown fur. Atop her hair sat a stylish fur and feather trimmed beret. Leather gloves and her buttoned half boots completed her outfit as she set off to walk the short distance to the castle alone, having persuaded Anna she was not in need of a chaperone.

This time at the gate, she was directed to the main door of the castle where she was made welcome and shown upstairs to a comfortable reception room. Surprise halted her motion when she realised it was not Rossington who rose from the chair to greet her, but John.

After an awkward moment, he drew her into his arms and held her close, looking into her eyes for a sign she was pleased to see him.

'Oh! I had not expected to see you,' Bella exclaimed. 'I have been wondering where you were. I have only just received the letter you sent from Cornwall, and I wasn't certain where to address my reply to. It has gone to Walborough House, so I suppose you have missed it.'

'I've missed you, and I've worried about you since Rossington and your aunt told me of what had occurred the morning after Deane's party. I'm sorry I wasn't there for you.'

'How could you have been? I, like everyone else, was distressed to hear of your nephew's sad parting from this life. Your duty was to be with your family. I must confess I didn't expect to be called before Rossington's papa or hear him speak to me in such an accusatory tone. It appeared as if everyone believed I was either yours, or his son's paramour and not in any way worthy to be amongst them. I fell apart a little. I felt vulnerable and quite alone.'

'I would not have had that happen for the world. If I had been there, I could have pointed out the error. Shall we sit down. I have much to tell you, some of which I hope you will see from my point of view and afford me some understanding.'

'You wish to take back your offer of marriage?'

'I wish no such thing! I love you. I want more than anything for us to be married.'

'Then what worries you?'

'Do you remember when I went on a tour of my estates?'

'At the beginning of August?'

'Yes. My last stop was at Hopston Chase where my racing stables are. My father bought the first thoroughbred and through careful breeding had a string of successful horses during his lifetime, but we have known little success since his death, neither winning nor finishing well in any of the most prestigious races. He was the one with the drive and expertise and replacing him has been difficult. I now have an excellent stable manager and trainer, and a small cluster of young thoroughbreds showing great promise. My intention was to overnight there, make an early inspection of my horses, then leave for London in the afternoon until I discovered by chance that Stillford was close by.'

'Not close enough for me to have had any particular knowledge of Hopston Chase. We had little social life to speak of beyond the outskirts of the village,' Bella explained.

'I confess I had not previously felt the need to venture into the surrounding area either.'

'But this time you chose to?'

'You called it a backwater. My steward said it had a fine church and nothing more of interest. My coachman said I would likely pass through Stillford and never notice I'd been there. I decided I would go and view the fine church.'

'Did you?' Bella said amused by his confession. 'And what did you find?'

'So much more than I bargained for. Let me see now. There was the resourceful young lad Arthur who hypnotised my horse with songs, a fine organist practising for a concert, his welcoming and gracious parents who asked me to stay for dinner, the opportunity to hear the wonderful concert in the evening, and afterwards, the wholesome supper I shared with everyone.'

'Who did you tell them you were?'

'John Becket.'

'The partial truth then.'

'John Becket is my name. The rest is a title.'

'But the rest is so much more. What did you imagine you'd find there?'

'I imagined nothing. I wanted to see where you came from.'

'And to see if my parents were backwater people with backwater minds who you could easily dismiss as non-entities, thereby convincing yourself I was unworthy of your interest.'

'You were in my head Bella, and I couldn't get you out of it. I needed a reason to go on seeing you. You fascinated me and I wanted to understand why.'

'And did you find a reason?'

'Of course, I did. It was staring me in the face once I met your parents. Your father is a wonderful intelligent articulate man, and your mother is beautiful, delightful to be around and more a lady than many who have the right to call themselves such. You are so like her which is why you reminded Rossington of someone he couldn't call to mind. For some reason Rossington and I have yet to fathom, your mama is the image of his grandmama and has mannerisms akin to his father.'

'How can that be?'

'We have no answer to that question as none of our imagined scenarios make sense and it is not now and never will be our intention to cause anyone distress by unnecessarily probing into the matter. Even when Randal and I stayed at Hopston on our way here from London, we made no mention of your mama's likeness to the Rossingtons.

'We did, however, stay an extra night to allow Randal to spend more time with your family and for me to have a conversation with your father.'

'What about?'

'I asked him for permission to court you and told him my intentions towards you were honourable.'

'Was he surprised?'

'No. I think my sweet Bella, he believes me to be the most fortunate of men, just as he believes he was equally fortunate when he met your mother.'

'I know I shouldn't speak of the details of childbirth in company but my Grandmama told me something of the life she had, living out on the moor at Belverhead Cottage. She gave birth to three of their four children there with only grandpapa to assist her. The ride to get help was too far and he wouldn't leave her on her own. They had each other which was enough for both of them.

'Grandmama said from the day she was married, she only left the cottage to go to church on Sundays and sometimes the weather was too fierce, even for that. Grandpapa drove down to the head gamekeeper's house once a week, to give his report and collect supplies.

'Their interactions with others were few. If you were thinking grandmama had an affair or was seduced, you are far off the truth.'

'We briefly considered it and discounted it as implausible but if, as you say, they lived so isolated, how did your mama learn to read and write?'

'I think grandpa taught her when she was a young girl and when they moved to work for Lord de Laurent at Follcliffe, mama took work in the house as a maid. Lady de Laurent had chosen to have a classically educated male tutor for her daughters, and mama sat in with them during their lessons for propriety's sake. She was allowed to learn alongside them. Lady de Laurent actively encouraged it. According to grandpapa she was something of a radical and campaigned for women to be better educated. They were a remarkably close couple and her husband let her have her way in most things.'

'She sounds a very interesting lady.'

'She was. She gave birth to another daughter when mama was fifteen and sadly died a year later, aged thirty-five, shortly after the birth of her son. Mama found it hard to be around the house when her ladyship was no longer there. The children were sent away to an aunt for a while and mama left to go and work for Lady Spiers in London. Grandmama and grandpapa stayed for a few more years until Lord de Laurent eventually remarried to give the youngest children a stepmother.'

'Did your grandmama work in the house too?'

'In the stillroom. She was very proficient at bottling fruit and making preserves. She'd had a lot of practice, isolated on the moor with not much else to do.'

'It must at times have been a very lonely existence,' John commented.

'Yet they never complained because they had each other and their children. Grandpapa had a deep love of the moor and only agreed to leave when it became absolutely necessary for their future. Grandmama would have followed him anywhere he chose to take them. They were devoted to each other then, and still are.'

'I have family letters for you including one from Shropshire, but I've left them in my bedroom.'

'Perhaps you should go and retrieve them for me, and I'll ask for refreshments to be brought in.'

'You're sure you don't want to come too?' he said playfully, stroking her cheek.

'I thought you promised my papa you only had honourable intentions towards me and if I were in a bedroom alone with you, judging by my response to your touch, I think our resistance to temptation would be severely tested.'

'You still love me then?'

'You should not doubt me,' she said. 'One kiss before you go.'

One kiss could last a surprisingly long time.

Lawrence was in the vestry with the vicar, Mr Joseph Powell, discussing church matters, with which he had some familiarity, when Lord Rossington walked in and was duly introduced to him.

'You are most welcome here Lawrence,' he said with an air of friendliness Lawrence hadn't expected. 'Mr Lang already speaks very highly of you. I hope you are settled and happy with the provisions made for you.'

'I am most happy for the opportunity to work with Mr Lang and play this wonderful organ. I never dreamt ….'

'You should have dreamt Lawrence and you must go on dreaming. Mr Lang has educated many a talented organ scholar and sent them out into the world to prosper, here in our great churches and cathedrals but also to study further afield in Germany, Austria, and Italy. This makes us truly fortunate as we have been sent copies of great works we might never have encountered otherwise, not only for the organ but also for the pianoforte and harpsichord.

'The Duchess, my grandmother stayed here often in the early years of her marriage. She is a very musical lady who gathered together a diverse collection of musical scores, most of which are stored in the castle music room.'

'Mrs Barker showed us around and gave me the opportunity to play the pianoforte,' Lawrence informed him. 'There is a cupboard full of bound and unbound music.'

'I don't suppose you would have the patience to look through it and sort it in some way, would you?' Rossington asked as if he had just thought of it.

'I can catalogue it for you if you wish, such that any piece can be more easily found as required.'

'That would be marvellous. I do have a suggestion for you if you're interested. I propose you move into the castle where Mrs Barker can see to your needs and you will have free access to the music room, not only the music but the instruments, which will also grant you plenty of time for practising, whilst not interfering with your education. What do you think?'

'It would suit me very well but what of my sister Bella? She is staying with me at the moment, and I must think of her comfort too.'

'Bella will come to the castle as well to be company for you, until she returns to London.'

'Is she returning to London?' Has she said so?'

'Not yet but I think she will when she knows you are happy to stay here without her. You should both come to dinner this evening with Mr Lang and Mr Powell.

'Walborough is also staying at the castle. You know him as John Becket.'

'John Becket who came to Stillford?'

'The very same. He was at Hopston Chase checking out his racehorses.'

'I don't know why he would have ridden to Stillford though. There is little to see besides the church.'

'He had a mind to see the church as it was recommended to him as worthy of a visit.'

'It is worthy of a visit,' Lawrence admitted, 'particularly if you have an interest in either church organs or monuments to the dead.'

Neither of which sounded to Rossington like pursuits which had previously held John's interest.

'Would you perhaps consider entertaining us with some music after dinner?'

'I would be happy to, I can't vouch for my sister who is very skilled vocally but is sometimes shy in public.'

'We will not press her then. I'll send someone to move your possessions over to the castle, where you can be comfortable, but for now I'll leave you to the vicar and Mr Lang.'

Bella was not impressed by the arrangements made for the evening.

'You expect me to dine with five gentlemen?'

'You can always escape to your room when the meal finishes.'

'What room?' she asked suspiciously.

'Lord Rossington has arranged for our belongings to be moved into the castle where we are to have rooms and be cared for by Mrs Barker. I have permission to use the music room whenever I want and to sort through all the music in the cupboard.'

'Wonderful news for you Lawrence but it will not do for me to reside at the castle as a single woman with two single gentlemen in residence too. I will make plans to return to live with Aunt Susannah, if you think you will be comfortable here on your own.'

'I think I should like to stay at the castle. I will never be without something to do but please come to dinner with me, just this once so I'll know what to expect.'

'Very well. I will take the opportunity to speak to Lord Rossington about an early return to town. As to what to expect, mama and papa have taught you all you need to know. You just have to remember not everything has to be done in a rush.'

'I do love you so Bella, and I'll miss you, but you have your own life to lead, and I don't need you to sacrifice your happiness for mine. I shall be twenty-one in a few months. I need to be responsible for myself.'

'Just promise me when a thought first comes into your head, you will not rush into immediate action but ask yourself the questions I taught you. Is it safe? Are you certain you will not be putting yourself in any danger? Is it appropriate? How will your actions be viewed by others? Is the time, right? Will you be causing a disturbance to those around you? And most important of all, can it wait until you have thought about it some more? Also remember to concentrate on your breathing and try to relax.'

'I will, I promise.'

'And you must write to me at least once a week.'

'That I won't promise because I will likely forget, but I will try to remember.'

'Honest at least. Come on then, we better get dressed for dinner. I must look my best if I am to be surrounded by so many gentlemen.'

Chapter Fourteen

Walborough led Bella into the Deane Castle dining room where she was seated comfortably with her friends to either side and Lawrence directly opposite, in the hope she would feel relaxed as the only female guest. With five pairs of male eyes all looking in her direction it was more unnerving than relaxing. She wore a high waisted slip of pale lemon silk with an overdress of sheer lace spotted with tiny white daisies, the hem elaborately trimmed with a wide band of gauze flowers, lace, and beading. The sleeves were short, tightly gathered and puffed. Her hair had been painstakingly formed into a twisted chignon decorated with pearls, leaving soft glossy brown curls to frame her face.

Walborough thought she'd never looked more beautiful.

The conversation got off to a slow start as the predominantly male company were wary of raising topics deemed inappropriate for ladies.

Walborough asked her if she had any further news of young Cuthbert Willis and in response, Bella immediately became animated.

'I have. Wonderful news in fact. He is now officially Cuthbert Foster, although he will no doubt continue to be called Cuddy by those who love him.'

'The adoption has gone through then.' Rossington commented.

'Indeed, it has, and instead of a childless couple longing for a child and a small boy longing for parents, we now have the happiest of families.'

'Miss Wrighton has recently been in London and having made a friend of Lady Goldsborough became involved in her work to find homes for young orphans,' Walborough explained, addressing the vicar and Hubert Lang.

'Do you have family in London, Miss Wrighton,' Mr Powell asked her.

'My aunt and uncle, Lord and Lady Bellingham.'

'And our brother Roderick will also be in London shortly,' Lawrence added. 'He is secretary to Sir Henry Leighton, and they will travel down to be settled for when Parliament sits in November.'

'I don't imagine I will see very much of him as he is kept busy,' Bella explained. 'He has hopes of a political career for himself in time.'

'Is he a Whig or a Tory?' Rossington asked her.

'A Tory.'

'Then he is a supporter of Lord Liverpool,' Hubert Lang suggested.

'He is an employee of Sir Henry Leighton and loyal to him. Sir Henry, I imagine, is loyal to Lord Liverpool as not only the leader of his party but as the Prime Minister. I see Roderick very rarely these days and when we do meet, we are more likely to discuss family matters. Wouldn't you agree Lawrence?'

'Roderick will have his views and he has licence to discuss them with Sir Henry, but his role is to support and promote Sir Henry's view and to keep to himself any knowledge he might have acquired pertaining to the government of the country, which might potentially be misused by others.

'Better to be silent, than to be seen as indiscreet or worse.'

'Then you have no idea of his view of Lord Liverpool as a Prime Minister,' Hubert persisted.

'All I can say is he is no Whig. If he were, I think his ambition would be severely dented by the disarray of that party at the current time,' Bella said hoping to end the discussion and move into something less contentious, but Hubert Lang surprised her with his next remark.

'Your brother is most fortunate, Miss Wrighton, to have a family who understand diplomacy and the need for caution in their speech, perhaps not entirely unsurprising when one has been privileged to meet your father.'

'Some would deem us to be educated beyond our purpose and wish us to be less forthright in our opinions, particularly in my case being a woman, but papa has always been most interested in developing our intellect and purposefully chose to treat us alike.'

'Mama taught you too,' Lawrence interjected, 'but you would always prefer to read than sit sewing.'

Bella laughed at her brother's observation.

'I admit I don't have mama's skill with a needle nor her creativity which she acquired from her own mama.'

Walborough, realising they might be moving into unchartered waters turned the conversation to other matters.

'Is it this Sunday Lawrence, when you are to be the organist at Holy Trinity for the first time?'

'It is,' Hubert interrupted before Lawrence had a chance to reply. 'I hope you will be able to stay long enough to appreciate how much he has learned in such a short time.'

Walborough left him in little doubt of his desire to hear Lawrence play again.

'I will gladly stay if Lord Rossington will bear with me for a few more days.'

Bella said nothing. She wanted to stay but the propriety of it bothered her.

'Miss Wrighton you must surely stay too,' Rossington said taking away her opportunity to say she was leaving. 'Your family will no doubt look to you for a detailed appraisal of Sunday's service.'

Still, she was uncertain.

'I should not wish to impose on your hospitality further.'

'You need have no fear of your visit being seen as a risk to your good name,' Rossington informed her. 'Mrs Barker has accommodated you and Anna in her domain, and she holds all the keys. Walborough and I are in the north tower with our valets nearby and Lawrence is in one of the guest rooms.'

'Then I will stay until Sunday. Beyond then I must look to make my way back to London and my aunt's house.'

Rossington had seemingly already made plans for their journey. 'We will all travel back together, Miss Wrighton. I am sure Anna will relish a trip to the capital to be your maid along the way.'

And to be her chaperone for propriety's sake, Bella realised, although by not mentioning it, Rossington implied there was no need for such concern as their aim was to protect her and not misuse her.

So, it was settled. They would leave on Monday, making one of their overnight stops at Hopston Chase, giving her an opportunity to visit her family before returning to London.

Since the usual etiquette was for the ladies to rise and leave the gentlemen to their port, Bella followed this pattern, excusing herself and intimating she would retire for the evening. Instead, she found herself ushered along to the music room where she was joined by Mrs Barker who sat discreetly at the back of the room as her chaperone.

Lawrence was happy to entertain and show his skilled fingering with lively music by Mozart which he followed with the slower more expressive piece. Bella was then persuaded to play a duet with him, before singing some familiar folk songs. After a quiet but intense discussion with Lawrence, she was persuaded to sing a long-standing favourite of hers, the words holding far more meaning to her now than they ever had before.

Lawrence introduced it.

'This next song, *Sweeter than Roses*, is from Richard Norton's play Pausanias. The music is by Henry Purcell and this delightful song has long outlasted the play.'

> *Sweeter than roses, or cool evening breeze*
> *On a warm flowery shore, was the dear kiss,*
> *First trembling made me freeze,*
> *Then shot like fire all o'er.*
> *What magic has victorious love!*
> *For all I touch or see since that dear kiss,*
> *I hourly prove, all is love to me.*

It was vocally demanding, but very successfully showcased Bella's fine voice and artistry. This time, Lawrence played the accompaniment on the harpsichord which he'd discovered had also been kept in tune, needing only a minimum of adjustment to satisfy his ear. She hardly dared to look at John as she sang it, recalling all too easily how a first dear kiss felt.

She knew how to give a polished performance, but she had not expected the four men to react so spontaneously as the song ended, by rising as one from their seats with cries of bravo and applauding generously.

Lawrence rose from the keyboard, and they bowed together to acknowledge their response.

'Why have we not heard you at Mrs Hepworth's soiree?' Walborough asked, 'when you easily outshine many of the participants.'

'She don't like to push herself forward,' Lawrence said drily.

'Oh! but you should Miss Wrighton,' Hubert Lang said encouragingly. 'Who was your teacher?

'Signor Bartolenti.'

'Ah, well that explains it. His real name is Frederick Bartle, a fine musician in his own right, who studied abroad for many years. When he returned to England, he discovered the fashion was for Italian music teachers, so he adapted his name accordingly. I understood he is inclined to be selective in whom he chooses to teach.'

'He made us sing and play for him before he would consider it. We learnt so much from him, we were sorry when he left. Mama was right then, when she said he was no more Italian than we were, despite him having an excellent Italian accent. He was very fussy about the correct pronunciation when we sang in Italian.'

'He is still teaching as far as I know.'

'He definitely is,' Lawrence confirmed, 'because he writes to mama on occasion and is often very humorous. Sometimes he ruefully admits to having to lower his standards to stay employed.'

'He always had a wanderlust. He could have had employment in any cathedral in the land being a fine organist, but he preferred the human voice and enjoyed developing it to its full potential.'

'Did you know him as a young man, Mr Lang?' Lawrence asked.

'For a while we were choristers together and were taught the organ by the same teacher, but as I said he had a strong desire to travel abroad and went his own way.'

'Which is what we should be doing now,' Rossington said firmly. 'Tomorrow morning at eleven, if you have the desire to watch, Miss Wrighton; Walborough and I are intending to race our curricles around the castle. Mrs Barker can advise you on a safe place to watch the proceedings. My greys against Walborough's blacks.'

'We might also step out from the church to view the event, Lawrence, so don't feel you will miss the excitement.'

'Thank you, Mr Lang. I should be sorry to miss it.'

The vicar felt the need to urge Lawrence to be cautious.

'Keep away from those offering odds on the winner if you have any sense. They aim to make a swift profit.'

Lawrence felt a little put out by what he considered an unnecessary moral judgement.

'My papa has counselled me well on the evils of gambling, and besides I don't have money to waste.'

The vicar would as happily have passed moral judgement on both Rossington and Walborough following their decision to race each other, feeling that in publicising the event, they were encouraging those with weak minds to lay bets and lose money they could ill afford.

He kept silent, however, knowing better than to openly criticise the leisure pursuits of the aristocracy when his position in society and his livelihood depended solely on their continued patronage.

When Anna drew Bella's bedroom curtains on the morning of the curricle race and pronounced the weather set fair, she rose eagerly from her bed and allowed herself to be readied for the day ahead. She would have preferred to go straight down for breakfast but had to wait for Mrs Barker to assure her that the gentleman were dressed and respectable enough to be in the company of a lady.

She was placed next to Lawrence who took reasonable care dressing himself, but too frequently showed a disregard for the state of his hair, which needed both cutting and styling.

'Shall I cut it for you later?' Bella asked casually, as she might have done at home, unaware of the embarrassment she caused him in front of Walborough and Rossington.

'You are kind to think of him Miss Wrighton,' Walborough said, sensing her brother's discomfort, 'but my valet Mr Ryder has taken it upon himself to perform this service for Lawrence after breakfast.'

Lawrence's glum look vanished at the exciting prospect of having one of the most coveted valets in the ton attend him. He wouldn't be at all surprised though if at that moment in time, Mr Ryder was not even aware of the offer.

Bella was in two minds about the curricle race.

'I own to being both excited and full of trepidation should one of you be injured.'

Walborough tried to reassure her.

'There is an element of risk attached to driving any vehicle at speed but neither Rossington nor I are reckless, and we value our horses too much to put them in harm's way. The castle was once surrounded by a deep moat which was filled in long ago when fortifications were no longer needed leaving a flat grassy area, wide enough to easily accommodate two curricles side by side. The land conveniently lies well below the double arched stone bridge which now leads to the main gate. Before we even start, I would say Rossington may have the advantage with his greys, but my blacks are bang up to scratch too. Over the years we are fairly evenly balanced in victories and losses.'

Rossington agreed, but Lawrence wanted to know more details of the race.

'How many circuits will you do?'

'Six. As this is a friendly challenge, the race will immediately be aborted should one of us suffer a mishap of any kind, which I might add is unlikely.'

Leaving the breakfast room later, Walborough held up Bella for a moment and whispered in her ear.

'You could give me a love token to improve my chances of success, if you wish to.'

She took out an embroidered handkerchief from her reticule.

'I can't take the credit for the embroidery which belongs to mama, but you may carry this as something I treasure and entrust to your safe keeping.'

'I will carry it next to my heart,' he promised and kissed her hand, which was as much as he dare do with servants wandering backwards and forwards.

The two competitors made their way to the stables to check their horses and see to their equipage whilst Bella and Lawrence returned to their rooms.

Lawrence was in alt when Will Ryder knocked on his door.

'If you would like to accompany me, Mr Wrighton,' he said with a formal bow, 'I can better serve you where I have everything I need to hand.'

Lawrence didn't need to be asked twice. He had never been ministered to by a valet before, so once settled in a chair and enveloped in a large sheet, he listened with eager anticipation to a very thorough explanation of the latest in gentlemen's hairstyles.

'Men of stature are choosing to wear their hair in the manner of a Greek warrior, or a Roman general as seen on the many statues from antiquity, with sideburns either short or long, hence the names Caesar, Titus, and Brutus. The Windswept is popular with younger men, poets, artists, and musicians when the hair might be worn with more length on top, curled and swept forward as if it had been blown by the wind to give a romantic look.'

All the while he'd been talking, Mr Ryder had been shaving him and applying warm towels to his face making it impossible for Lawrence to answer. He came to the conclusion a style had already been chosen for him and if it wasn't the Windswept, he'd be surprised.

'Now you sit there a moment and I'll see what I can make of your jacket. I doubt it's been pressed since you left home, has it?'

Lawrence no doubt looked sheepish beneath the towel his face was wrapped in and his reply was too muffled to distinguish. By the time Mr Ryder had finished with him he had learnt how to tie a cravat with style, how to brush and press his coat and the best way to polish his boots.

'You should try, if your situation permits, to wear fresh linen every day. Whilst you are here Mrs Barker will see it goes to the laundry for you. Otherwise, you can usually find a maid or a widow who will do washing and mending for you for a small sum.'

He placed a mirror in front of Lawrence and encouraged him to appraise his new appearance.

Lawrence who had throughout life rushed to dress with little thought of how he might look, seeing his new image in a looking glass, realised a little effort on his part might well be worth the result. He thanked Will profusely for the haircut and the advice.

Will smiled to himself as Lawrence walked out of the door head held high, in the manner of a gentleman, full of confidence to face the world outside. His father, had he been there to see him, would have been amazed.

Bella didn't see this wonderful transformation until it was almost time for the race to begin. Hubert Lang, feeling Lawrence's new look needed an outing, sent him to keep her company on the castle bridge where the race would start and finish. Quite a crowd had assembled to watch, anticipating some excitement to lighten their humdrum lives.

The usual touts were out, offering odds on the winner and taking bets.

'Who do you think will win Lawrence?' Bella asked him.

'If I were a betting man, I'd put my money on Walborough, but I imagine it will be very close.'

'Why Walborough?'

'I am in his debt after he sent Mr Ryder to turn me out so smartly.'

Bella laughed at his reasoning. 'You think it would be ill mannered of you to bet against him?'

'It would not seem right.'

'I must say Mr Ryder has indeed turned you out splendidly. Those young ladies over there are all giggling over you.'

Lawrence was unimpressed.

'I don't have time for giggling girls,' he said refusing to look their way.

'They must think you very handsome. You look more like Roderick now.'

'In what way?'

'You have the air of a young gentleman.'

'I'm just a scholar Bella. That's all I want to be at the moment.'

'You can be a handsome, well dressed, and charming young man as well. The two are not at odds with each other. I must confess, I like your hair windswept. It gives you a very romantic image.'

'Oh, do stop,' he said laughing, 'and let's position ourselves by the parapet. The race is about to start. Look here come Lord Rossington and the Duke of Walborough.'

Chapter Fifteen

Walborough came up to the starting point first and drew his horses to a halt beneath one arch of the bridge, all black elegance, apart from his pristine white linen and a silver silk waistcoat, whilst Rossington settled beneath the other, more flamboyant in his dark green cut away jacket, worn over tan breeches with a cheerful yellow and white striped waistcoat.

The crowd were noisy, remarking on the gentlemen's splendid outfits, on the magnificence of the horses and the sharp contrast of the black curricle against the yellow. They jostled for position, for the best view, excited and hopeful of winning their wagers.

A pie man came out to offer his wares, the beefy aroma too tempting for many to resist.

It seemed but a moment before the horses came out into the open and raced away down the track, side by side with nothing between them as they disappeared out of site around the castle walls.

Knowing when to expect the carriages to come through again was easy enough as the crowd grew excited and began to cheer for one, or the other, depending on their bet.

Bella and Lawrence crossed the bridge for a better view of the rapidly approaching horses, disappointed to see

Rossington ahead, Lawrence loudly cheering Walborough on.

'Give it time Bella. Stamina and pacing will come into play towards the end.'

She couldn't see how it would happen as all the way around until the start of the last lap, Rossington's greys were at least a head in front of Walborough's blacks. As the horses came round the final bend and back into view of the finishing line, they were side by side, until slowly the blacks began to move ahead, causing an uproar amongst the crowd and a feeling of excited panic within Bella's chest.

'I can't look Lawrence.'

'Of course, you can. Look Walborough in the eye as he crosses the finishing line first.'

He was ahead but it still seemed a long way to go, and her heart was in her mouth as he drew closer and closer, and Rossington was too near. A sudden surge from the greys and he would win. Walborough wasn't concerned. He knew his horses well and urged them forward in the final straight knowing they still had plenty of pace. The greys were magnificent but too new for Rossington to have them completely in hand and the race was easily won by a length.

Bella would have jumped up and down like an excited child if she hadn't known to show more decorum. It took the horses some distance to slow down and turn around before coming to a halt by the bridge where the combatants climbed down from their curricles and handed the reigns to their grooms.

'I thought I had you there,' Rossington said good naturedly.'

'You can still sell me the greys if you like,' Walborough said enviously.

'I don't think so. I haven't had much time with them yet.

Another race, another time and I feel confident I could beat your blacks.'

'I think so too,' Walborough said wryly, 'which was why I wanted the greys for myself.'

'You would have got them too if your mother hadn't called you away at the wrong time. How is she by the way?'

'Well, as far as I know. Still obsessed with me meeting every new debutante on the scene with either a title or a fortune as if either were of any importance to me.'

'Will you tell her of your plans?'

'No.'

'You have no qualms about what you are about to do?'

'None at all.'

'Are you still looking to discover more about Bella's mama?'

'I'm not planning to. If she is anyone's relative, she will be yours, though I cannot find a logical answer as to how that could be the case.'

'Neither can I.'

Neither of them realised how easily they had been misguided in the direction of their thoughts because the truth was beyond any reasonable man's comprehension, particularly when pertinent facts were not available to them.

The Marquess of Deane was rapidly coming to the conclusion there was only one answer to the mystery of the two Sally Fosters, yet he couldn't imagine finding anyway to prove his conclusion was right, nor could he decide who to approach first in order to test out his theory.

Asking the kind of questions, he wanted answers to, was going to prove hurtful to all those involved. He couldn't perceive of any of them having been involved in any malicious act, yet he felt certain a malicious act had been perpetrated.

In the end, he explained what he knew to his wife Martha, and asked her for her wise counsel.

'It seems to me Ivor, my love, that we should first go to this place Stillford and ask to speak to Miss Wrighton when you can also apologise to her as is your wish. She will surely know the whereabouts of her grandparents who may be able to offer some explanation for the burial of one Sally Foster and the baptism of another, both with the same birth date as yourself.'

'Then we shall leave as soon as you can be ready.'

'Where will we stay?'

'Daniel can look into it. He's proving himself to be highly efficient.'

Daniel was always extremely efficient and worked out the best place for them to stay would be Hopston Chase only a thirty-minute ride from the village of Stillford and somewhere they were likely to receive a welcome due to the closeness of their son to the Duke of Walborough, whose residence it was.

A week later they set out with just such an intention.

The Deane Castle party still had the forthcoming Sunday service to look forward to, although there remained a buzz around the place in the aftermath of the curricle race and the excitement it had engendered in the town. Bella, feeling she had not adequately praised John for his victory, persuaded him to take her out for a drive in his curricle.

'I had to be diplomatic yesterday morning and congratulate you both when the race finished but you did look magnificent coming down the straight inching forward all the time until you were ahead. I really wanted to shout your name and jump around excitedly when you crossed the line, but I felt the need to be more circumspect since Rossington is a good kind friend. Did you always think you could beat him?'

John smiled at her honesty and answered her question.

'I know my horses well and how much speed I can get out of them. Rossington's greys are potentially better racers but he hasn't had them long and has had few chances to really test them for speed and endurance, which is partly why we decided to hold the race.'

'You thought he might beat you.'

'Not yesterday, but he will in future. I suppose he told you I wanted the greys.'

'He did. He said your mama called you away and you missed the opportunity.'

'She had what she termed a small house party at Bascombe Hall, which she insisted I attend. It was neither small nor likely to provide me with any congenial company.'

'Debutantes?'

'No. Young ladies who are not yet out, aged sixteen or seventeen years, of good aristocratic families and some gentlemen of course who were told not to get in my way should I show any partiality.'

'And did you?'

'I was polite. I danced with them all. I responded to some very insipid conversation and left as soon as I could.'

'You prefer brazen ladies who accost you, mid ballroom?'

'Only one daring young lady. No one else has ever dared to approach me the way you did.'

'Are you so scary then?'

'Do you think I am?'

'No. I never thought you were scary, a bit aloof perhaps.'

'Hauteur. It keeps away those who I have no wish to engage with.'

'You had no wish to engage with me.'

'Ah, well that is not entirely true. I wanted to engage with you on a sensual basis and I knew I should not even contemplate it when I had no idea who you were and what our relationship might be.'

'Marriage was not on your mind at first, was it?'

'No. My family have expectations.'

'So, what has changed?'

'I fell in love with you and I can't imagine living my life without you in it. I have a special licence. I want us to be married by your father on our way back to Hopston Chase.'

'So soon?'

'Not soon enough, my sweet Bella.'

'Very well then. You are certain you will have no regrets?'

'I am, I promise you.'

Despite a coolness in the air, Bella felt all warm and cosy inside. When John drew the curricle to a halt in a sheltered grove and kissed her with more passion than he had on previous occasions, she felt extremely hot and never wanted the exciting sensations that built inside her to stop. John had no desire to stop either but he had a care for his horses and keeping them standing for long was not wise so they soon set off again.

'Do you want a taste of them racing?' he asked.

'Oh yes please. Randal built up some speed when he took me driving and I admit I found it thrilling.'

'You shall have your own carriage Bella and learn to drive yourself about.'

'I can manage a dogcart but I've never had the chance to drive anything else.'

'Do you ride?'

'I haven't since Roderick left home. Papa gave him our only decent riding horse.'

'Then you shall have your own horse too,' John declared. 'Now hold on and we'll race around the back of the castle before arriving at the bridge in a more sedate manner.'

Rossington watched them from a tower window, his emotions swinging from delight for them both and a fear that his friend was being led by his physical desire for Bella and hadn't properly equated the practical difficulties of raising her from her lowly social status to that of his duchess. He was virtually planning to marry her in secret, having no intentions of making any formal announcement in the newspapers and keeping her at Hopston for some time whilst he travelled to the capital, as necessary. He feared for Bella's happiness.

Bella was in love and blind to any difficulties that might stand in her way. John intended them to be married by her father for whom he had the greatest respect. He would not then turn round and treat her unkindly. She trusted him to help her find her way and prove herself worthy of him.

The Sunday service at Holy Trinity Church, Deane was always well attended but the Rossington family pews were frequently empty these days. Today was an exception. Lord Rossington sat with his guests, the Duke of Walborough and Miss Bella Wrighton who was accompanied by her maid Anna. Miss Wrighton, so the rumour went, was here to listen to her brother play the organ for the first time under the tutelage of Mr Lang.

They were an appreciative congregation. Their knowledge of the workings of the great organ might be slight in many cases, but they knew when it sounded uplifting and the Handel Voluntary being played by young Lawrence Wrighton was both new to them and exciting.

An anthem by the choir was always a popular interlude during the service, and the previously unknown piece by Bach was quite wonderful to listen to, even if it was in German, loosely translated by Dieter Meyer as *Jesus is my joy and comfort*. The intricate runs of notes on the organ played with perfect precision by Lawrence, and the long smooth phrases of the chorale sung effortlessly by the choir, held the congregation in awe, including Bella, Walborough and Rossington.

If they hadn't been in church there might have been a spontaneous round of applause. Instead, there was some quiet murmurings of pleasure as the service continued to its conclusion.

Lawrence modestly accepted praise from anyone who could get near enough to him to give it, the words of Hubert Lang being most precious to him.

'Wonderful, Lawrence, just wonderful,' which was praise indeed.

Dieter Meyer accepted without rancour that Lawrence was already more accomplished than he was and would soon usurp his position as sub organist, but he was all admiration for his young friend's ability. Between them they would go on to work together, Lawrence playing the organ, Dieter conducting the choir, to perform the great oratorios of Handel and Haydn for the glory of God and the heartening of those who would come to listen. In time, as their repertoire grew, they would establish a reputation for some of the finest musical performances in the land.

Bella knew she could safely leave Lawrence at Deane. He was in his element, amongst musicians who appreciated his gift and without rancour wanted to see him go on to become a true virtuoso performer.

Rossington thought of his concert schedule and planned to add more. The money raised provided scholarships and opened up opportunities for those who otherwise would lack the resources to pursue a quality musical education.

Walborough was delighted to know his initial understanding of Lawrence's ability had been correct and his patronage was not misplaced.

They went back to the castle happy and prepared themselves for goodbyes and onward journeys.

Stillford had never been as popular as it was on the morning of the sixth day of October in the year of our Lord, one thousand, eight hundred and fourteen. Walborough, Rossington and Bella, having arrived in a timely fashion the previous afternoon, had been accommodated in the Manor House and were now assembled with the Reverend Mr Wrighton, Mrs Wrighton and William Wrighton in the elegant drawing room.

The Most Noble John Selwyn, Duke of Walborough, of Bascombe Hall in the County of Oxfordshire, a Bachelor, was about to be married to Miss Bella Wrighton, of Stillford Manor House in the County of Hertfordshire, spinster, a minor, by special licence, by and with the consent of her father, Thaddeus Ignacious Wrighton, the Reverend Mr Wrighton.

A commotion outside the door temporarily halted the proceedings. A flustered downstairs maid peeped into the room.

'Begging your pardon Mr Wrighton but a gentleman is at the door with his wife. He says he's the Marquess of Deane.'

'Papa, here?' Rossington said confused by the untimely interruption. Shall I see what he wants?'

Thaddeus, as usual, offered a warm welcome and his generous hospitality to the unexpected visitors.

'Invite the Marquess and his Lady to join us Meg if you please. We can discover his purpose, I think, before we proceed with the marriage ceremony.'

It was the strangest situation of meetings, greetings and introductions, Rossington could ever remember. His father seemed to be on something of a mission, his purpose clear to him, his mother supportive and encouraging.

'I have travelled from London with my wife to offer an apology to Miss Bella Wrighton for my misjudgement of her character and family connections for which I hope she will forgive me. I would also wish to ascertain the whereabouts of William and Letty Foster who were at one time resident at Belverhead Cottage on the Belverdon Estate.'

Sally Wrighton rose from her seat and stepped forward, only to be struck dumb at the sight of the Marquess, or maybe not at the sight of him, just at the sheer presence of him, as if she knew him, as if she had always known him yet she had no recollection of ever having met him before.

'Are you Sally Mary Foster, as was?'

'I am,' she replied.

'Then,' he said, getting straight to the point as there was nothing to be gained by prevaricating, 'I have every reason to believe you are my twin sister.'

'Papa!' Rossington chided, 'how can you say such a thing?'

'Don't play the innocent Randal. You brought Miss Wrighton to my party for a purpose, didn't you? There is no need to deny it. You saw in her an image you recognised, perhaps not truly, unless you had already met her mother. Don't stand there now and tell me you haven't recognised the likeness of both mother and daughter to your grandmother. Here,' he said fishing a miniature portrait from his jacket pocket, 'this is her aged fifty. Tell me Mrs Wrighton is not of the same image.'

They passed it around and the likeness was undeniable but Rossington and Walborough already knew it to be the case.

'How came you by the conclusion Mrs Wrighton is your twin sister?' Walborough asked.

'There are facts you won't know which I will gladly tell you, but we seem to have disturbed you and can come back later.'

'Please stay,' Walborough pleaded. 'I am about to be married to Miss Bella Wrighton. Stay and bear witness with your son.'

If Lord Deane was surprised, he made no mention of it. He led his wife forward to where seats were offered to them and the service began without any further interruption. With no impediment raised and vows clearly spoken to each other, they were soon pronounced man and wife, and Walborough took the opportunity given to kiss his bride for the first time in public. The signatures of the bride and groom and some unexpected witnesses were added to the marriage record and everyone repaired to the dining room where a wedding breakfast was laid out, cook's renowned plum cake having been coated in white sugar paste and decorated with candied fruits, taking centre stage.

The discoveries made by Daniel Cunningham in Yorkshire were finally revealed some hours later and pieces of the puzzle became a little clearer.

'I see now where your conclusion has come from.' Walborough said thoughtfully. 'To understand the coincidence of dates and place of birth and to appreciate the uncommon likeness Mrs Wrighton has to Rossington's grandmama, that good lady would have to be her mother. It seems so logical now, it makes me wonder how Rossington and I never realised it for ourselves.'

'Vital facts missing,' Rossington responded, recalling their speculation as to the antics of the males in the family, which in truth had been hard to believe and subsequently been discounted.

'But how can it be?' Sally Wrighton asked Lord Deane. 'My mama and papa would never have been so cruel as to steal someone else's baby when their daughter died.'

'The thing is Mrs Wrighton, in the eyes of the law there is only you, baptised at Sawley as the daughter of William and Letty Foster. The child in the grave doesn't appear in any parish records. In normal circumstances the vicar would have gone to the grave as soon as he could and said prayers for the dead child. He would then have recorded the details of her short life under both baptisms and deaths in the register of the Church of the Blessed Virgin at Sawley.

'There was never any such record made. The only reason we know William and Letty had a baby who died aged ten days old, was because her father laid a small cross on her chest with her name, and the dates of her birth and death, carefully carved into it. Had I not decided to have all the bodies removed from the Belverhead graveyard and re-interred in the churchyard, none of this would have become known.'

'So, you want to see my grandparents and ask them what they know, or what they did?' Bella said, concerned they would be accused of some malicious act.

'If someone committed an evil act, I have a fair idea who it was, based on conversations I've had with my father, though why he would do such a thing. I can't imagine.'

'You think your grandfather was involved in some way?' Rossington asked his father.

'He was a heartless cruel man who ruled his family in a tyrannical manner. I haven't spoken to my mother yet but she was always afraid of him and I never liked him. The thing is I don't want to alarm your parents Mrs Wrighton. If it turns out you are my twin sister and we know it for certain, then I hope we might have a chance to get to know each other but I have no plans to disrupt anyone's family life unless it is favourable to all parties.'

'But how could you ever know it for certain?' Walborough asked.

'I don't suppose we ever will but circumstance seems to point to us having been born twins, even if we were never raised as such. My mama was at Belverdon giving birth to me. She could not have given birth to another child in the same time frame unless she carried twins and the likeness can only have passed down the female line at that point in time. My brother Frederick and my sisters Violet and Joan are all like my father who was the image of his own father. It's ironic that Richard and I, born two years apart, who both favour mother, were often mistaken for twins as boys.

'You believe my wife to be a descendent of the Duke of Aven?' Thaddeus asked Lord Deane.

'More so now than before, when it seemed the only plausible conclusion after Daniel Cunningham enlightened me with the facts discovered in Yorkshire. If perhaps I might explain.'

Since no one objected, he carried on revealing something of himself he had never spoken about in company before, unless he was deemed crazy.

'As a small boy when I had to spend time at Belverdon I used to feel strange, as if someone was close by me, but never truly near. It was as if a shadow sat on my shoulder and I could never reach it because it was nothing but a mist in time. I became almost afraid of it and was relieved when we stopped going there.'

'But it never left you,' Rossington butted in. 'You felt it again when we were at Belverdon recently. I asked you if it was a ghost and you said it was something ethereal. Where is the shadow now?'

'It's not a shadow anymore but a deep connection, a lost knowledge, a remembrance, buried for so long in the depths of my memory, released at last. Do you feel it too Sally?'

'It was a shock seeing you, sensing you as if......'

'As if we were once as close as two infants can be.'

They gravitated towards each other to hug and accept the bond that time and parting can never break. They would talk of their lives apart and realise how very alike they were in some ways, the same gestures, the same mannerisms noted by Walborough and Rossington.

Thaddeus was surprised, but not wholly, for he had accepted early on in his relationship with Sally that she was special, gifted more so than the servant class she lived amongst.

'Will you come to Tremar with your husband and meet the Duke and Duchess? It would be interesting to hear what my mother recalls of the day of our birth.'

Sally looked to Thaddeus as she had in all things since first meeting him.

'I think we can leave the parish in safe hands for a few days, if it is your wish to go.'

'I won't go if it will give you any hurt.'

How he loved her to think of him first and not selfishly seek to follow her own course.

'If it pleases you, we shall set forth with resolve and let the good Lord guide us.'

Chapter Sixteen

Bella said nothing and saw everything. If this was the truth, she was the granddaughter of both the Duke of Aven and Earl Wrighton. The Marquess of Deane, who must be her uncle, had stood witness at her marriage to the Duke of Walborough. She might have been elated but her thoughts were all for the beloved grandparents she knew, her uncles and cousins who might now be no blood relation at all. She feared for William and Letty, not knowing the truth of what had occurred so long ago. They had buried one child and raised another on the isolated moor above Belverdon. What truths had been hidden and what lies had been told?

'Where are you staying?' Rossington asked aware of little accommodation in the area suited to the status of his parents.

'At Hopston Chase. Your steward was obliging enough not to turn us away John, but no doubt now you will wish us to the very devil.'

'I would not be so ungrateful when I have been so frequently offered your generous hospitality. The house is large enough for Bella and myself to have some privacy and I would not see you and Lady Deane discommoded.'

'Nor would I,' Bella said firmly and I thank you for your earlier apology. You will, I hope, socialise with mama and papa for the evening and allow John and I to travel to Hopston ahead of you, to be settled before you arrive.'

'Better still,' her mother said, 'why not stay here with us since your son is already our guest? We have plenty of rooms to spare. They can easily be made ready for you in the time it takes for John to have your servants sent over.'

It was deemed the best solution by all, giving Sally Wrighton more time to spend with Lord Deane and his wife, as well as allowing the newlyweds all the privacy they'd hoped for on their wedding night.

The happy couple were waved off around an hour later to make the short journey to Hopston Chase where they planned to spend their honeymoon. Bella should have been living in a cloud of blissful happiness but her mind was still troubled as she sat beside her husband in the carriage.

'You seem to have fulfilled your family's stipulation of marrying well after all, although no one will know of it, unless some proof can be found.'

'I hope you will recall I was about to marry you without the knowledge that came to light this afternoon.'

'You knew something of it though, didn't you?'

'Nothing close to what might be the truth. I saw the likeness of your mother to Rossington's grandmama. There is a portrait of her on the stairs at Deane Castle which I've seen many times as well as having met her in the flesh on numerous occasions. It sparked a mystery Rossington and I were unable to resolve without speaking to your grandparents and how could we do that without potentially making people we cared about unhappy.'

'You chose not to pursue it?'

'We made a rational decision. If there is by chance any proof out there, which to be honest I doubt, where would we find it and whose lives would we mar by revealing it? Will your mama and papa be as happy now as they were before Deane revealed his suspicions?'

'Oh, I hope so John since they have always been there for each other, bound together in the deepest love.'

'And what of us Bella. Is anything changed between us?'

'Only that we are now married and I may call you husband. Did you expect ought else to change.'

'Possibly. You are aware of what is expected on a wedding night?'

'Mama explained what must happen and told me if I am in love and my love is returned, it will not be without some pleasure after the first time.'

'Then we have much to look forward to and little else to do besides.'

Oh, if only she had a fan handy to cool her blushes.

She expected to be placed at the opposite end of the table to John at dinner that evening but he insisted she sat beside him.

'How can I carry on a conversation with you or whisper sweet words in your ear, if you are so far in the distance?'

'Isn't it usual though?'

'If you have a table full of guests, then the gentleman entertains at the head of the table and the lady at the foot.'

'As in below you, beneath your foot?'

'Nonsense. You will not think of yourself as beneath me Bella, at least not socially. Whatever your rank before we married, you are now the Duchess of Walborough. You will cultivate your own circle of friends and choose what you wish to patronise or who to sponsor.

'You may be a part of any discussions which occur in any of my houses but I trust you not to be offensive to any of our guests. Not all men will allow women the freedom of speech your father does, but I look forward to us having lively discussions on any number of matters.'

'Then I shall aim to be diplomatic and sensitive to the fragile egos of men.'

'How will you deal with the spiteful words of women then?'

'I shall acquire some hauteur.'

'Will you, my love?' he said laughing.

The footman standing discreetly to one side smiled. The Duke had dodged so many women, cast hopefully in his direction, but now he had married the woman who held his heart in her tender hands, and he was happy. God willing, he would stay that way for the rest of his life.

John's thoughts were not on some distant time in the future but the here and now, contemplating how soon after dinner it would be reasonable to retire for the night. When the last plates were removed from the table, Bella swiftly put an end to his contemplating.

'These past few days have been tiring and with all that has happened today I think I will retire to my room and let Anna ready me for bed. Will you be long before retiring yourself?'

Oh, the wicked gleam in her eyes.

'Dismiss Anna,' he whispered, 'and I'll ready you for bed myself.'

'Shall we make a move then, my Lord?'

Her lord indeed. The minx would run rings round him and he didn't care as long as he could undress her slowly like a precious gift, touch and taste her soft feminine flesh, build her desire until she was ready for him to boldly make her his, and hold her replete in his arms as they slept until desire rode them, again and again.

He was magnificent, her John, a tender passionate lover and a bold stallion wrapped in the perfect male physique.

She would watch him rise from her bed naked, don his dressing robe and saunter into his room to be administered to by Will Ryder, blowing her a kiss in the doorway as if he hadn't already showered her body with them on waking.

They'd hardly stepped outside for a week, bathing together, eating their meals upstairs, reading poetry to each other, laughing and teasing, making long languorous love or simply responding to a rush of passion. Her body needed a rest and John knew it.

'We're going out today. Wear a warm carriage dress,' he'd told her.

The main stables were some distance from the house with only John's curricle, the paired blacks and a couple of riding horses kept in the stable yard behind the house. Jacob brought the curricle to the front door and John settled her comfortably into the seat with a blanket to keep her warm. He wore his usual dark riding attire with his greatcoat over the top and his hat perched at a rakish angle which amused her. He was no rake but he was definitely an ardent lover.

'Where are we going?'

'I'm taking you to meet some friends of yours.'

'Here at Hopston?'

'Wait and see. Are you warm enough? It's turned cooler these last few days.'

'I wonder why we didn't notice,' Bella said with undisguised humour.

'We were well lost to the world and will be again. I love you my darling Bella.'

'And I love you my dearest John.'

The stables were bustling with activity, horses being led here and there, stables being mucked out, saddles being cleaned, harnesses being polished, chattering and laughter heard all around, but no one idle.

They went inside to the harness room, where a young boy sat listening to the head groom.

'Arthur,' the Duke called to attract his attention.

'Mr Becket, Sir, I mean your Grace,' Arthur said flustered.

'Come outside for a moment Arthur. I've brought someone to see you.'

Arthur still somewhat overcome by his good fortune was wary but he soon realised he needn't have been.

'Miss Bella,' he said rushing towards her as he always had in the past.

'Not Miss Bella anymore Arthur. May I introduce you to my wife, the Duchess of Walborough.'

'You got married?'

'We did Arthur, last week, and I had no idea you were here.'

'Mam, dad and my brothers are here too, working for Mr, his Grace Becket.'

'You only need to say your Grace if you are talking directly to him and his Grace if you are talking about him. You don't need to add Mr or Sir or anything else.'

'I haven't seen him since he asked my dad if I could come and work here.'

'Are you happy here then Arthur? I know you always loved the horses, even if ours were nothing special.'

'Mr Lawton's horse was alright but he was mean with his pennies and made me look after him for free.'

'That wasn't well done of him,' Bella said with a smile.

'Mr, his Grace gave me a shilling. Mam put it to good use and saved some for later.'

'That was very generous indeed but he was well pleased with the way you cared for his very special horse.'

'I still sing to him before I go home at night. It soothes him. Mam sings to me too, now we're back together again.'

'We are going over now to see your mam and dad Arthur. Get your coat and you may come with us.'

Arthur, sitting between the two of them, chatted all the way about what he'd learned, which carriages he could now help to harness, what he could do well and what he was too little for. 'I'm good at polishing because mam taught me and cleaning the leather besides. I have to go to lessons too, lots of them, for reading and writing, learning about caring for horses, learning to ride a pony, scooping muck, but I don't like that as much,' he said wrinkling his nose.

John laughed. 'I don't know any lad who ever liked shovelling muck. Even I had to do it as a boy. My father said I should never entirely rely on someone else to care for my horses so he had me taught the same way you are being taught Arthur.'

The cottage, now being rented by the Briggs family, was set naturally in a small glade, back from the road, about halfway between the stables and the town of Hopston, detached and more substantial than the terraced cottage they'd lived in at Stillford. Arthur had his own small room, whilst his elder brothers shared a larger one.

They were expected, since John had sent a message earlier to say they would visit. Bowing and curtseying went on now they knew exactly who John was, respecting both his status as the Duke and as their employer. They asked particularly after Bella's parents and Lawrence, and she told them of his premiere as the organist for the Sunday service and how well received it had been. They congratulated the pair of them on their marriage and told John he was lucky to have found Miss Bella, which he readily agreed he was.

'Are you all happy here?' Bella asked them.

'We bless the day his Grace came to Stillford and our Arthur ran out to offer him assistance. Now will you come inside and have tea. Mrs Briggs has been baking.'

Mrs Briggs had always been fond of baking for as long as Bella could remember and her spiced and fruited griddle scones would have graced the table at every church concert such that you had to be quick if you wanted to get one. Today there was no rush.

John had a question for Mr Briggs.

'Mr Pike, my Head Groom, wants to put Arthur in a pony race with some other young grooms. I know he hasn't been riding for long, and there is no pressure on him to win, but he would like to see how he handles himself and his pony when racing, to inform his training. Would that concern you in any way?'

Mr Briggs was surprised to be asked for his opinion. 'What do you think Arthur?' he asked in turn.

'Mr Pike wouldn't ask me to do anything he thought was dangerous so I'd like to. It would be fun.'

'There you have your answer then, your Grace. My lad trusts your head groom to see him right.'

'Then we shall set it up and you will all come and watch. Now we should get Arthur back as Mrs Walton wishes to see him about his riding colours.'

'What does that mean,' Mrs Briggs asked.

'Each boy training to be a jockey will have an outfit in the Becket colours, black breeches and boots, white shirt and cravat, mustard waistcoat, and dark green jacket plus a tweed cap of black, mustard, and green check. Arthur's colours have been delivered and Mrs Walton will see to their fitting.'

'What a lucky boy you are Arthur,' Bella said ruffling his hair. 'We'll come to see you race your pony once it has been arranged.'

'You've done so much for the family John. How kind you are,' she said later, as they travelled home.

'I gave myself an advantage at the same time. Arthur is a natural with horses and he was dreadfully homesick when he first came here. His father and brothers are experienced carters and I have plans to extend the market at Hopston for the benefit of my farmers and the town residents. It made sense to offer them jobs and get them to move nearer to the stables for Arthur's sake.'

'What of Owen and his market trading?'

'Owen is not my concern. He's trading in my town, legally with some boundaries but making profits from his own farm when those profits could be made by my tenants. He is virtually without competition, and good for him for seizing the opportunity, but I will have the profits put back into my land and not his. There is also potential to bring produce and goods from other parts of the estate and further afield which is what Arthur senior and his sons are looking into at the moment with the help of my steward and land agent.'

'You aim to put Owen out of business?'

'Of course not, but he cannot have everything his own way. He is a tenant of Lord Bellingham but what was at one time a large estate is now considerably diminished and all but the village and an area east of the church has been sold across the years to my family.'

'I'm not sure how much he knows about ownership of the land around Stillford but he thought my father owned the Manor House and was surprised to discover he doesn't. Father rents it from Lord Bellingham, although the rent is nominal. My parents originally lived in the vicarage, rent free, with a small stipend and the money father had in the bank from his generous allowance which obviously stopped abruptly on his marriage. He sacrificed a lot to marry my mother.'

'He would do it again though, without question, to live his life with her. Of that I'm certain.'

'I'm worried now though. Will Rossington's papa want to take her away to live more like his sister and less like a poor vicar's wife?'

'To be honest my love, I don't think your mother would go. I can do a lot for your father if he wants preferment but I won't stamp on his pride if he's happy as he is.'

Chapter Seventeen

After two weeks of being together every day with many of their nights full of passion and tenderness, all in Bella's world seemed right. Then John left to go to London for a series of meetings. It wasn't that she couldn't have gone with him but he hadn't sounded enthusiastic at the prospect.

'You should stay here and continue your driving lessons and get more riding experience and I expect your father would enjoy a visit from you. I'll only be away for a couple of nights.'

The days seemed long, and the nights were lonely. A couple of nights turned into three or four.

Owen rode over to see her, unaware of her marriage and under the impression she'd become Walborough's mistress.

How should she answer him? John had made no official announcement of their marriage except to the servants so she too kept quiet and allowed Owen his say.

'Is this preferable Bella to my honest intentions towards you?' he said angrily. 'You know he's trying to ruin my business in Hopston, stealing my employees and setting up in direct competition to me when I had an agreement which was fair and honest. I knew it was a sad thing for you to go to London, allowing yourself to reach beyond your station and end up like this.'

'Like what Owen? Why don't you spell it out?' she said, angry that he could so misjudge her character.

'In respect of your father I won't say the words. I wanted you for my wife but now there can be nothing between us. You won't see me again.'

She didn't want to see him again and wondered at his respect for her father when he assumed he would have allowed her to become any man's mistress. She just wanted John to come home.

The house was the one delight she had as she waited for her husband to come back to her. Built in stone with three storeys of latticed windows, tall chimney stacks, and a fanciful curved roofline with parapets, many of its external architectural features had remained unchanged over the years. Internally it had been tastefully brought up to date. The French influence for more colour and delicate pieces of furniture, together with the removal of the original dark oak panelling, caused the large reception rooms to appear filled with warmth and light.

These were the rooms she loved, the music room being one of her favourites, although she could equally lose herself in the oak shelved library with its portraits of long dead Becket men and women, placed at intervals amongst the ancient leather-bound books. It retained the historic ambience of the house whilst maintaining a cosy welcoming atmosphere and was where she had spent some of her lonely evenings sitting close by a warming fire, reading.

On this bright morning, she had been out early to watch the young thoroughbreds being put through their paces, had received a driving lesson in the phaeton from Mr Pike, the Head Groom, and graciously accepted his praise for her rapidly increasing skill controlling the horses. She ate her breakfast alone, then walked for some time around the extensive gardens, asking questions of the gardeners when she saw a plant she didn't recognise, and sitting peacefully for a while to admire the intricacy of the knot garden with its pleasing scent of lavender and delicately perfumed aromatic herbs.

Returning indoors, Anna had tidied her hair and helped her change into an afternoon frock of spotted muslin decorated with bands of ruched ribbon around the hem. She now sat playing the pianoforte from memory. It had always been a gift of hers, a wonderful memory. Like anyone else she had to diligently learn pieces of music, but once they were familiar, she needed no score, even those with intricate fingering like the Mozart sonatas she favoured.

Outside the music room, servants had gathered quietly to listen to her performance. It could be called nothing else as she played Mozart's Sonata in A Major with skill and accuracy. The minutes ticked by as they waited for the third and final movement which was fast and exciting, *Rondo Alla Turca*, she said it was called, when she'd practiced it the day before.

John arrived home eager to see Bella, to be met with a dearth of servants in the hall and the sound of music coming from above. He ran up the stairs to find his progress halted by Mrs Walton, who put her finger to her lips and then indicated the audience outside the music room. Then it began, the dancing fingers, the bold striking chords, the thrilling sound moving towards a crescendo. He was as entranced as his servants.

'Is that my wife playing?' he whispered.

'It is.'

Lawrence had told him she was talented but he hadn't understood just how talented she was. He moved closer to the door not wishing to startle anyone. Music of such quality was to be enjoyed. He wouldn't deny his household the opportunity. When the piece finished with a grand flourish, the small gathering applauded without conscious thought. John made his way through them to join his wife, clapping enthusiastically as he walked towards her.

'You are home,' she said throwing her arms around his neck as if nothing momentous had just happened.

'I am,' he said and in time to hear your wonderful playing which has kept my servants inactive for the duration of it.'

'Oh! Don't be cross with them. Next time I'll close the door.'

'You will not, although they should not all neglect their duties at once. You have been hiding your talent behind Lawrence's excellence.'

'Lawrence can earn a living for himself as a musician and his talent needed promoting. I can only entertain.'

'You most certainly can, and you shall. Now tell me, how have you been?'

'Lonely. I missed you. Where have you been? It's five days since you left.'

'I know and I'm sorry. I had more to catch up on politically than I'd imagined and I would have written but I'd hoped to be back before the post could reach you. Did you spend time with your mama and papa?'

'No. They've travelled to Tremar with Lord and Lady Deane. Mama is torn between learning what might have happened in the past, and wishing she knew nothing, but she does know something, and must now learn all she can.'

'Do you have plans for the rest of the afternoon?'

'I might have had, but now you are home, I'm happy to forget them.'

'I must go upstairs and change. I'm dusty from the road. Will you come with me?'

'Can I be your valet?'

'You my love can be my valet and much, much more,' he said, capturing her lips in a mind drugging kiss and holding her close. I've missed you so much.'

Frantic undressing, passionate love making and a drowsy hour of lying naked in each other's arms restored Bella's confidence in John's love and his honest intentions as her husband. She told him about Owen calling to see her and his view of their relationship.

'You might think it wrong of me to have not sent a notice to the newspapers but these few weeks alone together have been precious to me. We will be inundated with invitations when we return to town, and first we must go to Bascombe Hall and enlighten my mother.'

'What if she doesn't like me?'

'If she voices such an opinion, then she is more foolish than I already perceive her to be. She was never as obsessed until my father died, then she thought the succession was vulnerable and urged me to make an early marriage and secure our line.'

'It's really too early to be certain, but something which should have arrived with regularity this week, is missing, so you may have very efficiently already secured your line,' she said shyly, 'although expectation and deliverance will be months apart.'

'What are you saying? You mean...'

'As mama would put it, your seed has settled on fertile ground and will hopefully flourish.'

'Oh, Bella, my dearest love, what a wonderful homecoming this is.'

'It will be if you don't take this news as a reason to leave me lonely in my bed in case you are driven to passion and do me harm.'

'Some adapting might be required but I have no wish to sleep alone or deny the passion we share.'

'Then, yes. This is a wonderful homecoming.'

Within a few days they were on their way to Bascombe Hall, the seat of the Becket family since 1720 when the grand house, built at the request of John's grandfather, had supplanted Hopston Chase as the family's main residence.

'You will find Bascombe Hall quite different to Hopston Chase. It's highly decorative with painted ceilings, grand staircases, tall mirrors, sculptures and elaborate wood carvings. In fact, most spaces are filled with some form of intricate decoration or pieces of fine porcelain. The reception rooms are substantial with gilded furniture and large framed portraits of past Dukes and Earls as well as their ladies and children.'

'Tell me about your mother.'

'She's more your Aunt Susannah's age since my eldest sister Esther is now forty. I was late arriving on the scene and I suppose having five daughters and an eight-year gap before her son was born have made her more anxious about the timely arrival of an heir.'

'Who is the current heir?'

'My cousin Nicholas, who is forty-two, married with seven children, three of whom are boys.'

'So, no shortage of heirs, but not as yet in the direct line.'

'Not as yet but we can be hopeful.'

'We should not raise our hopes too much for another few months. What are your mother's interests?'

'Like your own mother she is an excellent needlewoman and she enjoys listening to music although she is not proficient on any instruments. She likes to read but not anything too challenging. She enjoys the gardens and pleasure grounds to sit in or ride around but she has no interest in their structure or maintenance and she has not over the years shown any interest in remodelling any of the rooms in the house. She likes to entertain and entertains lavishly. Perhaps her forte is in the art of decoration for parties and balls which is a skill she is held in high regard for. We will allow her some latitude in that direction when we hold our first ball at Walborough House to formally introduce you to the ton.'

It was the first Bella had heard of it.

Lady Esther Becket, Duchess of Walborough had heard nothing of it either. Speculation aside, she had no wish to acknowledge her change in status to Dowager Duchess, until her son informed her of it in person. Since he had not, she would assume the tittle-tattle in the newspapers to be mere gossip.

'Read that to me again Sophia,' that noble lady said in a state of heightened agitation.

'But it cannot be true mama. It is only the gossips with their usual innuendo. Why upset yourself?'

'Read it to me again please,' she insisted.

'Speculation is rife as to the current marital status of the D of W who has been absent from town for several weeks. He is rumoured to have been married quietly in the country, at his Hopston estate. It is thought the M of D posted from town to be a witness at his marriage to the ML. VR was also present. The D of W was in town last week with VR but did not socialise, being there primarily on business matters. VR has since posted down to Tremar House. where his parents are hosting guests. The current whereabouts of the D of W is unknown.'

'This cannot be true, can it? Walborough is not secretive about his whereabouts. Who can this ML be? Do you recall anyone with those initials, a marchioness perhaps,' she said optimistically.

'No mama, but Lydia suggested it meant mystery lady.'

'Mystery lady? You mean someone we don't know and have never heard of. God help me if some upstart has trapped him by some indiscretion and a marriage has been forced upon him.'

'I think that unlikely mama. Walborough doesn't dally with those types of females.'

'Don't be naïve Sophia. You have to acknowledge that there are some unscrupulous ladies within society who would try to catch him that way.'

Lady Sophia wasn't convinced; her brother had been remarkably adept at avoiding any such encounters so far.

'If M of D is the Marquess of Deane and VR is Viscount Rossington, which seems most likely, I don't believe they would have attended any kind of havey-cavey wedding. Perhaps this report is all a hum and they were together for an entirely different reason.'

'Then let us hope so,' Lady Esther exclaimed.

Hope was in short supply.

The door to the drawing room opened and the steward Mr Peters entered and bowed respectfully.

'Mr William Ryder has arrived in company with several servants of his Grace, the Duke. The household is to be assembled at the main door in thirty minutes to welcome the arrival of the Duke and Duchess.'

'So, it is true then. Who is his bride?'

'I was not told, your Grace.'

'Then make any necessary arrangements and see everything is in place for their arrival. Is this the first you have heard of their impending visit?'

'It is your Grace. I understood the Duke to be at Hopston Chase until his return to town for the new parliamentary session.'

'We have not by chance missed an official announcement?'

'No, your Grace. I understand the announcement will follow.'

Her Grace felt she understood very little at that moment in time and prayed her new daughter-in-law would be graced with some virtues.

'Send Mr Ryder to me, Mr Peters.'

'As you wish, your Grace.'

If Walborough's mother thought she was going to get any information out of her son's valet, she was greatly mistaken. His household were a tight knit lot, who both served him, and admired him.

'Mr William Ryder,' Peters informed her moments later as the door opened and closed and Will stood looking suitably cowed and respectful in her presence.

'Who is she?'

'Who is who? your Grace.'

'Don't be obtuse and impertinent with me Mr Ryder. Who is my son's bride?'

'I am not at liberty to tell you, your Grace. I have been expressly forbidden.'

'Then I shall not greet her at the door.'

'As you wish, your Grace.'

'You do not intend to persuade me?'

'It is not my position to offer you wise counsel, your Grace, but some errors can never be adequately corrected.'

'Get out,' she said, her temper rising.

Sophia might not approve but she knew her place.

'It seems mama as if we must pay our respects to the new Duchess.'

'Lip service is all we will pay and Walborough will pay too, mark my words.'

'Beware mama it is not you who will pay. Walborough will not stand for any insult to his Duchess.'

'Pluck up your courage Bella and step out of this carriage with the same confidence you had when you walked across a ballroom floor and accosted a young man you didn't have any acquaintance with.'

'This is scarier.'

'Remember, stand tall and don't curtsey to anyone.'

'Not even your mother?'

'Not even my mother. Only to those who rank above you. She will in future be known as the Dowager Duchess of Walborough.'

Mr Peters guided them past the lowliest of servants, who curtsied respectfully, leading them at a brisk pace towards the door, where more senior servants were introduced by name and their position in the household clarified. Close by the door stood Walborough's sister.

'May I introduce Lady Sophia Ames, your Grace,' Mr Peters said as Bella stood before her. Lady Ames is his Grace's sister, one of identical twins.'

'How interesting,' Bella said smiling at Sophia. 'I'm pleased to meet you.'

'And this is my mama, Duchess Esther,' John said leading her forward. 'Mama this is my wife, Bella.'

'A wife Walborough? You are a little behind times in telling me of your marriage.'

He ignored her and turned to address his servants.

'Thank you for welcoming my wife to Bascombe Hall. I trust you will be as diligent in your service to the Duchess as you are to me. Mr Peters will see you all receive a guinea and an extra half day holiday but please don't all take it at the same time.'

There was a ripple of laughter and some words of thanks but John had taken his bride inside and everyone else filed in quietly behind him.

'Come Bella. I'll show you to your rooms,' he said aiming to avoid any animosity from his mother, at least until he'd had an opportunity to speak to her alone. 'I expect you would like to freshen up.'

'Can it wait a while, as above all things I would like a refreshing cup of tea?'

John merely glanced at Mr Peters and he went off to organise some refreshments.

'The drawing room then, I think. Mama, Sophia will you join us?'

Reluctantly they did.

The Dowager Duchess failed to heed her daughter's warning to be respectful, being wholly determined to make her displeasure in her son's hasty marriage known to him.

'You have been tardy in telling me of your marriage, Walborough. When and where were you married?'

'We were married three weeks ago, on the sixth, at Stillford Manor House, by Bella's father, Mr Thaddeus Ignacious Wrighton, son of the late Earl Wrighton, brother of Lady Bellingham and Vicar of St. Jude's. We met in London a few months ago.'

'Wrighton, you say? Would that be the disgraced and outcast son of Earl Wrighton?'

John stood tall and held her gaze, looking remarkably like his late father as he showed his undisguised displeasure at her carelessly spoken words.

'If you cannot offer your support mother you can remove yourself to Fensham Castle. If you offer another insult, you will be removed with immediate effect.'

'John,' Bella pleaded, 'I should like to be friends with your mother and sisters.'

'Then they must show respect to you and your family. It is my duty now to protect you as my wife and Duchess. I will not have you maligned, nor upset. Come, your tea can be sent upstairs on a tray.'

'Well done mother,' Sophia said as they left the room. 'I hope you like it at Fensham Castle. From what I recall of it, it's dark and dreary with a resident ghost.'

'Don't exaggerate, besides I will not be going there.'

'You intend to apologise then to the new Duchess.'

'I will do no such thing. Walborough owes me respect as his mother and marrying without telling me is not the way to show it.'

'Don't count on me supporting you. I think it the height of foolishness to challenge him. I have Caro to think of. Having a duchess to sponsor her will greatly improve her chances of making a good marriage. I will pay my respects to them both and then I'm returning home.'

Chapter Eighteen

Lucas Wainwright was coming home after six years of studying abroad in Italy. It had not been his desire to return to England but his esteemed father had died quite suddenly after a short illness, and he, being his sole remaining heir, had become the new Viscount.

His ship had docked, and he was expecting to be met by a lawyer who had made arrangements for him to travel on to their family estate, but either the ship had sailed into port early, or the man was tardy in arriving.

When he was eventually approached by a man who called him by name and asked him to accompany him to a nearby inn, he saw no reason to refuse. He followed him up a flight of stairs to an upstairs room where three men sat behind a solid wooden table and four more stood around the room. Nervous tension immediately engulfed him. They were masked. It didn't bode well.

He was surprised then to hear a cultured voice address him. Not ruffians after all, which made the situation appear all the more sinister.

He was encouraged to take a seat and did so when protesting seemed pointless, heavily outnumbered as he was.

Surprisingly, they aimed to set him at his ease.

'We should point out at once that we mean you no harm. All we ask is that you answer our questions as honestly as you can and when you leave here, tell no one of this meeting.'

'Who are you?'

'It matters not who we are for you will never see us again.'

'I have someone expecting me.'

'We have him in our care. You will meet up with him when you have answered our questions.'

'Very well then. What is it you wish to ask me?'

'Somewhere in the region of six years ago, you were at school with Hunter Harding Wrighton, a young man of the same age as yourself.'

'I was.'

'You were at one time his friend but severed the connection due to ….'

'Behaviour I found abhorrent.'

'Behaviour towards young women?'

'Towards one young woman in particular.'

'Would that have been a young woman by the name of Jenny.'

'Yes Jenny,' he said surprised to hear her name again after so long. 'I never knew her surname and by the time I found out what had happened to her, it was beyond my ability to offer any help, and as God is my witness, I wish I could have.'

'What was your understanding of his behaviour towards Jenny?'

'He seduced her and promised marriage.'

'How do you know this?'

'I didn't at first, in fact not for nigh on a year. We had a militia at the school for which we had a uniform, thought by Hunter to be dashing. He used to wear it on occasion to go out in town, said it appealed to the ladies. One evening when we were going home late, probably not very sober, we came across a young woman, cowering in a doorway. She had become separated from her party and was scared and unsure of where she was, being a visitor to the city, staying with friends, so she told us. Hunter, charming her, as he so easily could, offered to help her find her way home. He knew the city better than I, and at that time I thought him to be both honest in his intention and chivalrous. I trusted him to protect her.'

'He did not though?'

It was a bald statement hiding so much - disbelief, anger, sadness, and regret.

'No, he did not. At school I had no knowledge of his baser nature. He kept it well hidden. For the most part when I knew him, he appeared to have a natural charm and a generous nature, winning ways, used to his advantage when it suited him to impress. I honestly thought him a gentleman.

'We went home the next day for the holidays and I saw nothing of him over the summer. Since I didn't return to school in the autumn, going instead to Italy to stay with my aunt and uncle and begin my studies of architecture, it was almost a year later, when I was back home visiting mama and papa, that I discovered he didn't have a chivalrous bone in his body. He told me, as if it was an amusing tale, of how he had abducted her and kept her secreted away in a house in the country, leaving her for several weeks at a time with an older woman to keep watch over her.'

'Did he tell you she was pregnant with his child?'

'Not until he told me the old lady had unfortunately discovered a conscience, revealed his family connections and helped Jenny travel to London to seek help from his father.'

'Who generously took care of her until the child was born?' Lucas scoffed at the notion.

'Who detained her at his house, hidden in a cellar until the child was born.'

'What happened then?'

'I can only relate to you what Hunter told me when I met him quite by chance in Piccadilly near Hatchard's book shop.

'For old time's sake - for I had once thought him an amiable friend, we went to a nearby coffee house to catch up. He asked me about my year in Italy but he was not relaxed and stopped the flow of conversation in an instant when he stated without any show of emotion that he had a son. The mother, Jenny, whom he said I would recall, had died birthing him. It was only then when I discovered what had happened to her and how callous his behaviour, and latterly that of his father, had been towards her. His father, he whispered, was going to tidy matters up for him later that night. I admit to being horrified by what he revealed of his actions and his disinterest in his son, feeling a deep sense of concern for the child. I watched their house from the park and saw a woman come out carrying a baby in her arms. I was terrified she was going to throw the child in the river or commit another heinous deed so I followed her at a discreet distance.

'She walked for a while with purpose as if she knew where she was going. Then she stopped quite suddenly, turned to look around and placed the infant on the ground in a doorway, quickly moving on as two women approached. The baby let out a loud wail and one of the women picked it up and took it down the road to the orphanage. I contemplated approaching them and telling them who the child's father was but in truth I could not say for certain. It could just as easily have been a housemaid's unwanted child and I genuinely thought if it were Hunter's son, he was most likely safer there than with the Wrightons.

'After that I had little to do with Hunter. I was dedicated to my studies and returned soon after to live permanently in Italy having the freedom to follow my passion as I was not then my father's heir. The loss of my elder brother last year, and more recently my father's sudden demise, have now made me Viscount Wainwright.'

'I thank you for your honesty in relating the facts you are aware of in this tragedy. I should tell you Jenny was not without respectability. She was, as she told you, a visitor to the city, staying with the family of a school friend.

'They had been out for the evening with escorts but had by some misfortune witnessed a violent brawl and the fatal stabbing of a young gentleman in the street. In the general pandemonium which followed they become parted from each other. No doubt she ran like others to protect herself from harm. It seems that in retracing her steps and finding herself in unfamiliar territory, she panicked and became lost. She never arrived back at her friend's house, and her family never saw her again.

'A thorough search for her took place and extensive enquiries were made but there were few leads to follow. However, it is difficult to completely hide someone, and we have remained vigilant in our pursuit of justice.'

'How did you know about me?' Lucas asked, surprised they had ever heard his name in regard to Jenny's disappearance.

'We didn't. At least we had no idea you knew so much. We have over the past few years questioned every friend and acquaintance of Hunter Wrighton's we could find.'

'How did you know he was involved?'

'Early on Jenny wrote a letter to her parents but gave no address where they might find her and take her home to safety. Last year they both died when they succumbed to the winter vomiting illness and we found it amongst their personal papers.

'She said they should not worry about her since she was content living with her soldier Hunter Wild and they were going to be married.'

'But they never were?'

'Obviously not.'

'And they could not find her?

'No. She was not to be found anywhere and Viscount Wylde was not initially a subject of interest. Only a chance reckless remark made by a friend of his in a bawdy house gave us cause to suspect his involvement.'

'Do you have any idea what happened to his son?'

'He has since been adopted and is happy. We won't interfere. He was born out of wedlock and has no need to discover how unspeakably cruel his paternal family could be. We have seen him from a distance. He has Jenny's dark curly hair and blue eyes so something precious of her survives.'

'And Hunter?'

'Hunter and his father will pay dearly for the crime they committed against an innocent young woman.'

The coldness in his voice scared Lucas but they let him go as promised, directing him to the room where the lawyer sat nervously waiting. Together they went to the inn where they had rooms booked for an overnight stay.

Oh God! Lucas thought. He would never condone Hunter's behaviour but now he feared for his life. He wrote out a brief note. LOOK TO YOUR OWN SAFETY. He neither addressed it nor signed it and asked the lawyer to see it was delivered by an untraceable route to be handed directly to Hunter and no one else.

'Did you know who they were? Lucas asked the lawyer.'

'No, and I have no wish to, thank you. I think the lad has upset some quite sinister and ruthless people and will shortly live to regret it.'

Or die regretting it, Lucas thought horrified. Those men were cold and detached. Within a timespan he could not equate, they had searched for answers, unrelenting in their quest for the truth until they had latched on to a plausible answer and sought proof of their suspicions.

'Whatever you do, don't let anyone know who you are when you first pass on the note,' Lucas warned the legal man.

'I won't, believe me. I shall look to my own safety, above all things.'

Hunter Harding Wrighton, Viscount Wylde, was about to enter his rooms at the Albany when a small boy approached him and thrust a folded note at him, dashing off at speed before there was any opportunity to question him. Hunter held it at a distance in his gloved hand. It was dirty and crumpled but curiosity got the better of him. LOOK TO YOUR OWN SAFETY, was all it said. What was that supposed to mean? No salutation, no signature, just an idle threat from someone who thought to scare him. Once inside, he tossed it on the fire and thought no more of it. Probably from a disgruntled tradesperson he had chosen not to pay. How dare anyone imagine they could threaten him.

Sally Wrighton didn't feel as if she was going home when the impressive façade of Tremar House come into view. Home was with Thaddeus, her life with him, one of love, tenderness and compassion, a hidden life in a quiet countryside village, without exposure to the grandeur of the aristocratic life she appeared to have been born into. This had to be a strange homecoming, a first meeting with parents she should have had, but hadn't, if what Lord Deane believed was true, and she was in fact his twin sister.

It was as bizarre as it was enlightening, her response to the Marquess of Deane. She had never previously met him and knew nothing about him, yet upon first seeing him face to face she'd experienced a wave of emotion so strong it felt only natural to walk up to him and accept him as her brother, as if deep in her psyche she'd always been aware of him in some intangible way.

If they were fraternal twins, as he thought, they had not been destined to grow up alike but the resemblance of Rossington family members down the ages had long been noted. Even Thaddeus had to admit she had a look of her brother, now he'd seen them together.

'Are you worried about this meeting Sally?' Thaddeus asked.

'Not worried for myself but for William and Letty who have been my parents in my heart for all my life. How can I now supplant them with someone else?'

'I don't think you will have to,' he said hoping to reassure her. 'They will always be in your heart. You have room to embrace the Duke and Duchess as well if you wish it.'

She could not say what she had wished for in that moment of introduction.

There was no instant recognition and she saw wariness from the Duchess in particular who had her own doubts and regrets, realising if this woman truly was her daughter, she herself had been an unwilling pawn in her father-in-law's cruel power game. He had ruthlessly threatened her, knowing she was physically weak and close to exhaustion. She had been bullied, harried, sedated, and controlled until too tired and confused to fight any longer, she had buried the sorrowful memories of birthing this child in the deepest recesses of her mind.

A lost daughter for her own salvation.

She recalled now how fearful and anxious the Duke had made her, how he wore her down with his denials and the force of his personality until she had not known what was real and what imagined, terrified by the repeated accusation of hysteria and the threat of being incarcerated in an asylum to be abused by men of science with their dangerous experimental treatments.

In her weakest moments she had feared death and had no wish to recall those dreadful days again, yet she must try to remember. In truth, for the first time in almost half a century she wanted to remember and was encouraged to remember by those who loved her. Free from threats, she let her mind drift backwards through time, to the days of her youth when less than a year married, she had sought to give her beloved husband an heir. The past rose up and swept over her like the wash of the tide over craggy rocks, penetrating into deep hollows, flushing out the confusion, the lies, the pain, and the fear.

She had been happy in her marriage and had reached a plateau of contentment intent on having her baby in their London home, where a birthing room had been prepared in advance and the nursery newly decorated and furnished.

She had never planned to travel to Belverdon, bleak and unwelcoming as it was for most of the year, a man's residence without refinement, built within the looming shadow of the moor and constantly at the mercy of its moody, fretful weather. Thomas had refused to travel to

Yorkshire but his father had insisted he would be part of the shooting party with words of duty, respect and obedience wielded like weapons to force the issue.

'Bring the woman with you, if you must,' had been his final word, leaving Thomas with little choice but to take his very pregnant wife with him.

The past came to life again and the words began to flow from her in a torrent of long stifled emotion.

Thomas went out early. I woke in discomfort and the day began anxiously. It was too soon to be having my baby. I tried to rest but the pains kept coming and grew in strength until there could be no doubt. I feared my child could not survive. The room was dark. Heavy curtains had been drawn.

What time was it? Had night come so soon? Why was there no one familiar with me? Who were these women? The pains had been coming and going for so long I thought I would die from them but they kept me awake and alert. Then I was pushing and pushing and the baby's cries penetrated through the haze I existed in. A boy, they told me. 'You have a son.' Thomas would be pleased to have an heir. 'Send to Thomas to tell him,' I said.

The door opened and closed, yet I saw no one. I thought it must be over but the muttering and fussing went on, then the pains began again and the pushing and the cries began just as before but no-one spoke to me.
'Is it a boy or girl? I asked.
'Just the afterbirth.'
'Then what were the cries?' I asked.
'Just the boy wanting to be fed.'

The door opened again. He came in, the Duke, but he didn't approach the bed. They huddled around me and he went out again. How long did I lie there, confused, uncertain?
'Where is the second baby?' I asked. 'Let me see.'

'What second baby they said? There is but one child. You must rest now and sleep. Your son will need you to be strong. He is premature, very small, you must rest ….rest ….rest….'

And then I slept but I woke agitated, something was wrong. I knew it. I knew they lied.

The Duke came to see me again.

'Where are my babies?' I asked him. 'Was the second a boy or a girl?'

'You have only one child my dear, a son. You must rest now and keep up your strength. You are very weak. Don't risk your life by being unnecessarily agitated.'

He sounded reasonable, concerned even. I asked for my son.

'He's being cared for,' he told me. 'When you are stronger, he can be brought to you.'

'No, I need him now. I need to see him. Let me see him.'

I tried to get up but they held me down.

'Where is Thomas?' I cried. 'I need to see Thomas.'

'Thomas is doing his duty to our guests.'

I knew he would never put guests before me. They were deliberately keeping him away from me.

'Why won't you let me see him? What is happening to me?'

'You are letting yourself become hysterical. Do you want to spend time in an asylum, which is where hysterical women go?'

I was not hysterical. I just wanted to see Thomas.

'Drink this,' they said and then you can see your husband.' Everything went hazy and then I slept again.

When I woke, I was in a different room. It was light, the curtains were open. My maid came in to wash and dress me in a clean nightgown and a lacy dressing robe.

'Where have you been?' I asked her.

'They wouldn't let me in, my lady. They said you were asleep.'

'Have you seen my babies?'

She looked at me strangely.

'You have a son, my lady. Your husband will be delighted.'

'No. Listen to me,' I pleaded. *'There were two. I remember, but they didn't say if the second was a boy or a girl. They wouldn't let me see either of them. Help me, you have to help me.'*

'There is only the boy my lady. There is no other child. You must be mistaken, perhaps you dreamt it, thought you were going through it all again.'

I hadn't dreamt it. I felt the pain. I heard the cry. They were all against me. Why were they lying? Why were they keeping Thomas from me?

The door opened and I looked for my husband but it was him again, the Duke with his cold heart and cold eyes.

'Don't let me hear anymore talk of two babies,' he said in his harsh threatening voice. *'You are overwrought, hysterical. You know what happens to hysterical women.'*

'I'm not hysterical,' I insisted. *'Where is Thomas?'*

'He'll come later when you are calmer. You will not distress him with this fantasy.'

I must have slept again and when I woke, you came to see me, Thomas.

'Thank you for my son,' you said. *'Now you must take good care of yourself.'*

You wore a worried frown. I began to think maybe I had been delirious, maybe there was only one baby. I couldn't remember, my mind was fuddled. You fetched the doctor. I remember him examining me. He was concerned.

Thomas remembered too, recalling his own fear and anxiety upon hearing the doctor's hushed words of caution.

'He said I should take you away from there, somewhere quiet, and peaceful. He said the baby was small and obviously premature. He was worried and thought you had been given a sleeping draught as you seemed confused. He told me he feared for your life.'

I was ill, feverish. I thought I would die without ever seeing or holding my son. When I recovered, I questioned my own sanity. The Duke threatened me, said if I repeated that nonsense about twins again then he would have me committed to the asylum for my own safety. I was terrified. He didn't like me. He never wanted you to marry me. He hoped I'd die bearing your child and he could marry you to someone else, someone he could easily control.

'He certainly liked to be in control. He deliberately kept me from you which was bad enough but if we had a daughter as well as our son, why did he take her from us?' What reason could he have had? Whatever he did, he would have done it for his own gain, or a perceived gain for the family, though how denying us the raising of our daughter could be seen as any kind of gain.'

Thaddeus knew any kind of further speculation was pointless. They could not after all this time hope to understand the warped mind of Ivor Richard Rossington, the fourth Duke of Aven. He put into words the only reasonable way forward.

'For better or for worse we must travel to Shropshire to visit William and Letty. They will know their own truth, which might cast more light on the old Duke's state of mind.'

Thomas agreed. They must now look for any answers they could reasonably find but without question, they accepted Sally as their daughter. To Elizabeth, the Duchess it was a vindication of something she had once known, had perhaps always known in her heart, but for ever after been forced to deny. She had let go of the memory, let the child die in her mind so she herself could live and raise her son without fear.

'Perhaps Ivor,' she suggested, 'you might show your sister the portraits of her ancestors, since I can only think she is the child I thought I had given birth to, who was denied to me by my father-in-law.'

The tears came then and Thomas held her in his arms to comfort her. It was a good job his father was already dead because in that moment he was enraged enough to want to kill him for the torment he'd put Elizabeth through, for taking from them their firstborn daughter and denying them the opportunity to watch her grow from infant to child to woman. At the same time, he thanked God for keeping his daughter safe and seeing her raised within a loving family and married to a fine man.

Thaddeus thought he'd never heard anything so sad or cruel and he worried they hadn't heard the worst of it yet. The great irony of these recent revelations hit him. His sweet Sally had almost certainly been born a Lady, outranking him. None of it mattered of course. To him she had always been a Lady and whatever was discovered, she always would be.

Chapter Nineteen

The following announcement appeared in the marriage columns of newspapers around the country during the second week of November.

On the sixth day of October, by special licence at the house of Mr Thaddeus Ignacious Wrighton in Stillford, Hertfordshire, his Grace the Duke of Walborough to Miss Bella Wrighton. The ceremony was performed by Mr Wrighton, Vicar of St Jude's, at the request of the couple. Witnesses to the marriage were the Marquess and Marchioness of Deane and Viscount Rossington, amongst others. The newly married pair left after the ceremony to honeymoon at Hopston Chase, Hertfordshire.

By the time the news of their unconventional marriage became known, John and Bella were back at Walborough House. The Dowager Duchess whilst not being wholly committed to her new daughter-in-law, had at least ceased any hostilities, particularly when given the opportunity to host a grand ball with free rein as to the theme and decorations.

John was busy with his heavy schedule of responsibilities, and Bella had resumed attending Augusta Goldsborough's

Thursday afternoon gatherings of like-minded ladies. She also had endless fittings at the dressmakers, for a wardrobe deemed necessary for her new status, when she was usually accompanied by her aunt, whose judgement couldn't be faulted, particularly when there was no restraint on the cost. Having the freedom to shop without making much of a dent in her generous pin money, she frequented Hatchard's in Piccadilly and purchased books not generally associated with ladies of the ton, but which she had long wanted to read.

Of course, she had the Walborough House library she could search through, but newer books on scientific discoveries and some journals of adventures in far off places, were currently lacking in the catalogue. She also purchased new musical scores and song sheets she thought she would like to learn and perform, now she had an appreciative listener in her husband. She had even agreed to perform at Mrs Hepworth's next soiree, having been encouraged by both John and Rossington to demonstrate her talent, although she remained nervous as to what reception she might receive.

Anna had agreed to stay with her as her personal maid, and they would be seen walking together in the park when the weather permitted. No one cut her dead, nor was openly uncivil to her, but she knew they whispered behind her back.

There were those who considered themselves more worthy of being the Duchess of Walborough and thought John should have stuck to the rules and chosen a bride from amongst the daughters of peers. Words were spoken in secret but whilst the men felt he should have better towed the line, there were those who envied him his good fortune, for no one doubted their marriage was anything but a love match.

Perhaps that wasn't quite true, although the doubting appeared to be at home.

She arrived back at Walborough House, rosy cheeked from a walk in the park, to be told John would like to see her in his study, so she went to find him without delay.

'How are you?' he asked, which seemed a strange question when it was short of two hours since they had breakfasted together.

'Much the same as I was at breakfast, and you?'

'I'm troubled Bella. Have you grown tired of me?'

'What foolish notion is this?' she asked, confused by his unusually stern look.

'Not foolish when you have been seen kissing a fellow in the park.'

'Really! Who told you this?'

'Does it matter? Is it true?'

'That might depend on what you consider a kiss to be and what sort of a fellow it was?'

'You don't deny it then?'

'Aren't you curious to know who it was? After all he would have to mean something special to me, wouldn't he?'

He looked at her and frowned.

'What sort of kiss was it then?'

'I suppose you could equate the exuberant hug, and the peck on the cheek, and the embarrassment which followed, with Lawrence's reaction to my offering to cut his hair.'

Enlightenment struck John.

'You bumped into Roderick?'

'I did and I was so excited after not seeing him for nigh on a year that I'm afraid I did too boldly hug him, and kiss his cheek, which made him cross and he called me a hoyden.'

'Did he?' John said with a smile. 'So, you haven't tired of me after all?'

'How foolish you are. For one thing, Anna stood beside me, and for another, how could I ever tire of you?'

'Perhaps I've been neglecting you.'

'If you have, I haven't noticed. You've been busy, but I admire you for your diligence.'

'Should we put our heads above the parapet and attend some social functions together?'

'Only if you want to, although I do have some very daring new dresses which are all the rage.'

'You want me to stand around whilst other men admire your beautiful breasts?'

'No, but I want to dance in your arms and you can look all you want.'

'Did you invite Roderick to dinner?' he asked changing the subject before he found himself abandoning his work and taking Bella upstairs to admire all of her charms.

'I did, but he can't come until next week as he has evening engagements with Lord Henry, so he's coming on Tuesday when Rossington will be here as well, rounding up the numbers.'

She walked round the back of his desk and sat on his knee with her hands either side of his face.

'I love you, John Becket. You and nobody else. I should tell you perhaps that I never had the desire for any man to kiss me until I met you, nor would I want them to touch me the way you do, and I'll never tire of you, ever. She kissed his warm lips and for John that was all it took. Work was forgotten and his lady had all his attention.

The music room at Deane Castle had all Lawrence's attention. The floor was covered, in most part, with piles of music scores, neatly stacked according to the composer. These were then subdivided as vocal or instrumental which would later be further divided and catalogued according to which instruments and which vocal register they were arranged for.

He had cleared one side of the cabinet but the bottom six inches were taken up by a massive book which he found impossible to move, weighted as it was with a solid brass lock and corner guards. No light shone brightly enough to penetrate into the cupboard, and he feared holding a candle too close lest he should accidentally set the music in the other half of the cupboard on fire and begin a conflagration.

It looked nothing like any bound score he had come across before, so he ignored it, drew a wedge of manuscripts from the top of the opposite side of the cupboard and continued his painstaking appraisal of the music collection. Some excited him and he would sit down and sight read them, others held no interest at all. He catalogued everything, none the less.

His friendship with Dieter Meyer had grown to the extent that he had been invited to dinner with his family, who had two years past, left their German homeland to live in England, close enough to enjoy the company of their son, when it was convenient.

Lawrence had seen Dieter's sister Gisela in church and having spoken very briefly to her, was looking forward to getting to know her better. She was a talented harpist and understood how music could be a consuming passion. Dieter had younger sisters too and a brother, but Miss Meyer, the eldest, nineteen like Bella, was the one who'd caught his eye.

Had he but known it, he had caught Gisela's eye too, but Dieter kept this titbit to himself as he wanted them to have time to get to know each other before any commitment was made. A broken romance would all too easily ruin his working relationship with Lawrence and damage their close friendship. The dinner was a purely family affair but for the addition of Lawrence, and the hopes for him becoming part of their family in the near future, were as high as the regard they held him in.

Bella was also holding a dinner party, small but with the most congenial company. Roderick at twenty-four had grown in stature, mixing with men who shared his sharp intellect and his visions of the progress the country might make, if only it was taken in the right direction. Like his father, his ancestry was evident in his looks and demeanour. He felt comfortable amongst the aristocracy but greatly admired the common man who sought to advance himself through embracing fast-growing industries and innovative technologies, in a rapidly changing world.

His views married well with those of her husband and Rossington, views she had long shared with her brother, brought up as they were together, in a free-thinking household. The conversation was animated, the food excellent, the brandy indulgent. They retired to the drawing room and talked into the early hours when Bella finally gave in to her tired eyes and bid them all goodnight.

'Sleep well, my heart,' John whispered as she left him at the door.

She knew they would go on talking for hours and whether he expected it or not, Roderick's future was now secured with the patronage available to him as the brother-in-law of the Duke of Walborough. Friendship between the three men came easily to them. They were close in age, all classically educated, all hopeful of progress without the destruction of society seen in the French Revolution.

There would be a continuing shift away from the countryside to the towns and cities, bold men would seize new opportunities to bring them wealth and raise them in society, and those who only wanted to stand still would be left behind and pay a heavy price for their intransigence. Neither Walborough, Rossington nor Roderick Wrighton had any intention of being left behind.

Earl Wrighton on the other hand had no wish for anything in his life of idleness and debauchery to change. He was not a good landlord and honest complaints from tenants were readily brushed aside as whining and complaining. The latest ideas on husbandry were never adopted, broken tools were never repaired or replaced, work was never scheduled to improve run down cottages, damaged fences were not mended and barns were left with leaking roofs resulting in the heavy loss of valuable stored grain.

His tenants had finally grown tired of the neglect. They were angry, constantly ignored yet forced to pay rising rents to a profligate aristocrat. In desperation they gathered together to march to Belcourt and demand something be done.

The Earl listened and the Earl agreed something should be done with a sense of urgency.

'Leave it with me,' he said. They should have known it was too easy.

The Earl made certain something was done immediately. He saw their demands as an affront to his unquestionable authority. He had no compassion and no mercy. He sent his agent and some ruffians to throw them off his land -whole families: the old, the infirm, the pregnant, the young and babes in arms - their meagre belongings thrown into the street, smashed, and broken before their eyes.

The mood became ugly. They gathered for shelter in the *Soldiers Arms Inn*, angry, frustrated, feeling wronged. They worked hard and had not been unreasonable in their requests to the Earl, nor in their manner of asking for help, but now they wanted action.

They were not fighting men and had no idea how to get back at the Earl but a man sitting alone in the corner suddenly found himself well placed to take his revenge on a family he had long despised. He wore a dark caped coat, the collar turned up high, a muffler hiding much of his face. His hair was wiry and grey, straggly beneath a dirty and battered beaver hat and he spoke with a strange accent, not obvious to any of them.

'You want revenge?' he asked them.
'We want honest work and somewhere safe to live.'
'Then you shall have it if you are prepared to help me.'
'Who are you mister?'
'You have no need to know who I am. It will be safer if you forget you ever saw me once our task is complete. Will you help me for the sake of your families?'
Concern for what a man might be asked to do, was easily pushed aside, when poverty and death stared him and his family in the face. The Earl had left them with nothing to lose and much to gain.
'Aye, we will help you,' they agreed. What choice did they have?'
They had no idea at that point in time how little would be asked of them, nor how dangerous a man sat amongst them, a man used to killing. Granted it was mainly enemies of his country he dispatched, but to him the Earl of Wrighton and his misbegotten son were as deadly as any enemy and their crimes were perpetrated against their own countryfolk.
'Listen carefully,' he said as he drew them close around him.
'A travelling fair will come this way ……….'

Invitations had gone out to the Duchess of Walborough's ball. There were those who thought to miss it and show their disdain for a woman of lowly birth and those who would not miss such a prestigious event for all the world. Disdain was all very well but it didn't get your daughters married and with so many of the ton likely to attend, the ball was not an opportunity to miss. Prevarication in most cases ended in acceptance. Who after all would want their names excluded from the newspapers list of honoured guests?

Bella had been magnanimous and invited the Wrighton women to the ball, the men she knew would decline so she never gave them the opportunity. She worried no one would come and she worried if they did come, they would slight her. On her side, she had support from family and friends. Enough John had said to keep her comfortably entertained throughout the evening.

Her gown for the ball was exquisite, French gauze over a pink silk slip, trimmed with softly shaded silk flowers in a garland around the hem and a border of fine scalloped lace. The bodice was tiny, the sleeves short and puffed with lace trimmings. The slip peeping out below the gauze overdress was finished with a wide ruched silk ribbon of darker hue. Soft curls fell around her face and an abundance of silk flowers crowned her chignon. Anna tied the ribbons of her pink silk slippers around her ankles and drew on her elbow length gloves.

In a most timely fashion John appeared from his dressing room with a long thin box.

'These are for you,' he said revealing a single strand necklace of pink sapphires set in a minimal gold surround, stunningly beautiful and rare. He put them on for her, his warm hands against her bare skin. At his nod, Anna backed out of the room to leave them alone. His lips followed where his fingers had lain against his wife's satin soft skin.

'They are magnificent. Thank you,' she said lifting her face for him to kiss her lips, melting inside as she always did at his tender touch.

'You look every inch the duchess, my love. You will be the belle of the ball.'

'I am Bella,' she said laughing, 'and you my love will outshine all the men, even the Beau himself could not be turned out more perfectly and is not nearly so handsome.'

'Are you nervous?'

'I am, but I know you will never be far from my side. Your mama has excelled herself with the decorations. The ballroom is festooned with flowers, heady with perfume. I wonder where she found them all?'

'She raided all the hot houses at Bascombe Hall and had the gardeners cut a mass of autumnal foliage to be woven into garlands. Add to them some ribbons and bows and the room is transformed. Lamps glow behind them which heightens the scent and will no doubt send us all to sleep.'

'We will dance the night away. So far, I have saved you all my dances. You may give them away as you please except the supper dance.'

'And the waltzes, all the waltzes are mine.'

'Then perhaps we should go down as many of our guests have already arrived.'

They were announced and applause filled the room. The orchestra struck a chord and they stepped out onto the floor to begin the ball with a waltz, then gradually others joined in and there was colour and light, sweet music, dancing feet, romantic whisperings, and pure pleasure.

John danced with her cousins who felt fortunate to have been invited and introduced them to some young bachelors of good family. He spun her mama around the floor and danced a more sedate cotillion with his own mother.

Bella caught the eye of the Beau who generally caught the eye of everyone else, resplendent in black, his cravat a work of art.

'You seem to have skilfully matched your dress to the decorations,' he said, which she could not be certain was meant as a compliment. He had a cutting tongue and was too often rude, alienating many who had long called him friend, his star dimming somewhat, but by giving her a moment of his attention he had secured her future in society and vouchers for Almack's would soon follow.

John was relieved. Although Brummel's influence was rapidly on the wane, having alienated the Prince Regent, it still existed amongst those who revered him and sought his approval. If he had deliberately cut Bella, she might have found society more difficult to negotiate.

Many of the grand ladies of the ton having initially kept their distance, were watchful but not disrespectful. By the end of the evening most had at least briefly acknowledged her, and the relationship between her mother and Lord Deane had become the talking point instead. Curiosity abounded as those who knew the Marquess well, noted the likeness, and others pondered the notion that the very upright Deane, known for his deep affection for his wife, had finally strayed.

Sally hearing the rumours, made sure to stay close to her husband, dancing the waltz with him several times and enjoying his company for supper. She had no wish to see her brother maligned, yet they could not reveal the connection without more knowledge, and that, they would have to wait to discover.

Whilst the ton danced, flirted, and thoroughly enjoyed themselves at Walborough House, stealthily, under the cover of a moonless night, men dressed head to toe in black had reached a back door of Belcourt, Earl Wrighton's country house.

They had expected to have to pick a lock but the door opened easily.

What fools to leave themselves so vulnerable.

The light skirts had left and the servants were rounded up with little resistance to be loaded onto carts. Some went to the fair with the villagers, others were kept quiet and well out of the way. Four men lay stupefied, sated, and naked on rumpled sheets. The stench of sex permeated the air. Death stalked the room and would have his way.

Hunter Wrighton lay with one leg on his bed of depravity and one dangling over the side, his genitalia exposed. One sweep of a blade was all it took to deprive him of his manhood. It was a shame he couldn't appreciate what was happening to him, but he was virtually anaesthetised from strong liquor. It was almost certain he would bleed to death any time soon but they were not taking any chances. They dragged him outside and threw him headfirst down an old disused well.

The Earl, a cold unfeeling man, had no use for a warm beating heart. They held him down, cut it out of his chest and threw it on the fire.

His brothers, neither of them innocent of crimes a lesser man would hang for, were in the wrong place at the wrong time, too dangerous to leave alive, seen as collateral damage.

They had no moral compass, were as debauched as the Earl and his son, and unworthy of being the next Earl Wrighton. The people of Belcourt deserved better. They were given a quick death, their throats cut without remorse.

They might have burnt the place down, but the next Earl would bear the loss, hindering his ability to improve the lot of the tenants and estate workers. Instead, they piled the bodies of the three brothers on top of each other in the garden, doused them in lamp oil and set them alight.

No one could be found to bear witness to the crime. Some told what little they knew.

The fair had come to town and a jolly time was had by all, townsfolk, servants, and villagers alike. Some villagers, those displaced by the earl from their homes, enjoyed the night of merrymaking but were never seen again. It was thought they left with masked men before it grew light, maybe forced, maybe by their own will. Those who were left, drifted homewards as the sun rose, oblivious to what had occurred a mile away across the fields.

A sadly diminished group of servants made their way back to Belcourt on foot to discover what awaited them. Bloodied sheets, blood trails on the floor, blood dripped along corridors, blood smeared down staircases - leading them towards the hideous moment of discovery - to a vision of unspeakable horror.

It took time to realise what had been burnt on the fire that still smouldered well beyond the rear of the house - bodies, unrecognisable, black, charred and grotesque.

News of the murders reached London late the following afternoon and within a few short hours the story would headline all the cities newspapers.

EARL WRIGHTON MURDERED IN GRUESOME CRIME. SON AND HEIR MISSING

Read all about it.

They gave what details they could, naming George Wrighton and Thomas Wrighton as additional victims and were hopeful, so the article stated, of Hunter still being found alive, hopeful that he might have escaped the violence and be in hiding somewhere.

Newspapers sold in vast numbers as everyone it seemed wanted to know the grisly details, despite them being limited by what was deemed to be within the bounds of common decency.

The Wrighton ladies, staying at the home of Lady Dalyell after the ball, collapsed in shock as the details of what had occurred began to emerge.

There was a general air of disbelief amongst the ton. How could this have happened? Why were the Wrighton men so easily overcome? They might not have been universally popular and were actively disliked by many of the ton's distinguished families, but no one had thought them likely to come to harm in such a cold blooded and vicious manner.

There were reasons enough. Few would deny their hedonistic lifestyle, their disregard for the wellbeing of their tenants, their failure to pay their debts and the general unpleasantness of their characters.

If Hunter was found alive, he would be the next Earl but there was little optimism to be had as the search for him began. Few saw him as any different to his dissipated father and uncles. At twenty-one he'd already ruined the lives of several innocent young women, overcoming their resistance with his good looks and effusive charm. Inside he was rotten to the core.

It took three days to find his mutilated body and questions began to be asked.

'What wicked vengeance was this?'

Susannah and Thaddeus were shocked. How could this have been allowed to happen?

Quite easily it seemed when servants had no loyalty and harshly treated tenants had been cast out with nothing, so the story went. Many of the Earl's tenants were now missing entirely and their direction could not be traced. Then there was the mysterious man who had been seen in the *Soldiers Arms Inn*. Who was he? If anyone knew, which in fact they didn't, they were keeping it to themselves. The few servants, left to answer questions, spoke of armed masked men who forced them from the house at pistol or knife point. Others denied seeing anything. They were all at the fair and there were plenty to testify to that being God's truth.

Bella tried to console the widows and their daughters, but not everyone felt compassion for women they thought blinkered, who must have been aware of their menfolk's abhorrent behaviour yet ignored it.

'Such brutality to poor Hunter,' his mother wailed. 'How could anyone be so cruel? What had he done to deserve such a gruesome death?'

Plenty, Walborough and Rossington thought, and the punishment had likely been chosen to fit the crime. What that exact crime was, they could only speculate. As for the Earl and his two brothers, the only conclusion they could reach was that at some point in time, they had upset the wrong people, ultimately paying a heavy price.

Lucas Wainwright read all the details of the murders in the newspaper and was horrified. He sat in White's trying to deny his part in revealing the truth of Hunter's abuse of Jenny, and the abandonment of her child.

A man, quite unknown to him, came and sat in the empty chair beside him.

'A terrible business,' he said, glancing at the newspaper. 'I wonder what they did to die that way?'

Lucas closed the newspaper and looked the man in the eye, wary when all his senses were flashing a warning. Instinctively he knew to keep quiet.

'I have absolutely no idea,' he replied. 'As you say, a terrible business, but the family involved were not known to me. These past five years I've lived abroad and only recently returned to England.'

'Is it your intention to stay now?'

'I cannot. Once my father's affairs are in order, and I have appointed an agent to oversee the running of my estate, I must return to Italy to complete my studies.'

'Good luck to you then,' he said, and rose from his seat.

He was gone like a wraith in the night before Lucas could make any further comment.

'Who was that?' He asked one of the waiters.

'Viscount Seldon, a Major in Lord Wellington's army, 95th Riflemen, very highly regarded, crack shot and all that, never misses a target.'

Lucas shivered with shock and thanked God he was going back to Italy in a few weeks' time. Perhaps he was reading too much into an innocent situation and the Viscount had merely been passing the time of day but some instinct had made him afraid. Having encountered the cold look in his eye, he could quite easily believe the man was a skilled and ruthless army assassin. He would be more than happy never to be anywhere in his vicinity again.

Chapter Twenty

'So, they're blaming it on Luddites are they. Nonsensical if you ask me. Thought they usually broke up machinery in factories. No factories near Belcourt and these were cold bloodied killings, not vandalism.'

John was thoughtful.

'As usual Randal, a case of shifting the blame, although who is to blame in this particular case remains a mystery and most likely always will. Smacks more of some personal revenge to me, directed at Hunter and possibly his father, with the other two thrown in for good measure. Carefully planned, skilfully carried out and quite ruthless.'

Randal was of a like mind, convinced it had been an act of personal vengeance but for what specifically, he could not determine, which left some heightened level of concern within the family.

'Thaddeus, now being the heir, finds himself quite naturally perturbed. He had little affection for the men in his family but knowing they have all been brutally murdered is hard for him to accept. How might he now regard these atrocities in consideration of his religious beliefs? Whose vengeance will it be? That of masked men. Were they acting alone or guided by the hand of God who has taken away the wicked and put the righteous in their place? He never had any pretensions to be the Earl did he, nor thought it likely he could be, and he's not certain now if it's what he wants when the honour has come his way by such unexpected violence. Yet, if any of the brothers were cut out to be the Earl, Thaddeus was always the one. He has the intellect, the worldly knowledge, the compassion, and a devout loving wife to support him but Bella says he is not convinced it is the role for him.'

'Then Randal, I think we must convince him.'

In the end it was his loving wife, Sally, who convinced him to accept the responsibility.

'Caring for the people of the Wrighton Estates is as much God's work as preaching his gospel,' she told him. 'You can give back what has been denied them for far too long, and you have a son to follow you who would become a worthy Viscount Wylde. You can walk once again amongst men of rank, where you rightfully belong; live as you always should have lived, associate with men who can make a difference, who can change people's lives for the better, give back some pride to the Wrighton name, which has for too long been shamed.'

'Is it what you want Sally?'

'I want you to be happy and fulfilled. You have had the one but you've never truly had the other.'

'I had the important one, your love.'

'It would please me now to know you can have both.'

It would take away some of her guilt at having denied him the upward mobility he should have experienced in the church, even if it had been his wish to choose her over everything. Their love had sustained them but she would rejoice if he could also be the man of stature his youthful promise had projected him to be.

'If you are certain then, I will accept the title, but I fear what will happen to our community at Stillford.'

'Bellingham is of a mind to sell his outstanding land around Stillford to Walborough who can more easily have oversight of the church and those who live and work in the area. He will appoint a new vicar, and with the help of Hubert Lang, find an organist and choir master who can carry on the traditions we began of making music together.'

'What will Owen Lawton make of that I wonder?' Thaddeus asked, slightly amused. He liked Owen but he was inclined to be pompous at times and as for him marrying Bella, he couldn't deny he was relieved when Susannah had arrived to take her to London and out of his vicinity, despite the upset it had caused at the time.

'He will become Walborough's tenant,' Sally said, 'although how soon he will be aware of the fact is difficult to say. I cannot imagine he will be thrilled by the change.'

'How all our lives have changed Sally. Three of our children have left home, Bella has married Walborough and you my beloved are now a Duke's daughter and will be my Countess. We too will have to make changes after the funerals. Belcourt is noticeably short of servants and many of the tenants have left the estate. Walborough has generously sent his agent and some labourers to see what needs to be done urgently.

'The accounts have to be looked through, and various wills read, which will keep our lawyers busy. Then the women in the family will need somewhere to live and possibly financial support depending on what they are due to inherit. The estate has always been entailed and I can't imagine any of my brothers having any great personal fortunes, bearing in mind how free spending they were.'

'You will support them, when they would have done nothing to aid your children in similar circumstances.'

'I could not live with myself if I failed to protect them from hardship. I have dedicated my life to God's service and will not change my moral compass now.'

Sally hugged him tight.

'I never for one moment thought you would Thaddeus, which is why you have my heart and always will.'

The Rossington family were going to be at Deane Castle for Christmas. Lady Eliza, Randal's eldest sister was to be married to Lord Hugo Ancaster and had stated a preference for the service to be at Holy Trinity Church, historically the church of her ancestors.

Whilst marriage services were frequently short using the prescribed words in the prayer book, Eliza and her fiancé had hopes of hearing some special music to celebrate their nuptials. Lawrence and Dieter had been practising the chosen pieces for some time.

Since Walborough had already been invited as a guest, both he and Bella were to be at the castle over Christmas. It seemed logical that her parents and William would also join them, since Eliza was now known to be her mother's niece.

Lawrence wondered if Dieter and Gisela might join them for some of the Christmas celebrations, beyond being the musical entertainment.

'You are family now Lawrence. Invite some guests by all means,' Rossington said in a happy frame of mind, as they sat over dinner one evening.

He had arrived early, to be certain all was arranged in the manner his sister had requested, prior to the day of her marriage on Christmas Eve.

Later they went to the music room and Lawrence played some of his favourite pieces, plus one or two new songs he'd found in the cupboard, of a racier nature.

Rossington found them amusing.

'I expect they were popular with my great grandpa. He led a racy life. Have you seen his portrait in the long gallery?'

Lawrence denied having seen the painting. He hadn't roamed freely about the castle but he was happy to see more in Rossington's company. They were about to leave the music room when he recalled the heavy cumbersome book in the base of the cupboard.

'Before we go there is something you might help me with.' He pointed to the large book in the base of the cupboard.

'It's too heavy to move on my own and I don't want to damage it. Two of us might manage to get some purchase on it.'

Rossington was intrigued. He couldn't see it clearly but hoped it might be the old Bible he'd searched for in vain, with its tell-tale brass corners and solid lock. The music cupboard was the last place he would have imagined it to be. It was highly unlikely he would ever have noticed it hidden beneath the mound of music scores, even if he'd thought to look.

It was hard going but they managed to ease it towards the opening and between them lift it out gingerly onto the floor, **Holy Bible**, clearly imprinted on the front of the embossed leather binding.

'Well done, Lawrence. I've been searching for this for the past two months. The Duke is eager for it to be given pride of place in the library at Tremar. Apparently, it is exceedingly rare and valuable.'

It was also locked.

'I don't suppose you have any idea where the key is kept, do you?'

Lawrence didn't think he did until he remembered the key in the cupboard door which wouldn't turn the lock. He'd taken it out of his waistcoat pocket and placed it for safekeeping on a high shelf to one side.

Retrieving it, he held it aloft.

'I wonder if this is it,' he said and explained the circumstances in which he'd found it. The bow was small and decorated with trefoils, the shank and pin simple, not brass, but gold as were the corner guards and the lock when they looked more closely. No wonder his grandpa wanted it found and kept safely.

They carried the heavy book over to a table and tried the key, pleased when the lock sprang open. Rossington lifted the cover with great care, aware of its precious nature. Inside were two sheets of modern writing. He removed them and laid them on the table, turning over the frontispiece to reveal the first of three hand scribed pages, specifically for the recording of family births, marriages, and deaths down the centuries. He glanced down the page and read the final birth entry aloud.

Twins. Ivor Reid, Lord Rossington, and Lady Annabelle Sarah, born at Belverdon Lodge on the seventh day of September in the year of our Lord, one thousand seven hundred and sixty-eight. Lady Annabelle departed this life aged ten days.

Randal was astonished.

'So, it was true, grandmama did give birth to twins and he knew it all along. He caused her all that heartache and made her believe she was hysterical when she asked after her second child, all the while knowing he spoke a lie.'

'But the child didn't die,' Lawrence reminded him, 'so what did he mean by writing *departed this life*?'

They turned the pages to the one headed Deaths. There was no record for the death of Lady Annabelle Sarah.

'He never recorded her death,' Randal said mystified. 'Why then did he write departed this life? Was he uncertain of her fate? Did he care nothing for what happened to her after he denied her existence or did he just send her away to live with another family? Did the Fosters always know who she was?'

They looked to the two pages of writing. The first was some kind of confession.

I Robert Aston, being of sound mind but frail of body, do declare this to be my honest deathbed confession, dictated before my priest and my God.

On the eighteenth day of September in the year of our Lord, one thousand seven hundred and sixty-eight, I took the girl child, Lady Annabelle Sarah Rossington to the graveyard at Belverhead with the intent of carrying out the Duke's instructions to smother her and bury her body, but I could not, as someone was already there digging a grave. Panicked in case I might be seen; I left the child in the basket amongst the heather and made my escape. I returned to Belverdon and told the Duke the task was complete. He sent me away and told me never to return.

I did no harm to the child and she was alive when I left her, but I did have the intent to do the Duke's bidding and only God's will prevented me. I know not if she survived but I ask now for forgiveness for my willingness to comply with an evil man's intent, that my soul may rest in peace, and I might be granted God's almighty mercy.'

Signed, R. Aston and dated the tenth day of January in the year of our Lord, one thousand seven hundred and eighty-five.

The second was in the Duke's hand, signed and stamped with his seal.

So, Robert Aston is dead and buried in his forty-third year and I soon to follow him to the grave.

Weakness in his character might now be looked upon as a virtue as it seems I did not cause him to commit murder after all. At the time

I made my decision rationally without emotion for the future of our line. An heir is to be cherished and nurtured. The boy was weak and immature and needed all his mother's care. The girl would have been a distraction, a drain on her already weakened constitution. She was frail of mind and body, not a fit mate for my son but he made his choice and would not waver from it.

The girl child's fate appears to have been left in God's hands and I know not what became of her. There is the possibility she lives still but I have no knowledge of this truth or her possible whereabouts. I only recall that no live or dead child was reported as being found on the moor and thus the matter was closed to my satisfaction.

If a price was to be paid for the thought, not the deed, I have suffered it with a leg wound which will never heal, and constant unrelenting pain. I should have let them remove it long ago but was too full of vanity to allow it. Now what lay deeply buried in my flesh undetected but awaiting its moment, leaks its poison into my blood and I too will soon face God's final judgement.

I was a soldier in my youth and sent many a man to die for King and country in the name of God. I do not repent my decisions. I made them based on circumstances known at the time. As to the child, such was my thinking. The heir needed no rivals to his supremacy within the family. I did what I thought was best for the continuation of my line, for strength into the future, for the house of Rossington and the Dukes of Aven. I will not now be a hypocrite and say I have regrets.

Signed, sealed, and dated the twenty-first day of August in the year of our Lord, one thousand seven hundred and eighty-five.

'Good God, Lawrence, it really is true. Here is proof your mama is my aunt and we are cousins. He died the following June so he kept this knowledge to himself unto death.'

'Do you think the man in the graveyard was my grandpa and he found the child as he made his way home?'

'It seems likely, but we must ask him to be certain.'

Lawrence thought it a poor time to share this news.

'I think we must keep this to ourselves for now. Your sister's nuptials and the Christmas festivities can only be marred by the hurt these words will reveal. My mama must be told with great compassion that her grandfather, the Duke, cast her aside and sought her death.'

'You are right of course. It must wait until the New Year or beyond. We must not add further pain when recent tragedies have lain heavily upon us all.'

They put the Bible back in the cupboard, hidden as it was before and replaced the key on the top shelf. Rossington took Lawrence through to the family rooms and they sat comfortably in conversation with a glass of fine brandy and a large platter of fruit for supper, as their minds turned to more pleasant prospects.

'Tell me of Gisela, Lawrence. Is she to be your lady of choice?'

'I would like to think so, but papa's accession to the Earldom has coloured the Meyer families view of me a little, and they are concerned lest I might view their daughter in a different light now I have greater access to social events, and the opportunity to meet ladies with an aristocratic background.'

'All of which means nothing to you.'

'My world is always going to be my music. Gisela is a talented musician herself and we have so much in common, besides her being the prettiest lady I know.'

'She will meet your family and see how little rank and prestige matter to them. Might you invite all her family to the race on St Stephen's Day? I'm hopeful of beating Walborough this time. There is to be a feast out in The Yard for all who come to watch but they could join our family at the long table. Mr Lang and the Vicar will also join us after boxes for the parish poor have been handed out in the church.'

'I will ask them,' Lawrence replied, 'and hope they accept.'

Once Thaddeus had accepted his right and his desire to become Earl Wrighton, life moved on apace. The funerals of his brothers and nephew were a solemn affair with due pomp and ceremony. Mourners walked behind the horse drawn coffins to the steady beat of the drums as the band of the militia played a slow funeral march. There was no mausoleum at Belcourt so the bodies were interred in the church vault, beside their ancestors.

Despite the undignified way in which they had died, the funeral procession, the church service, the eulogy, and the committal were as dignified as they could be in respect of the women left behind. The new Earl had made an early start to weatherproofing houses and repairing barns, which gave hope to tenants where previously there had been none. They stood silently and bowed their heads as the coffins passed by, but their respect was not for the men inside them, but for the man who walked behind, who they now saw in the light of their saviour.

Since Sally was now the Countess Wrighton, she became elevated in society as a matter of course and it was in the interest of the former Countess and her daughters to be seen with her regularly at balls and parties. They had been left in financial difficulty by a will which offered much but could not be honoured, due to debts requiring to be paid, as was written in the first few lines of a long document. The Earl's intentions might have been to protect his family with financial sums and property but there was none to be had. Only an agreement between Thaddeus and the executors of the will allowed for some minor properties to be sold and annuities to be made available to them. His other brother's wives and children were left comfortable, if not wealthy, and Thaddeus felt no need to be responsible for them.

He and Sally moved into the townhouse for convenience being close to Bella, John, and Lord Rossington, as well as to Lord and Lady Deane. Roderick, now Lord Wylde, continued with his work for Sir Henry Leighton for the experience he could gain, but the balance of respect had evened out, and they became associates rather than employer and employee. Walborough had made plans to look for a borough where the incumbent was near retirement and might be persuaded to go early, such that Roderick could stand for parliament at the next election, but recent events had given him greater opportunities to consider, and it became less imperative.

Bella could not deny her happiness at the prospect of becoming a mother in the summer, but her mornings were now spent feeling nauseous to the point of being sick into the chamber pot. John was as helpful as any husband might be, but he had commitments and was often out of the house before she woke. To cheer her up he would bring her small gifts, some foolish to amuse her, some valuable to show her how much he cared, and occasionally the sweet treats she craved, like the soft sweet juicy Ottoman confection, lokum, fruit flavoured or with added dates and nuts.

They dined at home whilst she found the aroma of certain foods offensive and attended carefully selected evening entertainments where there was no risk of being jostled or bumped about by raucous merry makers. She sang for the first time at Mrs Hepworth's Soiree to the surprise and acclaim of the assembled guests, the song choice, *Sweeter Than Roses*, at her husband's request.

When it came time to travel to Deane Castle in Suffolk, their journey was planned with more overnight stops than usual due to her being enceinte and they stayed two nights at Hopston Chase, where they cheered Arthur on in his first pony race, before travelling for another two days to reach their destination.

Arthur didn't win the race, but no one had expected him to, being much younger and less experienced than the other competitors. Coming third was quite a revelation to both Walborough and his trainer who wouldn't have been surprised or disappointed if he'd come last, being more interested in the way he comported himself and encouraged his pony to make progress by the highly effective use of whispered words alone.

'I don't know what that pony hears in his voice, but he obviously approves,' John said to Bella later. 'Arthur Briggs is a revelation.'

Bella who had always thought him to be an enchanting boy with great promise could only agree wholeheartedly.

It was a hive of activity both within Deane Castle and the church, where decorations were being hung and flowers arranged. The music was well practised and the banns had been read three Sundays in a row. All was set fair for the marriage of two aristocrats who were deeply in love to be witnessed by their family and some invited guests.

Rossington found himself quite taken with Lord Ancaster's sister, Lady Rowena, when they were introduced for the first time. Since she was already twenty years of age and possessed of an uncommon beauty, being fair of face and figure, he wondered why he had not met her before at any of society's frequent events.

'Is your sister spoken for?' he asked his future brother-in-law as curiosity got the better of him.

'No. She chooses to live a quiet life with our grandmother who suffers much discomfort. Not that grandmama exerts any hold over her and hasn't frequently encouraged her to spread her wings. She regularly does so, but Rowena is comfortable at Lakedon and manages the household with great efficiency as well as being a lively and caring companion.'

'Where is Lakedon?'

'Herefordshire, close to the Welsh border. It's a substantial estate with a beautiful medieval manor house above a natural lake. Grandmama will undoubtedly leave it to Rowena but that isn't the reason she stays there.

'What is then?'

'She idolises our grandmother.'

Rossington couldn't think of any better reason for Rowena choosing to live there but it was a long way from where his life was. He would not easily find ways to spend time with her assuming she would want to spend time with him, which at the moment didn't look hopeful as she had disappeared from view.

'She will most likely be in the library if you wish to pursue her,' her amused brother informed him. 'I should warn you; good men have tried, to no avail.'

'I was merely intending to be sociable to a guest,' he countered and bowed before taking himself off.

Not to the library though. That would look far too obvious.

Chapter Twenty-One

In his short life, Cuthbert Foster had never looked forward to Christmas as much as he did this coming one. There was to be a big party at Oakley organised by Lord and Lady Bellingham which his new family would all be at, his great grandparents, his grandma and grandpa, his aunts, uncles, and cousins, and best of all his new mama and papa.

He knew he was a lucky boy to have found such a cheerful home to live in but now and then he wondered if he had other family, he knew nothing about.

He didn't like to think his real mam and dad had never wanted him, even it was probably the truth. Lady Goldsborough had told him his real mother had died when he was born and would have wanted him very much, but he knew she was only being kind the way Miss Bella was, because they wanted him to be happy.

He was happy now playing out in the field with a brightly coloured ball his new great grandpa had given him. He liked going over to his house because there were other boys his age living nearby and for a while, he would have playmates. Great grandpa was also good at carving and made him model soldiers to play with. He had four now and hoped to get another one for Christmas.

He wandered absentmindedly towards the little lane that ran along the back of the field. Sometimes he would see a man's head above the hedge as he walked past and sometimes just a hat. Today he saw no one but he heard what sounded like a cross between a bark and a whine. He knew he wasn't supposed to go out into the lane but curiosity got the better of him and he squeezed through the hedge to see what was making the strange noise.

It was a puppy with a grey speckly face and large floppy ears. It looked at Cuthbert and then ran off up the lane. Cuthbert followed, and around a corner he came across a man sitting on the grass banking.

Cuthbert looked him over. He had red hairy whiskers on his cheeks like many a farmer and wore leather breeches and a woollen jacket. He looked as if he might be tall as even whilst sitting, Cuddy had to look up at him to properly take in his features. In a rare moment of trust, Cuddy sat down next to him.

'Is this your dog?' he asked.

'Do you like dogs?' the stranger asked in return.

'I like the dogs at the farm but they must work, so I can't play with them. I think I should like a dog to be my friend,' Cuddy said honestly.

'This one is an English Setter pup. He needs someone to adopt him.'

'Don't you want him then?' Cuddy asked surprised.

'I would love to keep him, but I have to go abroad soon, and I'm not allowed to take him with me.'

'Could I adopt him then? Cuddy asked hopefully, as the pup licked his hand. 'I don't think mama and papa would mind because they adopted me.'

'Did they?'

'From the orphanage in London. Miss Bella was my friend. She was kind to me and read me stories and took me for walks. She asked me if I wanted to be Adam and Jane's little boy because she couldn't keep me even when she wanted to.'

'Why was that?'

'She wasn't married.'

'So, you came here.'

'Miss Bella brought me for a visit to see if I would be happy. She said I could go back to London if I wanted to, but I love Adam and Jane and now they are my mama and papa.'

'Then you are happy to be living here?'

'I am, but I would like to adopt your dog if I can.'

The man smiled at him.

'Then you shall. Take him with you now, for I must go.'

'Will I see you again?'

'I cannot promise to. Off you go now before you are missed. I would not wish your parents to be worried.'

Cuddy reluctantly prepared to leave with the puppy in his arms.

'Who shall I say gave it to me?' he asked.

'Your uncle. Say your uncle gave it to you.'

Adam was confused.

'Which uncle gave it to you Cuddy?'

'The one with red whiskers, he had lots of whiskers.'

'Not your uncle Henry then or Thomas or Daniel?'

'No. Can I keep it though, the puppy?'

'I don't see why not. He will be good company. We had put it about that we would like to find a puppy for you. You will have to think of a name for him and learn how to look after him and train him to behave well.'

'I can do that, though I might need you to tell me how.'

Adam ruffled his hair and hugged him tight.

He was such a delightful boy and they felt truly blessed to have him for their son.

'The man didn't frighten you did he Cuddy?'
'No, he was a kind man.'

Major Lord Benjamin Seldon and his companion, Captain Linus Willoughby made a strategic exit from the district, bound for London, then the coast and France.

'Are you content now?' Willoughby asked his friend and comrade in arms.

'Satisfied enough. In a strange twist of fate, Cuthbert has landed in the bosom of his real family. At least part of it. The new Earl Wrighton has long been estranged from his family but his daughter Bella was recently launched into society by his sister, Lady Bellingham. Bella, it appears, was the one who suggested this putting together of Cuthbert and the Fosters through her involvement with Lady Goldsborough's charity. Bella's mother Sally Wrighton, now the Countess, was a Foster before her marriage. Adam is Bella's cousin on her mother's side. Hunter Wrighton was Bella's cousin on her father's side.'

'Who did you tell the boy you were?'

'His uncle.'

'Possibly a good thing then that the boy is never likely to see you again and if he does, wouldn't recognise you as yourself.'

'I don't know. They say blood will out and he wasn't the least bit wary of me. Sat down next to me as calm as you like when I set most people's hackles rising.'

'When you ain't being sinister, you're the best of men to be around. The boy must have seen the good in you.'

'He is absolutely adorable Linus. Jenny would have been so proud of him.'

'As long as he doesn't grow up to be like his father.'

'I doubt it. Hunter had the worst possible example set for him; his son will have the best.'

'Ironic, don't you think, that if Hunter had married Jenny, Cuthbert would now be the Earl.'

'Probably not Linus, because if Hunter had married Jenny or treated her with some respect, he would still be alive.'

'Ah, yes, I suppose so. I understand you wanting to eliminate Hunter and his father, but why the other two?'

'It's simple enough Linus. If either had inherited the title, there would have been more of the same debauchery, despoiling of innocents and ill will towards honest tradesmen and tenants.

'The youngest brother on the other hand is a man of God with a reputation for goodwill to all men and he has a fine upstanding son. Kinder I think for everyone to skip the middle brothers as heirs. Don't you agree?'

'The law wouldn't, but I would never argue with your instinct when it has kept us alive all these years, and dead men tell no tales.'

'Indeed, my friend, nor can they make up lies to convict the innocent and someone innocent would surely have taken the blame for the Earl's death if either of them had lived to tell the tale.'

'Come then, let us be on our way. We have our orders. Say goodbye to England. Who knows if we'll ever see her shores again.'

Scouring through the burial records of churches within the vicinity of Wrighton House was a time-consuming task, particularly when the writing was not always as clear as it might have been.

There was many a Jenny, but not the one he had been tasked with finding and not one within the timeframe given. A vicar noticing the painstaking nature of his search and his eventual disappointment, offered a few helpful insights. There were, he said, too many bodies to be interred and not enough burial places. Some were transported out of the parish and buried elsewhere. There were new graveyards opened up but even they were getting short of space. Had he considered if the girl had been buried in a pauper's grave. If so, the parish clerk might help him with that.

Jenny had been far from being a pauper, but she might have been seen in the light of one given the circumstances surrounding the end of her days. She was three weeks shy of her seventeenth birthday when rough handling during the delivery of her son had caused her to bleed to death. She had been taken to be buried in a cart with her name and age chalked on the cheap wooden coffin. No funeral service had taken place as far as he could discover.

That was as much as he knew, told to him in the greatest secrecy. He had taken on the challenge to find Jenny and it had been a long road of discovery, a painstaking endeavour to seek the answers his employer sought, to right a wrong and bring a loved one home, sadly not alive as had first been the hope of her family, but now in death if he could locate her burial place.

It took another month of going from one place to another, finding a few names that gave him pause for thought – Jenny Hunter and Genny Wylde, but the ages were wrong and he persevered until there in front of him was written Jenny Syce aged sixteen years and eleven months, buried in the Drury Lane burial ground in the parish of St Martin-in-the-Fields, the position and the number of the burial plot stated, and the name of a vicar. Perhaps a few words were said over her grave after all.

The disinterment took place under the cover of darkness, the remains placed in a lead lined coffin to begin the long journey to Northumberland; its final destination, Beaton

Magna, the home of Viscount Seldon, where a grave had been prepared.

A winged angel at prayer stood watching over it, and the upright stone was thus inscribed:

In memory of a beloved daughter and sister,
Jennifer Ellen Syce
1792 -1809
Aged 16 years and 11 months.

Blessed are the pure in heart, for they shall see God.

Details of the reinterment service were sent to France via a coded letter which was eventually received by Major Seldon whilst on reconnaissance duties. Napoleon had been forced to abdicate in April, to live in exile on the island of Elba and the King restored to the throne, but those whose job it was to keep their ear to the ground, remained vigilant.

Despite defeat at the hands of the coalition, Napoleon was still preferred by many of the French people to Louis XVIII, and many in the French army were eager to have him back in command. It was not quiet, and it was not over. Seldon and his few chosen men disappeared into the background on a watching brief, whilst knowing if they were caught in France out of uniform, they would all be shot.

The marriage service joining the Right Honourable Hugo David John, Earl of Ancaster, bachelor, to Lady Eliza Violet Rossington, spinster, was over, and the celebrations had begun in style. Uplifting organ music had filled the church and now softer tones provided a background to the wedding breakfast. Dieter had organised a string quartet to entertain the guests and accompany the dancing later. Now enjoying the status of guest with his sister, he wandered through the milling throng in search of Lawrence.

'Come Dieter,' Lawrence said jovially when they eventually found each other, 'fill your plate. The food will be quite exceptional. Where is Gisela?'

'I thought she was with you but it appears not.'

They let their eyes roam around the room until they settled on Dieter's sister in conversation with Bella, Duchess of Walborough.

'Starting at the top, I see,' Dieter laughed.

'She is my sister. I would hope the pair of them become friends.'

'Your family are very gracious Lawrence. We have not always been made to feel so welcome.'

'Then you should be. Are the rest of your family coming to the race on St Stephen's Day. It should be exciting.'

'It seems so. They are excited, and a little overwhelmed by the inclusion.'

'My family have not changed since they have been elevated in society. My papa is still a man of God who cares for his parishioners. He just has a lot more of them to take care of now, as both their spiritual guide and their landlord.'

'Will you take Gisela to wife?'

'If she will have me, but I'd like to get to know her more before I ask her. I want her to be certain she will be happy with the life I aim to lead. There is no point pretending I will ever change.'

Dieter laughed at him.

'I wonder if you realise how much you have already changed, how much more confident you are, not only as a musician but as a gentleman. You might still be impulsive at times but more frequently you are thoughtful and take your time. Contentment has made you less agitated.'

'You can thank Bella for that. She always did know how to calm me. Besides, I have few restrictions placed on me now and am mainly asked to do exactly what pleases me anyway.'

'A joyous life we lead Lawrence. Come, shall we join our sisters?'

Bella was the height of elegance in a high waisted cream dress of embroidered gauze over silk, with ruffled bands of ribbon and lace on the bodice and sleeves. A full frill at the hem was decorated with a band of silk flowers and vine leaves, the same adorning her hair, pinned high on her head with soft curls around her face.

By contrast, Gisela wore a pink gown which set off her dark hair, simple and unadorned but for three bands of pleated ribbon around the bottom of the skirt. The difference in wealth would be obvious to anyone observing them standing together, but the conversation between them was warm and friendly.

Walborough was equally warm towards her as he came to collect his wife, wanting to introduce her to more of the guests. Bella excused herself to go with him, and Dieter, realising he could leave Lawrence and Gisela alone together, also excused himself to go and speak to Hubert Lang.

Lawrence might have been a blind man for all he noticed the intricacies of feminine costume. All he saw was Gisela's sweet face framed with dark curls. All he thought about was kissing her sweet lips. He had not previously felt any attachment to the girls or young ladies he'd met, and the desire he felt now, was both new and exciting. He knew he must be patient; marriage was for life. He would not risk making the wrong decision.

Gisela had easily fallen in love with Lawrence, a kindred spirit, but her parents had warned her of late to be cautious, and not assume he still had marriage in mind.

They might have gone immediately upstairs to make music together, instead they stood and talked.

'Will you go to London now that your parents are living there?' Gisela asked him.

'What for?'

'For the opportunities.'

'I have all the opportunities I want here, making music with Dieter.'

'Will you stay living here at the Castle then?'

'For now, but I would hope to have my own establishment at some time. I cannot forever be dependent on Lord Rossington.'

'Where will you go then?'

'Not far. I wouldn't want to go far.'

'Have you….'

'Have you seen the music room?' Lawrence asked knowing it was unlikely.

'No.'

'Would you like to see it. I can go there anytime I like.'

Of course, she wanted to see it, and be alone with Lawrence.

He took her hand in his and off they went. Lawrence stole a sweet kiss when no one was around. Impulsive as ever, he decided waiting was futile.

'Lawrence is smitten,' Walborough said later when they re-emerged from the music room.

'Gisela, equally so,' Rossington said with a smile. 'They will do well together, she's a fine musician in her own right. Tomorrow we must have some music in the evening since we are blessed with so much virtuosity amongst us.'

'I must be watchful of Bella as she is likely to tire with too much activity. Perhaps I can persuade her to rest a while in the afternoon.'

Rossington looked at Walborough strangely.

'Are you trying to tell me something since I've never known Bella to be anything but full of energy?'

'With God's blessing Randal. I am to be a father in the summer.'

'Well that I must say is wonderful news. Do you intend to make it known?'

'Not at the moment, Bella is still wary, but I thought you should know.'

'I'm honoured to be the first to hear the news. Uncle Frederick, I feel sure, would say Bella is very well proportioned for childbearing.'

'Let us hope so. I could not bear to lose her.'

'You truly love her then?'

'Did you doubt it?' John asked surprised.'

'I was concerned when you made no announcement and left her behind at Hopston.'

'I just wanted her to myself for a few weeks and to be well and truly married before I told my mother, so Bella would be confident and not cowed by mama's attitude which I knew would be critical of her parentage.'

'She appears to have come around now,' Randal observed.

'Before she had the support of my sisters in encouraging me to make an early marriage. Now they have turned their thoughts to marrying off their own daughters and being at loggerheads with one's brother's wife, is not the best way to secure sponsorship of the highest level for them. Pragmatism, plus discovering how easy it has been to like and admire their new sister-in-law, have mellowed their views.'

'So, all is well in the Becket family.'

'Esther is still depressed in her spirits and goes to Lowen's grave every day, but only time will ease that sorrow. If I didn't have Bella to keep me cheerful and you my best of friends, I think my spirits would also be low.'

'You would think the Wrighton women's spirits would be deeply affected by the loss of their menfolk in such sudden and dramatic circumstances yet they show no sign of any genuine mourning. They seem almost relieved now they know Thaddeus will support them.'

'Turning a blind eye does not mean you are unaware. To know you are married to a lecherous, loathsome man cannot sit well in any woman's mind, but no doubt they were all powerless to do anything, lest they were mistreated themselves.'

'Speaking of mistreatment. I should tell you I have discovered the whereabouts of the family Bible, or at least Lawrence uncovered it and we retrieved it from the music cupboard together. I can see how it might be valuable as the key, lock and corner guards are in fact gold and it is written in an elegant, illuminated script. In itself, it is in excellent condition, considering its age, but the callous behaviour it reveals inside is simply unbelievable.'

He related to John the contents of the two handwritten statements and the birth record.

'You haven't revealed this to anyone else?'

'No. Both Lawrence and I thought if the information is to be revealed, it must be done sensitively, maybe never at all. I thought to go alone to Shropshire and speak to Bella's grandparents. Their story, I suspect, will be one which I now believe will only do them credit.'

Chapter Twenty-Two

Christmas Day was one of religious observance, everyone attending the church to celebrate the birth of Jesus Christ, generally behaving in a sober fashion until the feasting and drinking began. It was followed by lively conversation, games and later an evening of fine music. The women mainly retired before the men, who sat up for hours drinking and talking, taking the opportunity of a large gathering of family and friends to air their views on political matters, voicing their hopes, their fears, and their deepest concerns but thankful that for the first Christmas in a long time, the world was mainly at peace.

St Stephen's Day was set fair for the guests at Deane Castle to enjoy the best of outdoor entertainment. The sun shone dazzlingly low in the sky, the air was fresh but not too cold and the winter market stalls had brought the townsfolk out in numbers as they filled the Yard to buy seasonal treats. They tried their luck throwing wooden balls at metal ducks, firing arrows or pistols at distant targets, or testing out their strength with a giant mallet, in the hope of winning a few coins. Others were even daring enough to have their fortune told by a gypsy dressed in the rich colours of her hastily erected tent, crossing her palm with silver, or in many cases a farthing, to hear what future she saw for them in her crystal ball.

Walborough and Rossington were at the stables preparing for their second race around the castle walls and as usual bets were being placed on who would win. The odds seemed to be in favour of Walborough since he had won the previous race, but he knew it would be much closer this time around, and he couldn't be certain of gaining another victory.

Bella was wrapped up warm to watch the race from the bridge; Lawrence, Gisela, and Dieter standing close by. She'd given John one of her garters to carry as a love token for good luck, which he thought more challenging than helpful.

'How am I supposed to concentrate on driving when my mind will be on where this garter is usually to be found?'

'It will urge you to win and after the race I will allow you to put it back where it belongs.'

'In private, I hope,' he said laughing at her saucy look.

'Most definitely in private.'

'What if I lose?'

'You cannot lose to my mind as it is a race between men of equal skill. We already know the greys are potentially faster horses. If Rossington runs them well, I suspect it will be very tight at the finish.'

'How perceptive you are, my love. I shall endeavour to win and hope for a prize from you, even if I lose.'

'My garter must needs be returned,' she said provocatively, turning up her face for his kiss, a moment of sweet pleasure, before he left her to Anna's care.

Anna had fussed over her and dressed her stylishly in a cherry red high-necked dress of fine woollen cloth matched with a warm coat and a fur beret. Admiring glances were cast her way as she stood waiting for the race to start. The band, resplendent in red frogged jackets and white trousers, with their instruments polished and gleaming in the sunshine, entertained the crowd playing popular Christmas Carols until the church clock was nigh on eleven. At the first chime of the hour, the race would be started, and the two men would spring their horses hoping for a good get away.

Whether it was the pleasant weather or the joy of a holiday which drew the large crowd, Bella wasn't certain, but the atmosphere was full of excitement and tension. All eyes were on the two curricles with total admiration for the immaculately dressed drivers and the magnificent horses as they almost flew around the course. As they began the last circuit the crowd grew noisy, cheering for one driver or the other to *come on,* in hope of them winning their bet. It was neck and neck all the way which built the tension to a near frenzy of shouting. No one was certain who had won as they crossed the finishing line beneath the bridge, all waiting eagerly for the result to be announced.

'My Lords, ladies and gentlemen, the winner ….. by a nose is Lord Rossington.'

Cheers of joy and sighs of disappointment followed. Walborough and Rossington congratulated each other on a tight race, fairly run.

'The greys are quite wonderful. Only my mother could have managed such atrocious timing that she demanded I leave town just when Freddy Farquhar's creditors finally caught up with him, making it necessary for him to find substantial funds in a hurry.'

'I wouldn't have known about them being for sale if Uncle Frederick hadn't given me the hint. He wanted them himself, but didn't have the blunt, so thought I should have them instead. Not an offer I was inclined to turn down.'

'If you choose to sell them, remember I have first call.' John reminded him.

'Well as to that, I heard of a very promising pair of chestnuts likely to come up at Tattersall's within the month. Uncle Frederick will keep you informed should you be interested. Expensive, but could be even better than my greys.'

'Then indeed I am interested.'

'Thought you might be.'

Despite the loss, John was in a good mood all afternoon and particularly so when he returned Bella's garter to her, prior to going down to dinner. A lady should definitely have a husband who was naughty in the bedroom, she decided, having been in receipt of very sensuous and intoxicating kisses whilst in a state of semi undress before Anna administered to her sartorial needs.

John was of the same mind when it came to his wife. He adored her and worshipped her body, softly rounded and feminine, her flesh so responsive to his touch. Her initial shyness, when faced with the intimacies of the marriage bed, had faded with her understanding of the pleasure they could give to each other.

He thanked God for the good fortune which had come his way when a bold country girl had ignored convention and sought to converse with him in Lady Creighton's ballroom.

With undisguised pride in his beautiful and charming duchess, he led her into the dining room, feasting, drinking, and merriment being the order of the day, and well into the early hours of the next, when weary but happy they sought their beds.

Festivities of some kind went on for the whole twelve days of Christmas, after which those guests still at the castle, journeyed home.

Rossington wasn't returning to London immediately, having made plans to go to Shropshire and seek out William and Letty Foster, hopefully to find the answers he needed to finally resolve the mystery surrounding Sally Mary Foster's birth.

Without any general hoo-ha, Sally Wrighton had been unconditionally accepted into the Rossington family over the course of the Christmas holiday. The facts were thin and fragile, but the family likeness was unmistakable, especially on the occasion when she stood on the stairs near the portrait of her mother, the Duchess.

As for being like her brother, this became increasingly obvious as they spent more time together. They were different too but odd little family traits had been passed down to both of them.

The Marchioness of Deane and the new Earl Wrighton looked on with fascination. Thaddeus put his thoughts into words.

'In my heart I have regrets for what they have missed over the years but had Sally been raised as the daughter of a Duke it's unlikely we would have married with my prospects, and our marriage, I can never regret. She has been the delight of my life, together with our wonderful children.'

'And she will go on being so Thaddeus. Ivor will not seek to upset your life. All he will want is to have greater closeness, by letter, from visits, from meeting up in the ballrooms of grand houses.

'He is not a selfish man but a thoughtful and caring one. He was deeply sorry to have upset Bella, but I think seeing her unexpectedly might have confused his mind in a way he didn't understand as he wasn't very rational for a few weeks until Daniel's research cast a strange new light on matters.'

'I don't know if we will ever be party to the whole truth of what happened forty-six years ago. I don't think I even need to know, as it must by its very nature be hurtful to my darling Sally.'

'Then we should not now press unduly for disturbing answers,' Lady Deane said compassionately, 'when we can be happy that a brother and sister, separated for so long have now found each other.'

'Amen to that,' he said.

Amen or *so be it*. Yet it was not to be, or at least not for a while longer.

England January 1815

Rossington would have easily understood their sentiment had he been privy to their conversation but having discovered the shocking truth of his great grandfather's cruelty and deceit, was now determined to have the fullest picture of the events surrounding the birth of his father and aunt. To that purpose he journeyed to Shropshire alone, arriving at Oakley Park late in the evening having broken his journey twice on the way. Bellingham's servants were ready and waiting for him since his valet and his own personal servant had travelled ahead for the final few miles.

William Foster, for many years now the Steward at Oakley, was the first to welcome him to the house. Bella had told him her grandfather was sixty-five years of age and still very sprightly which appeared true as Rossington would have thought him to be in his late fifties if he hadn't known better. He was also articulate and refined in his speech.

'I understand you wish to speak to myself and my wife and if the time would suit, I propose we meet in the library tomorrow morning after breakfast.'

And so, it was arranged, but Rossington had no wish for them to spend the night in a worried frame of mind.

'I would point out to you immediately that I come as a friend of Bella's and only wish to ascertain a few facts which I think you might help me with, about your time at Belverdon.'

'I see my Lord. Then we will be as helpful as we can.'

'If possible, whilst I am here, I would also like to see the boy Cuthbert as I have gifts for him from Bella and her husband. Could that be arranged?'

'Would you like me to send word to the farm for them to come here or would you prefer to visit him there? It's about a twenty-minute ride from here.'

'I'll go there. You can send a message to expect me if you feel it would be beneficial.'

'I will, or Adam might be out somewhere and would be sorry to miss you.'

The library at Oakley was not large but comfortably appointed with elegant, padded sofas arranged around the fireplace where a log fire gave off a goodly heat.

Letty Foster was anxious. Rossington saw it straight away as she came into the room and her hands were shaking as her husband introduced them.

'Please be seated and do not worry. I only want your honest version of events which took place when you were young and newly married. You have nothing to fear and I might be able to answer questions you may have long wanted the answers to as well.'

'Is it about Sally?' Letty asked as if she'd always known someone would come one day to probe her mind.

'It is Letty, but first let me tell you what I know and hopefully you can fill in the rest which will end a mystery and grant peace to everyone involved who is still alive.'

He told them of the disinterment and reburials of those previously laid to rest at Belverhead, of the two girls both named Sally Mary Foster, of a buried cross and a christening, of the words written in the Bible and the statements they'd found and finally of Sally's unmistakeable likeness to the Marquess of Deane and his mother, which led them to honestly believe she was born his twin sister.

'My grandmother when asked about the birth of my father said she thought she gave birth to two babies, but everyone denied it and implied she was hysterical and heading for an asylum. My grandfather kept the child from her and instructed Robert Aston, who worked at the kennels, to take her away and dispose of her.'

There were gasps of horror and William began to tell of his remembrance of that sad time in their young lives.

'Our sweet daughter Sally died in her sleep, we know not what of, and I took her to Belverhead and dug her a grave, placing a little cross within the bindings we'd wrapped her in. My intent was to see the vicar and ask him to record her birth and death and when he could, say prayers over the place where she lay which I'd marked with a shower of pebbles. I was coming away from there when I heard the familiar sound of a baby crying and thought myself a little crazy, but it persisted and there in a basket amongst the heather lay another baby girl, like a gift from God. And she was heaven sent, for she was the perfect child in every way, but don't think we claimed her easily. We were torn, knowing by right she wasn't ours to keep but afraid for her survival, for who abandons a baby on the moor if their intent is not for it to perish. If I hadn't found her, animals would have discovered her scent and devoured her.

'I had no idea when I took her home what Letty would think, what she would say. The child was small, smaller than our own sweet Sally, but she had not been neglected since birth, was clothed and wrapped in a good warm blanket. She was hungry though and once Letty fed her our decision was made. We would do our best to keep her alive and safe and if no word spread of a missing child, we would claim her as our own.

'Belverdon was quiet, the moor was quiet, the guns were silent and the baby continued to wake each day and cry to be fed. She needed Letty's milk and Letty needed the child to suckle. I couldn't have separated them once a bond had grown between them so we raised her as our own and loved her as if she were our own.

'We never told her how we'd found her because how can you tell a child she was left out on an isolated moor to die.'

'You can't. Her husband and brother will decide what if anything they want her to know. Whatever that is, it will not change how she feels about you, nor how Bella loves you. If you feel able to cope with the situation, then the aim is to become one extended family.

'Your Sally is now Countess Wrighton, a Lady by marriage. Only the family need to know she was born Lady Annabelle Sarah Rossington, twin sister of the Marquess of Deane, granddaughter of the Duke of Aven.'

'We should let her decide,' Letty said feeling they were denying Sally the right to know the truth. 'She has always been strong. If she hadn't been, she would never have survived.'

Her grandfather is dead. He can't hurt her now.

'Do you agree William?'

'Letty has a point and perhaps we are being overprotective. Thaddeus will know what to do. He's always known what to do for her to live a life of fulfilment, even at his own expense, although he'd likely deny he suffered any loss with Sally by his side.'

Rossington could only agree. Thaddeus and Sally were a most devoted couple and their love had survived society's disapproval to shine undimmed down the years.

'Will you stay and take some coffee with me?' he asked. 'Bella speaks so highly of you; I'd like to get to know you better.'

'Just for a while then. We do have work to do.'

'I know, but Bellingham said I had a free rein to distract you, so I feel we are on safe ground. Perhaps you will also tell me a little about Adam and Jane.'

They passed the time amiably as William and Letty told him how they had raised their whole family in love, with a respect for hard work and education and a desire to take what honest advantages from life they could. In the afternoon, Rossington set off for their grandson Adam's farm and the Oakley stables nearby.

Cuthbert, who was most days outside playing with Whiskers, the dog he'd named after the uncle who gave it to him, was the first to see Rossington approaching and rushed inside to tell his mum.

Bella had sent a generous bag of presents, toys for Cuthbert and knick-knacks for Adam and Jane, which kept everyone busy to begin with, and broke the ice. Whiskers the dog lay well behaved at Cuthbert's feet.

'A Setter, is he?' Rossington enquired.

'An English Setter,' Cuthbert told him. 'My uncle gave him to me to adopt because he had to go abroad and couldn't take him with him.'

'I don't think he was your uncle, Cuddy,' Jane said.

'He was. He said so,' Cuddy insisted. 'He asked me if I was happy here, and when I said I was, he smiled. He was tall and had bushy whiskers at the side of his face. I sat down next to him and he didn't mind.'

'What was he wearing?'

'He had black boots up to his knee, brown leather breeches, and a brown coat. His hat was a bit squashed in.'

'Did he wear a cravat like Lord Rossington?'

'I didn't see because his collar was up.'

'Did his boots have a cuff around the top like mine?' Rossington asked him.'

'No, they was just black.'

'Military do you think?' Rossington wondered. There had been talk of Cuddy's father having been a soldier, but no one had ever put a name to him.

'I don't know. Cuddy would like to think he has other relations, but we know of none. If the man he spoke to really is his uncle, why not come in and say hello?'

'Perhaps he just came to see if Cuddy was happy and settled.'

'Then it would have been helpful if he hadn't unsettled him and made him wonder about his parents again.'

'You are my parents,' Cuddy said out loud and ran out into the garden with Whiskers.

'Oh dear! Sometimes he's so quiet I forget he's there,' Jane said remorsefully.

'He'll be alright,' Rossington assured her. 'Maybe a mysterious uncle isn't a terrible thing to have and the dog he gave him is quality bred. He loves you both and for him that is everything. For once in his life, he has a home, a loving family, and prospects. Bella was wise to think of bringing him to you.'

No one was going to argue on that point. Adam and Jane felt their lives were now filled with a contentment previously denied them and knew Bella's thoughtful and caring outlook on life had been responsible for their good fortune.

'Will you thank her for the lovely presents when you next see her?' Adam asked. 'Cuddy often speaks of her.'

'Is she happy now she's married?' Jane added.

'Of that there is no doubt. Be assured, Walborough is a very attentive husband.'

After a pleasant and relaxing few days at Oakley, Rossington began his journey home with much to occupy his mind. No fault could be laid at Wiliam and Letty Foster's door. If they had not taken the foundling child in, she would surely have perished, as had been her grandfather's intent.

He could not fathom the mind of a man who could so easily make the decision to deprive his son and daughter-in-law of a child they would have cherished. His written rationale for committing the deed was absurd since wet nurses and servants a plenty would have been available to take the strain of those early months of motherhood, it not being uncommon for a Lady to see little of her newborn infants until they were weaned.

A tyrannical nature, no finer feelings, and a desire for revenge when crossed seemed to be a fair summing up of his great grandfather's character, a trait thankfully not seen in any of his descendants who valued tolerance and forgiveness above retribution. Ideals which didn't prevent them from ever making mistakes but left them more open to seeing reason and accepting the error of their ways.

He hoped he was a reasonable man, thoughtful in his dealings with others, a good friend and companion. He hoped for some personal happiness but as yet he had no prospective bride on the horizon and with so many examples of love matches around him he would not in the foreseeable future, contemplate settling for anything less.

Chapter Twenty-Three

Rossington's journey home from Shropshire turned out to be more tedious than expected when lost for a time in thick fog, he was forced to seek overnight lodging in Herefordshire, considerably delaying his arrival back in town and leaving his temper somewhat frayed. Now relaxed and enjoying an intimate family dinner with John and Bella and possessed of a full understanding of the circumstances surrounding the birth of Bella's mama, he was able to give a plausible account of the way events had unfolded at Belverdon forty-six years ago. The way forward, however, was not fixed in his mind.

'I would value your views on how I should now proceed.'

Bella was the first to comment.

'Mama is already aware that her grandfather denied her existence and most likely sought her death. For all his professed reasoning it was a foul, cold-blooded and spiteful deed. I think she must now have the right to know the truth and fully regain her place in society. Equally, William and Letty's true daughter should have her short life recorded in the church records.'

John was in agreement with his wife.

'With sufficient evidence to hand, it should not be an impossible task to have the records amended. Your mama was rightly born Lady Annabelle Sarah Rossington. She might easily adopt her birth name again as Sally is a frequently used variant of Sarah, particularly when a daughter is named after her mother and grandmother, which makes his subsequent actions even more unfathomable.'

'In truth, John, he named her after two women he had no affection for. He hated his wife Annabelle and never wanted Elizabeth Sarah Reid for his daughter-in-law, considering her family to be socially inferior despite her father also being an Earl. He eventually accepted her when he realised what a fortune she would bring to the marriage, the Reid family having been a canny lot with their finances. In all other matters he ruthlessly dismissed them as boring because they chose to live quietly and responsibly at their country estate.

'He did all he could to keep Elizabeth apart from her parents after her marriage, although Thomas found ways to get around his father's edicts, which no doubt rankled.'

'And what of William and Letty, how do they feel about the records being corrected?' John asked.

Randal did not foresee any problems.

'They have always known Sally wasn't their own child. Whatever happens to the records, she will always be to them their beloved daughter and no one would dispute their right to remain her beloved parents. My grandparents will only seek to have more engagement with her and her family since they are now happily aware of having a son-in-law and four grandchildren they previously knew nothing of. We must hold a full family gathering, I think as soon as it can be arranged. I'll speak to papa about it.'

It seemed a sensible solution to all three of them. If Sally was to be told the truth, which now seemed most likely, she should be surrounded by those who loved her, blessed as she was with the love of her newfound birth family as well as the caring one in which she had been lovingly raised, who would all look to the future rather than dwell on the past.

To this purpose, in late February, a large house party was held at Bascombe Hall, the advantage of its geographical position providing similar travelling distances for all those invited and an abundance of bedrooms available to the guests and their entourages.

Bella pondered for days over the distribution of the rooms, not wishing to create an aristocracy versus commoners' situation, yet adhering to some level of precedence.

John had an idea that he thought might suit.

'What if you accommodate them generationally. That way at least if the younger generation are rowdier, the older generations will not be kept awake half the night.'

'Oh, what a marvellous idea. I've never done anything on this scale before. I would be all at sea without your help.'

'I doubt it, my love, but I have been to a great many house parties over the years and the young can get just as grumpy being told to be quiet all the time as the elderly can get being denied some peace.'

'It will work this, won't it?'

'Of course, because everyone wants it to for your mama's sake.'

'Who would ever have imagined the Fosters mixing freely with the Rossingtons when they were once so far apart in status?'

'In social status possibly, but William Foster was born with a good brain, and the ambition to better himself. The old vicar of Sawley taught him to read as a boy and he acquired a natural understanding of the cycle of nature in his youth from living on the moor and working with his father which subsequently made him an excellent gamekeeper. Once he left Belverdon he was fortunate enough to find himself employed by men of vision and compassion who didn't judge him by his birth but by his knowledge, skills, and efficiency. To rise from apprenticed gamekeeper to steward of a substantial house is some achievement even with family support. Randal was easily impressed by his quiet efficiency at Oakley.'

'How do you know all this when you haven't met him yet?'

'Your mama told me and Randal backed up all she said.'

'Who shall we sit him by at dinner?'

'The Duke of Aven I think, they are of an age and will have Sally's childhood and the wild moor to talk about and they are both grandpas.'

'This is going to be very interesting.'

The whole weekend was busy from the moment the first carriage arrived bearing Rossington with his parents, the Marquess and Marchioness of Deane, to be followed shortly after by the Duke and Duchess of Aven. The new Earl Wrighton, Thaddeus, and his Countess Sally along with their youngest son William came next, and then began a steady stream of arrivals. Roderick travelled from London, Lawrence, and Gisela, now engaged to be married, from Deane Castle and its environs. The Fosters forming quite a convoy from Shropshire arrived safely together in the late afternoon with the delightful Cuthbert, adopted by Adam and Jane, now six and as adorable as ever. Bella was delighted to welcome them all to Bascombe Hall.

She still found it hard to accept the reality of her ancestry now it was plain she was not, by blood, the granddaughter of William and Letty Foster, whom she adored, but of the

Duke and Duchess of Aven, who were virtual strangers to her. She was still a Wrighton, but apart from her immediate family, no other Wrightons were on the guest list since they had not been favourably involved in her mother's life until very recently. The Rossington family were present in greater numbers since the Duke and Duchess had four other adult children besides Sally and the Marquess.

It was years since so many Rossington's had been together in the same house, especially the cousins Randal saw infrequently due to them still being engaged in the process of education. They had all come to meet the lady, Lord Deane claimed to be his twin sister. It was not surprising to discover most of them were initially both curious to meet her and sceptical as to the truth of the matter.

The dinner on the first evening after everyone's arrival was a splendid affair, the food courtesy of Walborough's greatly sought-after chef, the decorations Bella's, with some inspiration from her mother-in-law who also graced the proceedings being currently resident at Bascombe Hall. The seating plan seemed to have worked if all the animated conversations were anything to go by and William Foster, initially panicked to find himself seated next to the Duke of Aven, discovered him to be a fine conversationalist whose knowledge of Belverdon and the moor was vast, despite the length of years since he had stepped foot on the estate. The Duke, William soon discovered, was also quietly in command of all situations.

'Tomorrow, you, Letty, Elizabeth, and I with sit down together as parents and you will tell us of our daughter Annabelle Sarah and all you can remember about her growing up. Tonight, is for revelations, fine musical entertainment, and dancing.'

The story was told to a mainly astonished audience, the evidence related, the facts honed down to be precise and indisputable and then there was the basket. Letty had retrieved it from the back of a cupboard, dusted it off and brought it with her to give to the Duchess. The blanket Sally had been wrapped in was neatly folded inside it, cream wool with a cotton binding mitred in the corners, only a little stained and worn in places as she had soon grown too big for it to adequately cover her.

Elizabeth, the Duchess took it out and unfolded it. She peered at all the four corners.

'Can someone bring me a magnifying glass. My eyes aren't as sharp as they used to be.'

A quizzing glass was quickly produced, and she looked again in more detail at the corners of the blanket.

'There, she said, pointing to one particular corner, 'the R for Rossington, I had it embroidered on all the layette for our first child.'

Once you knew it was there it was easily seen but the stitching was fine and the mitre formed the upright of the R such that the squiggle at the side of it could have been taken for anything, wayward stitching coming easily to mind. Certainly, Letty had never noticed it, but then all her attention had been on keeping the child alive.

Sally stared at both the blanket and the basket.

'God must surely have wanted me to survive if this was all the protection I had from the elements and the wildlife.'

William aimed to reassure her.

'Fate or God took me to the graveyard that day at about the same time as Robert Aston was heading towards it. You cannot have been there long before I found you. Our tragic loss meant Letty was well placed to care for you and you filled a hole left by our daughter's failure to thrive. For all we pondered over your parentage, I don't think for one moment we ever imagined you to be a Rossington, for why would a family so well set up in life, feel the need to abandon a child so heartlessly?'

'Why indeed?' the Duke said, sick at the thought of his father's perfidy.

'He might have justified the act to himself, but such an unnecessary and pointless crime can never be forgiven, and we can only be glad to know she fell into the hands of a loving couple who kept her safe and well and nurtured her to womanhood to become a fine wife and mother.

'Please raise a toast to Lady Annabelle Sarah, born Rossington but now Countess Wrighton, who is back where she belongs in the bosom of her family, adored by her husband and children and a credit to both the parents who created her and the parents who raised her. And to William and Letty Foster, for their never ceasing, tender loving care of a foundling baby.'

Glasses were raised and a general mingling began, when questions were asked and answers given, of wrong steps, confusion, and conclusions slowly drawn until the last piece of the puzzle had fittingly landed in its rightful place.

There could be no further doubt. Sally Wrighton had been born Lady Annabelle Sarah Rossington, daughter of Thomas and Elizabeth, then the Marquess and Marchioness of Deane at Belverdon on the seventh day of September in the year of our Lord, one thousand seven hundred and sixty-eight, and records would be legally amended to place her firmly back on the family tree.

Sally marvelled at the new relatives she was introduced to, brothers and sisters and their spouses, cousins, nieces, and nephews. She worried that her Foster relations might be neglected, the three brothers she'd grown up with and their children, but it wasn't the case when her daughter and son-in-law, the Duke and Duchess of Walborough, led the way in ensuring everyone felt welcome and comfortable.

'Well, my love. I think our little gathering has proved to be successful,' John said to Bella as everyone gradually found their way to the ballroom where a concert would precede dancing and a masterpiece of a supper. With her husband's arm firmly around her shoulders, she could only agree with him, and finally felt able to let out a huge sigh of relief.

Lawrence and Gisela had organised the concert, playing a selection of popular pieces themselves as either solos or duets, but they had also persuaded both Sally and Bella to participate.

Walborough sat with Rossington and marvelled at the talent on display.

'You couldn't buy a ticket for a better concert than this,' John said proudly.

'I'll give you two complimentary tickets for the next concert at Deane Church,' Randal replied. 'It's already sold out since my protégé is proving to be a phenomenal success. How is yours doing?'

'Young Arthur? Give him chance. He has to grow up a bit before he can compete with adults but he's already the undefeated champion of all the grooms and trainee jockeys at Hopston Chase on a pony, and such a likeable lad they don't seem to mind him always being the victor.'

'Who would have thought talking and singing to horses would prove to be such a winning combination?'

'It's quite a rare gift he has. I've never come across anyone else having such an affinity with horses, and he has such a thoughtful pleasing way about him.'

'It was a lucky day for Arthur and his family when you rode into Stillford out of curiosity, but not so for Owen Lawton. How has he responded to discovering you've purchased the land he farms?'

'I've encouraged him to go on maximising the use of the land and given him a position in Hopston organising the markets to increase sales and introduce new products. Mr Briggs and his boys now work with him, instead of for him, which surprisingly seems free of friction. It would have been foolish to have wasted his particular talents.'

'And the church?'

'The new vicar is excellent as is the organist and choirmaster Hubert Lang found for me. The music society goes from strength to strength and the community seems happy enough with the change.

'A schoolroom is being built behind the church and when it's finished, I'll employ a teacher.'

'You might get some resistance to the children attending when families need them to work for a wage however small.'

'I know but they must learn of the importance of education to their children's futures. The land won't sustain them forever in a changing world. On my other estates all have basic schooling until they are ten, mainly during the winter months with a long break in the summer for the harvest. Children born on my estates will no doubt go to the towns when they're older to find work. Education I hope will give them a little advantage to be more than itinerant labourers.'

Randal was thoughtful.

'Fate, it seems, has opened up new opportunities for Bella's family too. Roderick and Lawrence are now young gentlemen with prospects and William will go to Oxford when he is of an age, and no doubt excel like his father.'

'Roderick, I might add, is currently quite engrossed with your delightful sister Annabelle. Of course, their heads could just be close together because they're discussing the wonderful programme of music.'

'She's not yet seventeen. Papa won't want to see her married yet a while.'

'They may stay close. Roderick will need time to establish himself as Viscount Wylde and Annabelle can gain more experience and spread her wings a little. It wouldn't be a bad match if it ever came to pass, but they are now known to be first cousins, which may give them second thoughts about contemplating marriage.'

Thaddeus, Earl Wrighton was also viewing proceedings with a watchful eye but he had never seriously worried about Roderick being successful. His sleepless nights had generally been over Lawrence whose impulsive behaviour as a boy could have easily led him into danger and might have but for his love of music. Finding a tutor for him on a modest income had been hard but they had been fortunate in securing the services of Signor Bartolenti, mainly because he had been impressed by Bella's voice. Since he was also a fine pianist and organist it had worked out well all round and Sally had joined in the lessons too, finding and extending the range of her own fine singing voice.

Looking at Lawrence now it was hard to see him as that same impulsive boy. He had found his niche in the world, had all the manners and charm of a young gentleman of fashion and had fallen in love with a delightful and talented young lady. As a musician he flourished, confident now of his ability and having a sound understanding of where it would take him.

If he was still a little impulsive and obsessive at times it would be because he had found a new piece of music he wanted to learn how to play and would continually study it until he'd mastered the notes without anyone putting obstacles in his way, except perhaps to persuade him to eat.

Having Walborough for his son-in-law was all he could ever have hoped for. He hadn't wanted Bella to go to London but now he was grateful that his sister had whisked her away, even if he had questioned her motives for doing so at the time.

In less than four months, God willing, he and Sally would become grandparents and his grandchild would be the son or daughter of a Duke as his wife had been, unbeknown to them until recent events had uncovered the truth.

They had discovered so much in the past months and learned of behaviour far beyond normal understanding, the hand of fate, or God's mysterious work?

Even he, with his Bachelor of Divinity, had no convincing explanation for what had occurred both in the past and more recently in the Rossington and Wrighton families; gruesome deaths, new beginnings, lives turned upside down and the promise of a new brighter future.

Darkness and evil dwelt in the minds of men who might outwardly appear affable and charming. They had their motives, their desires, their truth, but he could not easily fathom their iniquities.

He had never wished for any harm to befall any of his brothers, yet in recent times he had prayed with increasing regularity for them to live more through the Lord, and less through the devil.

He had never sought to become Earl Wrighton, nor imagined circumstances where he might find himself inheriting the title. Certainly, his mind would never have conjured up the horrible fate of his siblings, murdered in their own home, along with his young nephew.

Now that the honour had come his way, he saw God's purpose more clearly and relished the opportunities it gave him to move freely in the social world he'd been born into, to trade thoughts with men of greater understanding and to raise the families on his estates from the darkness into the light, with hope instead of despair.

All God's children, he believed, should live in hope.

Cuthbert Foster, who had made his way around the ballroom with both hope and purpose, came to sit beside him and wish him goodnight as it was almost time for him to go to bed. Thaddeus, having been introduced to him soon after his arrival with the Fosters, had felt instantly drawn to him, since he'd experienced the same separation from family at birth as his Sally. His strength of character and determination, plus a delightful personality, had seen him through those early unsettled years and now with good fortune, he was comfortably settled and happy.

'Have you enjoyed yourself today with all the other children?' Thaddeus asked him.

'Yes, thank you, but I miss my dog. Mama said it would be unkind to make him travel so far and we wouldn't want to lose him on the way. That would make my uncle sad.'

'Which uncle?'

'Uncle Whiskers. I know that's not his real name but it's how I remember him. He said he had to go abroad and gave me his dog to look after and now I'm worried about him. Would you say a prayer for him to keep him safe.'

'Why are you worried about him?'

'I don't know, but I can't help thinking of him, and mama doesn't like it if I talk about him because he is only a stranger who gave me a puppy to care for, not my uncle at all.'

If a prayer would help the boy feel more settled in his mind, Thaddeus wasn't about to deny him the comfort.

'Put your hands together like mine then and we'll pray for him together.'

'Heavenly Father, hear our prayer for Uncle Whiskers. Keep him safe from harm wherever he is and bring him home again when the time is right. Bless him with good fortune in all things and thank you for sending him to give Cuthbert his sweet puppy. Amen.'

'He'll be safe now won't he,' Cuthbert said happily, giving Thaddeus a kiss on the cheek.

'I'm sure he will,' Thaddeus agreed, and wondered who it was who had given Cuthbert the puppy he adored. There was every possibility the boy did have an uncle but if he did, no one had the remotest idea who he was.

Chapter Twenty-Four

The whole purpose of Major Lord Seldon's current existent was for no one to have the remotest idea of who he was, or where he was. He'd been tasked with a secret mission for months, inactive save for sending coded dispatches to London whilst observing all that went on along the southern French coast between Nice and Marseilles. He wasn't alone. His small company of chosen men from the 95th Rifle Regiment were embedded around the area too, disguised doing ordinary jobs, shacked up with women leading ordinary lives, inconspicuous, monitoring and recording the movements of ships and boats in the Mediterranean Sea between the mainland and the coast of Elba. They were on permanent alert, believing something would eventually happen, if they had judged their target correctly.

Napoleon Bonaparte had been defeated, yet he was not a prisoner as such. He had no gaolers. He retained his status, in title only, and ruled his own small island, subject to the terms of the Treaty of Fontainebleau, meant to spend the rest of his days there with a pension from the King of France. He had not been idle in the months since his arrival on Elba. He had built roads, improved mines for their income, and revitalised the schools and legal system, taking charge of everything as a sovereign should. He was a man of action, a man with an ego, a man who had reached great heights but reached too far, a man who had less than a year since, been undisputed Emperor of France. In the opinion of Major Seldon, such a small island would not keep a man of his stature, caged for long.

The coalition forces who had defeated him and forced him to abdicate, leading to the accession of the Bourbon King Louis XV111 to the French throne, had met in September at the Congress of Vienna to realign borders and reduce the risk of new powerful alliances arising, thereby limiting any future threat to the peace of Europe. They argued amongst themselves and made little progress.

Napoleon, able to entertain visitors from France, received regular intelligence of their wrangling for territory and power and fearing himself at risk of being moved to a more secure destination, saw an opportunity to put himself forward once again as the man of the people, assured by his great vanity of the support of the army once he landed on French soil.

On the night of the twenty-sixth of February, whilst the coalition were sufficiently distracted and suspicious of each other's motives and demands, Napoleon took them all by surprise.

Those set to guard him, if it could be called guarding, were absent on other business and with his tiny fleet of the brig Inconstant, four small transport ships and two feluccas, he slipped away from Elba during a masquerade carnival, accompanied by a force of around one thousand men, landing with little opposition to his plans on the southern coast of France, between Cannes and Antibes.

'So, it begins again,' Major Lord Seldon said to Captain Linus Willoughby, 'and where will it lead us to, this time?'

'To death or glory, I expect, because they failed to properly confine him whilst allowing him too much control. I doubt they will want to make the same mistake again.'

News was slow reaching London, nothing coming by mail, message or express delivery until a letter arrived from the French coast indicating Napoleon was marching towards Lyons. The London newspapers were more intent on giving full and detailed reports of rioting through the streets of the capital in angry demonstrations against the Corn Bill. Railings were torn down, windows and shutters broken, and a general rampage only halted when military patrols were put in place.

The first official bulletin of the events in France was published by ministers upon receipt of dispatches from Lord Edward Somerset dated the sixth and seventh of March confirming Napoleon had landed at Antibes at the head of about one thousand men and that troops had been sent to oppose him at Lyons. *'Perfect tranquillity,'* so the dispatch stated, prevailed at Paris.

Tranquillity also prevailed in London as other news took precedence. This was a French matter; they saw no reason to be alarmed. Balls and parties took place as usual and the social whirl continued uninterrupted.

A further report on Napoleon's escape from Elba was printed on Sunday the twelfth of March stating:

'he escaped from the commissioners by which he was surrounded and it was understood, most vigilantly watched and by some effort he landed with at least one thousand men on the south coast of France.'

'In other words,' Walborough remarked to Rossington, 'no Englishman was to blame for his audacious escape. They should have argued less amongst themselves and seen to it that he was confined somewhere more secure. Let's hope the French army subdue him before he gets too far. He's been declared a rebel and a traitor and his arrest ordered so the law should deal with him before a call to arms is required.'

'One would hope so,' Rossington agreed, but neither of them was overly convinced.

Bella into the sixth month of her pregnancy felt she had enough to do without being particularly concerned about the political situation in France. John was assisting her father with the management of his new estates, ensuring experienced men were employed to fill positions where negligent managers had been speedily removed from their posts. Belcourt had been thoroughly cleaned and closed up since the gruesome murders of the Wrighton males, with only a minimum of dependable servants left in residence as caretakers. Her father wished to concentrate his efforts of ensuring the estates finances were in better shape, and leaning towards prosperity, before he considered living in the grand mansion.

The needs of his tenants and villagers for a sound roof over their heads and reliable work to keep their families from hunger, were greater than his and Sally's need to be living in splendour. Wrighton House in Mayfair was in fact more than splendid enough for their current modest way of life.

They were frequently at Walborough House, in any case, as John and his agent went through the estate accounts with her father to find savings and better investments.

When her father arrived for a meeting, so did her mother, and they enjoyed each other's company as they had done before Aunt Susannah had taken her to town.

They oversaw the purchasing of a layette for the baby and the redecoration of the Walborough House nursery together. Bella learned about being in labour and what she should expect in the birthing room.

Sally had never wanted her daughter to be surprised by the natural events in a woman's life but she kept her explanations positive and emphasised the joy of holding your own child in your arms for the first time, rather than the pain and effort likely to be involved, knowing fear and anxiety did nothing to alleviate any kind of discomfort. Bella was not consequently unduly alarmed at the prospect of giving birth. She was too busy learning how to be a duchess with a constant list of tasks she set for herself. John was amused by her list and regularly teased her about it.

'You could cut those tasks in half or even quarters if you would only remember to send a footman to Hatchard's to order and collect your books and ask tradespeople to call here instead of going to them. They will be more than happy to oblige you.'

'I know they will but I enjoy browsing through the books and seeing what new wares are on sale in the shops. I haven't grown accustomed to having assistance always at hand.'

'What have you grown accustomed to then?'

'Sparkling conversation, soft lips, warm hands, waking up every morning with you beside me, being deeply in love and feeling cherished.'

'A very promising list, my love and a copy of mine. Promise me you won't overtax yourself with other matters. I don't want to restrict you in any way but I don't want you unnecessarily weary either.'

'I will have a care for myself and our child, do not fear.'

'Then I will trust in your common sense but don't forget it is my duty as your husband to take care of you.'

'You take care of me very well. I have a whole host of people looking out for me. I couldn't be better cared for.'

'Are we cramping your style?'

'Not really and it's such a pleasure to have mama and Aunt Susannah close by to keep me company when you are busy.'

'Your aunt needs keeping busy. She's all too well aware of Wellington having gone to Brussels to take command of the allied forces and cannot miss mention in the newspapers of the increasing number of troops to be seen marching towards the coast. Your cousin Matthew is set to leave any day now and she had hoped his fighting days were over.'

'Will it come to a fight?'

'I think it must. How else is Napoleon to be stopped when he is raising more troops with every passing day?'

'Can we win?'

'We have the best commander in Lord Wellington and we did have the finest army before much of it was disbanded last year after Napoleon's abdication, when our soldiers were brought home and returned to their civilian lives. New recruits will need to be drilled and that of course takes time. Will we have enough time to be fully prepared to meet the French army once again? That I think is the big question. Meanwhile in Brussels the social scene continues in a lively fashion and parties and balls go ahead as planned, as if all life was a holiday.'

'Shall you wish to stay in the city or will we go to Bascombe Hall as planned?'

'The summer is nigh upon us and you will find the countryside more restful and less formal. Your mama, papa and William will come too and Rossington if he so wishes. Your aunt and uncle plan to go to Bel Manor next week to see Matthew's family settled there for the time being but may join us later. My mama is already in residence and no doubt my sisters will arrive at some point with their families. We might even see Lawrence and Gisela and perhaps

Roderick for a short stay so you will not be without company.

'I confess I have a longing to explore Bascombe Hall and all its treasures. I hope you intend to be my guide.'

'I will, of course, be available to you although I must spend a little of each day working with Harry Keats to keep on top of my correspondence. I hope you will like what mama has done with the nursery at Bascombe. She has been most eager to have everything ready for you when you arrive so you may be comfortable.'

'I am not planning to be cossetted and confined until our child is born. I don't appreciate being bored. Six weeks of idleness will not do for me. I shall want to see something of the estate and walk a little each day for the freshness of the air, should the weather permit.'

'It shall all be as you wish with no tyrannical dukes anywhere in your vicinity.'

'You are likely to be the only duke in residence. You are never tyrannical and I would never keep you purposefully away from me. You may be as close at hand as you wish and make yourself known to our child at the earliest moment. I'm not planning on being long in labour.'

'You're not?' John said sceptically.

'No.' She affirmed.

John wasn't about to argue with her but he thought she was under some kind of misapprehension about the length of labour from what he'd heard about it. Pacing up and down for hours outside closed doors in a state of anxiety, seemed too frequently to be the fate of husbands, whilst their wives laboured hard to deliver their child. He hoped he might stay calm but he knew he would grow worried once the event was upon them as he waited to hear his son or daughter was safely born and his wife unharmed by the experience, God willing.

Rossington, having arrived to join them for dinner, put paid to any further thoughts on the matter, maudlin or otherwise, as he had planned another trip and wanted to tell them all about it.

'News has come through that William and Letty now have the go ahead to bury the remains of their baby daughter Sally Mary in the churchyard at Sawley, next to her grandparents. I have agreed with my papa and Bella's mama to go as a representative of the family to offer support. I will drive to Shropshire and collect them from Oakley Park. We can then travel on to Yorkshire together, stay a few nights at Belverdon Lodge and go as a family to meet the vicar at the Church of the Blessed Virgin, to complete the sombre task and finally put right the wrongs of the past.'

John and Bella were sorry to see him go but wished him a safe journey when he left them at the end of a pleasant and relaxing evening together to prepare for his journey north.

It was to be a strange return to Belverdon for William and Letty, guests at the Lodge in the company of Viscount Rossington, when once they had been lowly servants of the Duke, his great grandfather. They had spent the first eleven years of their married life living on the estate but never before had they been privileged to see the inside of the Lodge, nor wander the grounds with Lord Rossington as if they were on an equal social footing when society would still view them as being far apart in status. William had for many years viewed the buildings from high on the moor, but the distance had deceived his eye, and he now knew Belverdon to be far roomier than he had ever imagined.

'You say your father plans to sell the estate?'

'He was of a mind to but I'm not convinced he will now, at least not immediately. Coming here always unnerved him as if he knew something bad had happened within these walls yet he never had a clear understanding of what that might have been. He has no use for it as a hunting lodge.'

'If it isn't used as a hunting lodge, what use might it have?'

'There you have the dilemma, William. What other use could it have? It's not pretty inside, the gardens are nothing special and the weather is frequently awful. As for the cottages up on the moor, most are in a dreadful state after years of being neglected.'

'It's thirty-six years since we left and they were in need of repair then. There was nothing to keep us here compared to the chance of greater prosperity if we moved on.'

'How did you manage when you had young children, being as isolated as you were?'

'I don't suppose we thought we had any choice but to make the best of it. Complaining rarely got you anywhere and we were happy at the cottage as long as the supplies were delivered regularly.'

'You loved the moor and the wildlife,' Letty reminded him. 'You were reluctant to leave even when you knew we had no alternative but to look for somewhere else to live and work.'

'I suppose I was. I loved its wildness, knowing it could never be tamed, knowing it generously supported life but also had a wild destructive streak. I loved its changing moods, the colours of the land and sky, the wind and the rain and the earthy scent which followed a storm. We never had much in those days, but we were happy knowing we were playing our part, until my role was effectively axed and we knew it was time to move on.'

'Would you ever contemplate living here again, in the lodge, not on the moor, taking care of it, overseeing what needs to be done both in the house and out on the moor.'

'Not now as old age takes its hold on me but if you wanted someone for that role, I know who the right man for the job would be. Adam's older brother Henry is the one in the family who would cherish such a role, who listened as a boy to our son Robert's tales of life on the moor. He has never lost his interest in that unique environment whereas Adam loves the softer landscape of meadows and rivers.'

'Perhaps I should talk to him before I leave the area and consider what might be possible. We should take the carriage up to the High Road and cross the moor tomorrow on our way to Sawley, to remind ourselves of its wild beauty, if that would please you.'

'I would like one last look before we leave the area,' William agreed. 'I doubt I'll ever come back this way again.'

He had been born on the moor, survived life's hardships, absorbed what knowledge he could, grown from child to man, married his beloved Letty and raised his family in challenging circumstances. He had not been unhappy in those youthful years but there had been no prosperity attached to his position of assistant gamekeeper. The necessity to feed his growing family had been the deciding factor in leaving Yorkshire for a life at Follcliffe where his knowledge and work ethic had been highly valued bringing its own rewards and the furthering of his education. They had dwelt in a larger house, in more comfort and he'd had the respect of those who worked under his guidance.

Moving to Oakley Park had been an entirely different challenge. Sally had married Thaddeus and with new family connections they had begun to thrive in a beautiful part of the country, sheltered from hardship by the generosity of Lord Bellingham who saw to it that he was taught how to become a steward, by a man of wisdom and knowledge, who was edging swiftly towards his retirement.

They had not looked back, only forward. Those early days of hardship were behind them. They had never returned to the moorland graveyard, nor to Sawley Church where they had been married and baptised several of their children.

Once it had been a regular venue for the Foster family, travelling down the track in the horse drawn cart, when the weather permitted to hear the vicar preach on a Sunday and meet up with friends and Letty's parents, both long gone now. The old nag had given them good service until she'd collapsed one day and died making the children mournful for several days.

The horses drawing Lord Rossington's comfortable carriage were spectacular in comparison. Letty thought everything about him was spectacular as was the whole Rossington family. Sally, whom they had raised to be a fine woman, wife and mother, or Annabelle Sarah as she was now officially known, was back in the bosom of that noble family, the sister of the Marquess of Deane, Lord Rossington's aunt. It was almost beyond belief but the evidence of her aristocratic birth had been there all along, hidden from sight, waiting to be found.

William, who had painstakingly made a little cross for their own dear Sally, carving her name and the dates of her short life on it, had never expected it to surface again but by chance it had and now it lay once more with the last mortal remains of their firstborn daughter in a small wooden casket, ready for reinterment. They had come full circle. She would be buried again, beside her ancestors, but this time she would have a small, engraved stone to mark her final resting place, to record her name, when she was born and when she had died, hardly a life at all.

They stood now with Lord Rossington before the graves of the Foster family of Belverhead, Greater Belverdon in the County of Yorkshire as the vicar spoke the words of the burial service and they shed a tear in sorrow as the small casket was placed in the ground and they scattered soil and flowers to cover it before the gravedigger came to make good the ground.

'May your loved ones now rest in peace for all eternity,' Rossington said, when the vicar left them to return to the church, all too aware of the undercurrent of sadness felt by William and Letty at such a poignant moment in their lives.

'She was the sweetest baby,' William said reminiscing, 'like an angel, perfect in every way with wisps of fair hair and blue eyes that held your gaze. Letty put her in her cot to sleep when she was just ten days old and we went to bed ourselves but Sally never woke up, never cried again, lay cold in the crib I'd made for her, still and silent and we couldn't understand it, we couldn't bear it, we wept for our loss and were distraught.

'When I found the baby in the basket, all I remember thinking was, *the Lord giveth and the Lord taketh away*. He had given us Sally and taken her away again to dwell in his heavenly kingdom, and then it was as if he had given us another girl child to replace the daughter we'd lost, so I took the foundling home to Letty and we loved her as if she was our own child, whilst always knowing she wasn't.'

'She would have died if you hadn't found her in a timely way. I can't profess to have any understanding whatsoever of what was going on in my great grandfather's mind to cause him to callously deny his granddaughter's existence and charge someone with the task of murdering her. As for making my grandmother believe she was hysterical and threatening her with the asylum, it doesn't bear thinking about.'

'Yet he recorded her birth as a twin in the family Bible, which seems odd,' William reminded Rossington.

'Then never allowed anyone to see inside it for he must have known what questions would arise if anyone ever saw what he'd written. All I will say is that whatever his intention, God saw to it that his granddaughter didn't die and was raised by kind loving people, who did all they could to keep her safe, who nurtured and encouraged her to grow into the wonderful Lady she is today for which you will always have our deepest gratitude and her family's love.'

'And we can only be happy to learn of her birth family and know them to be kind loving people who bear no resemblance to the old Duke who caused so much misery.'

They journeyed back to Belverdon and then left the next day for Shropshire and Oakley Park, where William and Letty's lives would go on much as before, but their children and grandchildren would never know poverty, having the benefit of a close connection to the powerful Rossington family, and the generous patronage which would become available to them down the years.

Chapter Twenty-Five

Rossington travelled back to London to spend a few days with his parents and relate to them the successful outcome of his emotional journey to Belverdon and Sawley Church. After a few days much needed rest, and some pampering from his mother who thought he looked weary and in need of some tender loving care, his carriage took him south to Tremar to deliver the very heavy family Bible to his grandfather, where it would be given pride of place in the library, to be permanently displayed in a glass topped case designed specifically for the purpose.

The Librarian, thrilled by the magnificence of the Holy book now in his keeping, would henceforth open the Bible at a different page each week, generally choosing one where the text was positioned within a painted decorative border enhanced with gold leaf.
Occasionally there was a full-page illustration, beautifully coloured, depicting a scene from the Bible, but these were thinly spread throughout the old and new testament. The fact it was still in such excellent condition was considered by that learned scholar to be due to its having been hidden in the bottom of the Deane Castle music cupboard for so

long, free from any damp air that might have mildewed its glorious pages.

Leaving Tremar after a delightful week with his grandparents, who remained sprightly in their country retreat despite their advancing years, he set off for Oxfordshire and Bascombe Hall, arriving there as promised without much ceremony in the second week of June.

Bella, close to giving birth, found her activities were seriously limited by feeling ungainly and needing to rest more frequently. John had no wish to confine her in any way if she felt well, but insisted on her always having someone beside her as she ascended or descended the stairs, a request she hadn't chosen to argue about when it seemed a sensible precaution to take.

The company they had recently welcomed from both sides of the family had mainly returned home feeling they could only be in the way as the birth became imminent, and suddenly the house seemed too quiet. Her parents and John's mother were still in residence as was Harriet, his middle sister, but she would admit to being bored when John was frequently hard at work with Harry Keats, trying to get all estate matters up to date so he could devote himself entirely to her and their child when it was born.

Lord Rossington's arrival at Bascombe Hall was consequently very timely.

'How wonderful,' she said, as he was shown into the drawing room where she reclined on a chaise longue. 'Please come and distract me from anything to do with babies until this one decides to make an appearance. I'm not feeble and my brain is functioning perfectly well so some challenging conversation would be an absolute pleasure. Everyone but John is fussing over me as if I'm about to break, and he's working hard with Harry Keats, holding meetings with agents and advisors on estate matters, and other business he feels to be essential at the moment.'

'Shall I take you driving at a very sedate pace around the park tomorrow?' he asked in his usual charming manner.

'Oh, would you? And can I get out and walk for a while too?' she asked eagerly.

'Providing the ground is even. I'm not prepared to face John's wrath if you should have an accident.'

'I won't. I might look like a duck waddling along but I am quite steady on my feet.'

'Then at a sensible time in the morning we shall venture out, but now, for the sake of politeness, I should make my arrival known to John. I presume he's in his study.'

'Either there or in the library. It seems to depend on whether they need the map table or not.'

The days passed more pleasurably with Rossington around to keep her company and walk with her in the gardens. They talked, played chess, and gambled at cards for small stakes and John would join them in the afternoon for tea, seeking assurance that she was not overtaxing herself.

'Randal is a conscientious watchdog whilst also keeping me entertained,' she told her husband so you may rest assured I will come to no harm in his company. In fact, the entire household is very watchful. I sometimes wonder how grandmama managed on her own up on the moor at Belverdon. It must have been wonderfully peaceful.'

No one saw fit to mention her grandmama was in fact the Duchess of Aven and not Letty Foster who held such a special place in her heart. John knew she still found it hard to assimilate the change to her ancestry as far as the bloodlines were concerned. As to love, that deep emotion for William and Letty would never falter.

'They only watch out for you, my love, because they care, having taken you to their hearts,' John was quick to reassure her.

'I have not asked them to restrict your movement in any way. Dr Hayes, who came to us most highly recommended, asked that you should remain as active as possible and get plenty of rest and fresh air. Having spent some time, in his youth, amongst the native tribes of the Americas, he noted that wives continued to live an active life until their birth pains began and frequently gave birth alone with good outcomes, consequently he is not a believer of lying in bed when it isn't necessary, a practice which I think can only please you.

'Randal, being generous with his time, is willing to aid you in remaining active whilst also seeing to your safety outside.'

'And I am most grateful to Dr Hayes and Randal, feeling fortunate to have my dear friend here when he is always so affable, entertaining and charming, as is mama, who gets secret updates from him so she doesn't appear to be constantly fussing around me.'

'Does anything get past you?' Randal said laughing at her candid assessment.'

'Not much and I would appreciate it if when everyone gathers for dinner, the conversation is more natural, maybe even a little contentious, sparkling maybe. Something interesting must be happening somewhere.'

It was, but they were not about to worry Bella with the knowledge of it. Matters were moving to a head in Europe, although Wellington was hopeful of not having to make a move until he felt fully prepared for battle.

News coming from the army's headquarters in Brussels was generally several days behind the event, even later in some of the newspapers, so none of them sitting around the dinner table that evening, enjoying the fine cuisine and more illuminating conversation than had been the case, were aware that Napoleon and his army had already seized the initiative and crossed the border from France into the Southern Netherlands.

Wellington's troops had been put on immediate standby for a rapid move whilst the Duchess of Richmond held a ball, an evening of gaiety, attended by many senior British officers and their families, some of them never to dance again, as death sat heavily on their shoulders. A battle had become both inevitable and imminent with little time for manoeuvring. Orders were dispatched and a weekend of bloody fighting began with the outcome far from certain.

At Bascombe Hall, on the morning of Sunday the eighteenth of June, Bella rose early from her bed after a restless night marred by persistent niggling discomfort. Heading for the chamber pot she was startled by her waters breaking as she crossed the bedroom floor.

The time had come at last for her to bring a new life into the world. A kind of pandemonium reigned until John calmed everyone down and took charge. They settled her in the room next to the nursery where she had chosen to have her baby with a nurse, a nursery maid and Doctor Hayes on hand, who had been conveniently in residence at the Hall for the preceding few days.

There was a lot of talk about first babies taking their time and not to expect much to happen straight away but Selwyn John Charlton Becket, the infant Marquess of Bascombe was apparently unaware of this capacity for long windedness on his part, being born at four minutes past two in the afternoon without any fuss, a strong healthy boy to begin their family. John was thrilled, particularly when he was told by a cheerful Doctor Hayes that Bella was sitting up in bed nursing the child and he could see her and his son whenever he wanted to.

The family who had gathered around to keep him company during what they had all expected to be a prolonged labour, congratulated him on his heir and sent him straight in to visit with his wife.

'Bella my love is everything all right with you?' he asked, as he sat down in a chair swiftly provided for him beside the bed and took hold of her slender hand.

'I'm perfectly well, if a little tired. Would you like to hold our beautiful boy now?'

Of course, he would, feeling truly blessed, knowing he was now the proud father of a son and heir.

The nursery nurse handed Lord Selwyn to John who stared at him in awe, so small and so perfect.

'You are so clever my love, a son at our first attempt.'

'You played your part too, very efficiently, if you recall.'

'I recall very well,' he said gazing warmly in her direction. 'Our honeymoon was a constant delight to me. I doubt I'll ever forget how entrancing you were, how you captivated me, how loving you were.'

'You were quite magnificent yourself as I recall.'

John smiled at her winsome face. They would enjoy those heights of passion again but for the moment they had the undeniable pleasure of making their firstborn son known to the family who waited patiently outside, eager to make his acquaintance.

'Are you ready to receive your parents, my mother, Harriet and Randal, who all wait outside in breathless anticipation?'

'Send them in. I haven't made them wait too long. Even I was surprised by how swiftly our son came into the world although Doctor Hayes seemed of the opinion that my labour started in the night with those annoying pains that kept me awake.'

'You never said they were pains,' John chastised.

'I didn't want you to worry.'

'You should have told me.'

'There was no need when you were sleeping peacefully and there was nothing you could do. But now, why don't you just kiss me?'

He gave his son back to the nursemaid and took his wife in his arms, kissing her with reverence and a profound sense of relief that she was safe. He'd waited anxiously, trying to stay on top of the nervous tension riding him, kept occupied by Randal who knew him so well, Randal who would be as eager as his family and Bella's parents to see his Godson.

'Shall we let them in now my love?'

'Of course.'

'Then you must get some rest.'

'I promise I will. I'm quite tired and could easily fall asleep right now.'

As Bella had laboured to bring new life into the world on that Sunday in June, far away across the English Channel at a place called Waterloo, sons, husbands, and fathers in their thousands gave their lives desperately fighting for their countries.

London would learn of it soon enough via Wellington's written account of the battle, published in the London Gazette on the twenty-second of June, the newspaper also carrying a list of the dead and wounded British officers, shocking and sorrowful in itself, but recording only a small number of the thousands of men whose sightless bodies littered the battlefield, leaving behind mothers, widows, and fatherless children to grieve for them.

Lord and Lady Bellingham would scan the list with only a sense of relief for it was hard to be joyful when so many lives had been lost. Their son Matthew was thankfully not one of the officers listed as dead or wounded.

Thaddeus Ignacious Wrighton, hearing of the victory some days later along with everyone else at Bascombe Hall, found his belief in God sorely challenged when he learned of the numbers of men who had died on both sides. Alone with John in the library he voiced the questions disturbing his peace.

'Did they die because it was God's purpose or was it for the vanity and ambition of one man? They rise these men, bold in their conquests, seeking approval and finding it, at least for a time and then they are gone, leaving death and disaster in their wake. How long will it be before another such man comes along with dreams of ruling the world and making so many pay the price for those dreams?'

John was thoughtful.

'I cannot say Thaddeus. It seems that all we can hope for, if one does, is that we have the best commander to see us through, because we are always too late in seeing the evil as it grows, appearing benign whilst it spreads its tentacles unhindered, vicelike, and unrelenting. Is God testing us, do you think, asking us to deliver ourselves from evil?'

'I don't know John, but in this case the price we have paid for deliverance seems unnecessarily harsh.'

For most people, their thoughts were only of a great victory, of heroes, dead or alive and glory on the battlefield. If the tragedy of the dead didn't touch them personally, they would not overthink it, their lives progressing unhindered. Life went on as usual in the capital and for the most part, society barely skipped a beat. Noble families drifted back to London in the autumn for another round of parties, balls, and soirees, presenting their daughters at court and exposing them to the vagaries of society, optimistic of them making a good match in their first season.

Bella found herself once again standing on the edge of Lady Creighton's ballroom but this time she was well established as the Duchess of Walborough, the mother of the heir to a Dukedom, her proud husband standing close beside her. Across the room she saw a man she didn't recognise, standing alone.

'Who is that?' she asked John.

'Lord Seldon. He has an estate in Northumberland, Beaton Magna, I think it's called. He's ex-military, a Major in the 95th Rifles, served valiantly at Waterloo so I've been told, and was commended some years back for bravery above and beyond the call of duty bringing him to Wellington's notice. Now Bonaparte is finally subdued, he's resigned his commission to manage his estate. He's waiting for his friend Linus Willoughby so don't even think of going over there and making conversation with him.'

'I wasn't going to. My aunt once told me it's bad ton.'

John looked down at her with an amused smile.

'And when did that ever stop you doing anything Bella Becket?'

'Never since I first saw you, my beloved John.'

'So, what do you think of him?'

'Who?'

'Seldon?'

She glanced his way, noticing his imposing stature, his air of confidence and his snugly fitting breeches.

'He's very handsome, and military men always know how to dress well, even out of uniform. No doubt he'll cause quite a stir amongst the ladies. Have you met him before?'

'No, and strangely I haven't come across anyone else who recalls ever having met him before.'

'Looking like that you'd imagine people would easily remember him, women in particular.'

'Looking like what?'

'Very manly,' she might have said, but chose to say, 'dark and mysterious.'

'Why mysterious?'

'As you said, whatever his past, no one seems to know anything of it, although other military men must have some knowledge of him, Wellington for one and his fellow officers.'

'I expect they do but fortunately he isn't our concern. The next dance is a waltz and you've promised it to me.'

'I promised you all my dances except the two Rossington has, leaving you to choose whether or not you want to give any away.'

'You know very well I'd rather keep them all for myself,' he said fascinated by the rise and fall of soft tender flesh above the deep decolletage of her exquisite dress. However, I may have to take you home early as the cut of your bodice is far too enticing and holding you in my arms is far too inviting, and it is getting late, or should I say early, as it's already well past the midnight hour. Let's go home,' he urged, holding her closer than was likely to be considered proper in a ballroom by some of the high sticklers.

'We've only just got here,' Bella said laughing at his optimistic look. 'And what of Rossington? He's expecting to spend the evening with us.'

'He can find his own woman, there are plenty of eligible young ladies available for him to dance with. I doubt he'll even notice we've gone, nor anyone else for that matter, now we're no longer single and eligible. An old married couple, past our peak?'

'What nonsense, we are still very much at our peak.'

She rose on her tiptoes to whisper in his ear.

'Next Autumn will prove it when we have a brother or sister for our beautiful boy.'

'Truly Bella? How wonderful,' John said scarcely able to conceal his delight at such welcome news. 'Even more reason to go home early and celebrate.'

Bella was pleased by his enthusiasm for a night alone together but persuaded him to delay a while. She was dressed in her finery, a magnificent creation of the palest green silk and tulle, shimmering and floating in the candlelight whilst John was looking supremely handsome in his form fitting black evening dress, not a man in the room able to challenge him for bold masculinity, nor sartorial elegance. She wanted to be seen with him, to be envied for her good fortune, to be admired in the same ballroom where once she had been left on the sidelines, ignored and desperately unhappy.

She had been ruthlessly whisked away from her country home by her aunt, for a season she had no craving for. She had hated everything about London society and was determined to return home as soon as possible, back to her ordinary life where no one looked at her and then turned away in disdain, their aristocratic noses in the air.

Plagued by boredom she had crossed the ballroom with purpose to engage in a conversation with a young man who stood alone, watchful and uneasy. She wouldn't deny he was impressive from afar, but he was something else entirely when she stood close by him. Even when he'd made it obvious he had no wish to converse with her, those tender feminine feelings of optimism and desire, severely tamped down by her aunt's lectures on her woeful prospects, had skipped unwarily through her mind.

If Rossington hadn't chosen to befriend her that same evening and keep her in John's proximity as the days and months passed by, then the chance of love blossoming between them would have been unlikely. Now she could bask in his generous love and make merry, for they were young of heart and here in the midst of high society they might in all honesty play the starstruck lovers upon their worldly stage.

'First,' she said with a teasing smile, 'you must waltz me around this dance floor, for it is beyond intoxicating to be held in your arms, to feel our bodies touch, as the music thrills and there is no one else but the two of us in thrall.'

'Then, my love,' he said with breathless delight, 'let me always have you to hold tenderly in my arms, and let me worship you always with my body, and love you forever with every beat of my heart.'

'And be the perfect answer to all my dreams of true love and happiness ever after.'

'It shall be so,' he said as his lips brushed against her soft cheek.

The polite world watched them with envy. The waltz ended with a courteous bow and they might then have crept out into the night but Rossington had arrived and John remembered what a kind and thoughtful companion he was and how, but for his determination to befriend Bella, they might never have got together. They could not in good faith leave him to spend his evening alone, even if the ballroom was crowded. They owed him more than indifference to his need for the company of dear friends.

Rossington led Bella onto the dance floor and John stood watching them, friends first and now known to be cousins, easy in each other's company. Other close friends gathered around him, and conversations began.

His wife was spoken of with admiration and affection. He couldn't be prouder of her than he was in that moment of understanding, when he realised she had stolen his heart, in this very ballroom on such a night as this, a sweet ingenue who had all too easily confused and delighted him with her unconventional approach.

Now she truly was the belle of the ball and he was the fortunate man who adored her and could call her his own. There was no need to hurry home. They could enjoy the evening dancing the night away, enjoy the company of dear friends and hear all the latest gossip.

Much later, as dawn heralded a new day, they would retire, weary but happy, to climb the stairs to their bedroom, hand in hand with time enough to indulge their youthful passions before they slept, undisturbed, blissfully unaware of the house awakening, as the day began and the Duke and Duchess of Walborough's servants went cheerily about their work, content to know the future of the noble house of Becket was on solid ground, safe and secure into the next generation.

Printed in Great Britain
by Amazon